# MERCY HOUSE

# MERCY HOUSE

LUBOV LEONOVA

# Contents

"You've broken too many rules already."
"These rules broke me first. So, now it's my turn."

- Lubov Leonova

Excerpt from *Mercy House*

# 1

# A Promise

Aring. Its tiny diamond gleamed, causing Lana's heart to skip a beat. Rendered speechless, she kept staring at it.

"So, what do you think?" Oliver asked, bringing her attention back to the summer cafe. "Will you marry me?"

*Damn...* Lana batted her eyes, her clouded mind trying to process what just happened. She took a glass of water and took several gulps. It helped her to pull herself together while Oliver patiently watched her from the opposite side of the table. In the bright sunlight, his hazel eyes shimmered with hope. They sat on an open patio of the student cafe, and the day outside was wonderful – the cloudless sky stretched above, and the smells of blossoming lilac filled the air. *And why did he pick such a nice day to ruin our perfect friendship?*

The waitress in a white apron neared their table and clapped her hands in excitement. "Congratulations!"

Lana gave her a hesitant look. "Erm... can we make an order?"

The waitress knitted her eyebrow and turned to Oliver. "What would you like to order? We have a special dessert today – a chocolate cake with seasonal berries. Half-price for the students."

He smiled at her. "I like specials. Bring us two pieces of cake, please. And two coffees, black."

"Will do." She threw Lana a disapproving look before leaving. Now it was clear that the student community would soon figure out about this awkward proposal. *And why did Oliver put himself into such a situation?*

Oliver folded his hands, letting the open velvet box with the ring rest on the table. "I once heard that if you really love someone, you can't imagine the rest of your life without this person. Each time I wake up in the morning, the first thing I think of is you, Lana. And it's the last thing I think of when I fall asleep. I just want to be with you. Always."

"Oliver, I just... I had no idea you thought of me in that way," she finally said. "I wasn't ready for it."

His face became concerned. "We've known each other for a year. Isn't it enough for you to become ready for more?"

*For more?!* Lana gave him a hesitant look. "Oliver, I really appreciate you. You are very kind, and I can always rely on you as a friend and my study partner. Honestly, our friendship became a gulp of fresh air after I almost drowned."

"Are you still heartbroken?" He asked, a worry written on his face.

Lana pressed her hand to her chest. The memory of her unfortunate romance didn't cause her heart to ache, not even slightly. However, there was no place for new love there. Maybe Oliver was a great guy, however, there was no sparkle between them. *Something must be wrong with me,* Lana thought with regret. *Am I attracted only to bad guys? Or guys in uniform?* Oliver was a complete opposite of the man she used to love so madly – raised in a strict religious family, he was kind to everyone, always respected her boundaries, and knew what to say to cheer her up. Well, except for today.

"Lana, please, say something," Oliver said, gently taking her hand in his. Only now, Lana realized how cold her palms were. "What bothers you that much?"

She exhaled nervously. "You are a terrific friend, Oliver, but I'm afraid I can't meet your expectations."

"It's about my family, isn't it?" he suggested.

*A family...* This excuse sounded much better. "Yes. I don't know much about your family, but your parents are religious, so they'll hate me if they learn about my past. I wasn't a saint, Oliver. As you know, I had a forbidden romance with a man in my hometown."

"Trust me, they won't care about that."

"Because they are so forgiving or because you plan to hide me from them for the rest of our lives?"

"Neither."

Lana narrowed her eyes at him. "What do you mean by 'neither'? Do they hide a terrible secret that is bigger than all my sins?"

His voice was laced with sadness. "Exactly."

His answer sparked an intrigue in her chest. It's been a while since she felt that way... who knew, perhaps Oliver wasn't too dull husband material after all?

"Okay... If it's a family mystery, I must know about it before considering marriage."

"Fair enough," he agreed, taking the velvet box with the ring and twisting it in his hand. "But before I tell you, I must know you'll never tell anyone about it. Ever."

"You know that you can trust me," Lana assured. "I can keep secrets. Also, you already know mine, so –"

"It's serious, Lana," he interrupted in a hushed voice. "If someone outside our family learns it, we are all doomed."

"Is it a classified case?" she teased.

"Yes."

Lana knitted her brow. If it was some sort of game Oliver played to tickle her curiosity, it worked. After all, despite all her efforts to move on with her life, she still had a soft spot for mysteries. That's why she couldn't resist pushing him. "Then you must tell me. After all, we are supposed to trust each other fully before tying the knot."

He gave her a sincere look. "You are right. It isn't fair to invite you into our family without telling you the whole truth. However, I also see that you aren't ready to become my wife."

"As I said, I need more time. Marriage is a huge step for me. I need to be sure that I'm ready."

He nodded and placed the velvet box on the table between them. "Let's change our agreement, then. We can call it 'the ring of promise' instead. If you wear it, it means that you give us a chance and don't look at other men. And with time, when you are ready, we can get engaged."

Lana shifted her eyes to the ring and then back to his pleading face. "Why don't you just call it 'dating?'"

"Dating is against my religion."

She sighed. Apparently, her best friend simply wanted to ask her to date him but he couldn't help himself making things so complicated. "Alright, I can consider a promise. Although I don't think we need a ring for that."

"I want to do it in the right way. You know, I've never had any serious relationship before, and I've been saving myself for my future wife."

*Saving himself?* Lana pondered. Well, it explained a lot – unlike most men she had met on her way, Oliver was always keeping distance. Not for once, he attempted to kiss her. His modesty was one of the significant things that prevented Lana from considering him as a boyfriend. Who knew, maybe he needed Lana to wear this ring as permission to make a bolder move? If so, she was ready to give it a try.

"Fine," Lana said, extending her left hand. "Let's do it."

His face brightened as he pulled the ring on her finger and kissed the back of her palm. "I'll never break your heart. I promise."

"I promise it, too." Lana admired her new jewelry, getting used to the sensation of the metal on her skin.

The waitress came back, and Lana didn't miss a chance to wave her hand with the shining ring on it. It felt nice to give her the pull to spread rumors about their new relationship status.

When they were left alone, Lana savoured a piece of cake. It was heavenly good, and its soft chocolate dough melted in her mouth. Even though losing a friend was unfortunate, she might enjoy discovering a new side of their relationship. Maybe now Oliver would stop being so shy and act like a man. Her man. *Interesting, how would it be to kiss him for the first time?*

"Okay, let's discuss our study project," Oliver said.

Lana gave him a puzzled look. "And forget about your family secret? No way!"

He furrowed his brow. "It's not safe to talk about it now – there are too many ears."

Lana looked around. His point made perfect sense – at this time of the day, the cafe was bustling with the students who gathered here for their lunch. "True. Let's go to my room, then."

"Let's do it after we finish with the project," he suggested. "Not to get distracted."

Lana gave him an amused smile. Perhaps, there wasn't a mystery and he only needed an excuse to visit her chambers and time to make something up. Well, then, she could pretend to play his game. "Alright. We can 'do it' whenever you are ready."

"Thank you," he said with a small smile, then started explaining the details of the project they had to deliver to pass their final exam.

Lana barely listened. Despite her best efforts, architecture appeared to be one of the most boring subjects she had ever studied. However, when Oliver spoke of it, his eyes shone with passion. *Gee, he really is in love with his work,* she observed. *Will I ever fall in love with my life just like him?*

Not that Lana hated her new life. She had nothing to complain about – here, in the capital, women were allowed to choose so many suitable options for their careers – they could become teachers, professional cooks, artists, musicians... Being an interior designer was quite a new area, and Lana appreciated this opportunity. After all, she chose a path of building her own life instead of getting married and raising kids with the man who would never respect her. Unfortunately, this newly found freedom didn't ignite her heart as it was in Triville, when she was investigating real crime cases. *Something is definitely wrong with me,* she concluded.

"Lana, are you listening?" Oliver asked, pulling her out of her daze.

"Of course," she replied with a nod.

"Then we must collect a group of at least ten students."

She blinked. "For what?"

"Okay, I see you're a bit distracted." He pointed at her ring of promise and smiled. "It's okay, I'll repeat. For this project, we need to provide a presentation for the prospective students to earn some bonus marks. We can join forces and do it together, then share the marks. It will let us earn enough scores to qualify for the scholarship next year."

"My father has already covered all my studies expenses. But if you need my help, I'll happily do it."

"I really appreciate it. It will help release the burden from my family."

Lana knitted her brow. "Hold on. You were working part-time all this year, saving for your studies."

"I had some expenses, too." He glanced at the ring that he had given her.

*Shit, how much did he spend on this piece of jewelry?* The idea of wearing a massive part of his earnings on her finger weighed heavily on her chest. "Olive... you didn't have to buy it like that. Anyway, this proposal has been postponed –"

"It doesn't matter how much I spent," he interjected. "It matters how much we can do now. Together. And as I said, we can earn enough scores to get a scholarship."

*He really is serious about being an independent adult.* Lana could only support his decision. "Okay. Where shall we start, then?"

"I was thinking of preparing the fliers and placing them in the hall room of our campus. You know, the students who are thinking of applying come here to check it out, so they can become interested in having a special educational tour."

"A tour?"

He nodded. "I want to do it in a creative way. Instead of giving a boring presentation in a dusty classroom, we can take the group outside and show them the city."

"It's a brilliant plan!" Even though Lana wasn't too passionate about this profession, it wasn't that bad when Oliver was by her side. This guy never ran out of ideas.

He waved his hands, explaining her role. "Middle Lake has so many landmarks, and I thought you could do a bit of research and choose the most interesting places that we can show."

"Consider it's done," Lana assured him. The thought of spending the evening in the library, checking on the history of the buildings, didn't seem attractive; however, she was ready to do it. For the sake of their new mission and to help Oliver with his marks. Then, in the moment when he would be satisfied with her quality work, he might eventually kiss her and become more than just her friend.

# 2

# Back to Passions

The sun generously lit up the morning streets of Middle Lake city. Spring was in the air, and hundreds of blossoming trees decorated their path as the group of students strolled after Lana and Oliver. His promotional fliers had worked well, and they managed to gather sixteen prospective students for their city tour.

Lana did her part of the job, too. In the college library, she had learned about the stories of some old buildings, and she planned to make their route very interesting. She also took her time to shop for a pretty summer dress to impress Oliver and pull him out of his shell. Today, she wore a flirty pink dress with charmingly open shoulders. So far, Oliver hadn't paid it any mind, but at least her efforts weren't fruitless – her looks captured the attention of the prospective male students. Lana didn't doubt some of them would consider applying for the city development architecture program.

They stopped at the crossroad where the street made a turn to the old trade avenue. A two-century-old building of the bank stood in the middle, surrounded by puffy pink cherry trees. There was a man on the crossroad. He wore a black guardian uniform, and he was about her father's age – with gray hair on his temples and wrinkles around his blue eyes. His presence made a bitter-sweet sense of nostalgia wash over her. *Damn... I miss being around the guardians.*

Seeing them approaching, the guardian stepped forward, lifting one of his hands to block their way. "You can't go there."

Lana curiously looked at his shoulder. A golden dragon embroidery was complemented with two stripes. "Is anything wrong, Captain?"

"This street is closed today," he explained, his voice carrying an official tone. "You have to choose another route."

Lana shifted her eyes to Oliver.

As usual, he preferred to refrain from arguing. "No worries. I guess we need to cut this from our program –"

"Let's discuss it first." Lana pulled Oliver by his elbow before he agreed to comply with the order. She led him ten steps away and lowered her voice. "We can't just turn back. That bank is important for our presentation."

"You heard the man. We can't go there."

"Are you always following the damn rules?"

"Yes."

Lana breathed out through her nose. His obedience to the law was exemplary, and sometimes it was annoying. "I'm pretty sure we can sort it out. Just give me a minute to convince him."

He frowned. "Why are you always so stubborn?"

"It's just the way I am," she said with a playful smile. "If you want to marry me for real, you must get used to it."

He exhaled a sigh. "Well, maybe, but –"

"Plus, the students need to see the inspirational example of how not to give in to difficulties," she implied before Oliver ruined the momentum with his indecisiveness. "If they see how we handle it, or at least try, they'll be more encouraged to sign up for the program. And the more people sign up, the more points we'll earn. Right?"

He gave it a brief thought before replying. "Well, I guess it won't hurt to try."

"Thank you!" She planted a kiss on his cheek and rushed back to the guardian.

When Lana approached, the man in uniform still stood in the middle of the crossroad, his hands crossed protectively. "Can I help you, young lady?"

"Lana," she introduced herself with a small smile. "Ah, you talk just like my father. He is a guardian captain, by the way. Just like you."

His face brightened with curiosity. "Is he?"

She nodded. "He serves in Triville, a small town in the northeast. His name is Bernard Morris."

He scratched his chin covered with a gray bristle. "I guess I heard something about that town. It must be a quiet place, though."

"It is, but troubles can happen anywhere."

"True."

"You see, I'm a future architect," she continued, "and I really need to show one building to that group. You see, that old bank was robbed 12 times during its two-century history. And the last time it happened was last year. What are the odds this crime will be repeated this year?"

"The chances are high. That's why we closed this street today."

Lana gave him a pleading look. "I just hope you let us there for fifteen minutes. I worked so hard on preparing the speech about the robbery that took place a year ago. If I deliver it at that building, it might bring more awareness to these guys. And I dare to think it might help prevent future crimes."

He glanced at the empty street, then back to Lana. "Fine, you have ten minutes. If you notice anything suspicious, please get out of there as soon as possible."

She smiled. "I really appreciate it, Captain."

"Captain Harrison," he clarified with a smile. "Good luck with your project, Lana!"

"And how exactly was this building robbed?" One of the students asked in curiosity after Lana had revealed the history of this landmark.

She waved her hands in explanation. "That's a good question. They have special crystal sensors, and the security guard is constantly watching the hall. They are all strong and educated mages who can freeze you with a single finger click. When the mysterious crime happened last year, the guardians couldn't resolve the case. You see – no one was hurt, and no one could describe the criminals. They only discovered the robbery at the end of the day when the cashiers were checking the gold inventory after closing."

"Then they must have been hypnotized," someone suggested.

"Not really." Lana walked along the porch, capturing all their attention. "Usually, when people fall under hypnotic charm, everyone experiences different kind of illusions. However, all the witnesses' reports match, which means they never were charmed."

"What about the energy traces?"

"They had been erased," Lana explained in a mysterious tone.

Oliver took a step up on a wide stair, taking the spotlight. "Yes, we like talking about the guardians and criminals, but let's not forget that we came here to discuss the architecture." He gave Lana a strict look before shifting his attention to the group of students. "This building was designed by one of the most famous architects – Hofstongen. He created this unforgettable old style that we call 'Gothic.'"

Lana stepped aside, covered her mouth with her palm, and let out a yawn. Sometimes it was hard to imagine that this subject could spark any interest in anyone. However, when Oliver talked about the architecture, his words piqued the students' attention. *And why is this subject so boring for me?*

Even after a year of studying, Lana still had a strong desire to fall asleep each time she had to listen to a lecture about the local architecture styles. She only managed to accomplish this project because she chose buildings based on their criminal history. *It was a good compromise; however, adult life isn't supposed to be all fun,* she reminded herself.

Before the gloomy thoughts about the boredom of adult life started creeping in, Lana looked around the street to distract herself. Her gaze stopped at the carriage at the corner. It had been parked there since they arrived, and the coachman seemed suspicious. He wore black clothes and a hat. His unfolded newspaper covered the lower part of his face as he periodically glanced at them.

Lana blinked. As a person who loved mysteries, Lana knew one thing – with time, criminals got smarter, and with the calm environment, business owners got less cautious. Who knew, maybe the bank decided to hire less security guards, hoping that the same crime won't happen again?

Oliver slightly poked her elbow. "Okay, we're done here. Let's go."

"Sure." Lana took a heavy sigh and glanced at her pinkish-red time crystal. *Almost noon.* She promised Captain Harrison not to be here longer than ten minutes, and her time was up. She had to leave all the foolish thoughts about the mysteries and return to her real life.

# The Robbery

Irida lurked behind the corner of the building, watching the carriage parked near the bank. Since its arrival, no one had walked out of it. The coachman sat on the horse, lazily glancing around as he read the newspaper.

The street was almost deserted, with only an organized group of students disrupting the calmness. They chatted and raised their hands in question to their guides: a tall young man and a young woman with flaxen hair and a dress that was a bit too revealing. Irida guessed that the coachman was waiting for them to leave.

"So?" Walter asked.

She turned to him. Walter, a guardian with attentive blue eyes and dressed in a black uniform, looked at her inquisitively.

"Patience," Irida teased him. It had been a while since they arrived, and Walter couldn't wait to catch the criminals who were planning to rob the bank. It was amusing to see his disappointed face when he didn't get the answer he had expected.

Walter took her elbow and squeezed it, not too hard, but enough to assert his dominance. "Don't you dare play games with me!"

She narrowed her eyes at him. "Trust me, of all the people I might play with, you are not one of them. No offense. You're just not my type."

"How subtle!" He pulled her closer. "Listen, thief –"

"I'm not a thief!"

"You were caught attempting to rob the jewelry store," he reminded her. "And if I recall correctly, you made a deal with the Captain to avoid arrest."

Irida rolled her eyes. "I remember our deal. That's why I led you to the people planning a bank robbery. So, you can relax."

"I'll relax after it's over."

"Anyhow," she pointed to the corner of the street where the carriage was parked. "So there are your thieves. Once that group of students clears their path, they will enter the bank and take the money. Your job is to catch them red-handed."

"Right, about this group of students... What are they doing here?"

Irida took advantage of the moment when he eased his grip and took a step back. "I don't know."

"Last night, you mentioned that these robberies are well-planned, scheduled at a time when no one would interfere. Where did this group come from?" Walter eyed her suspiciously. "Was it your doing?"

"Me? What?" Irida gasped at the accusation. "I swear, I have nothing to do with it! It must be just a coincidence."

"A coincidence, huh?" He remained unconvinced. "That gang executed this robbery operation last year. And like today, there was no one in this street. If they are that skilled at organizing, then what's happening now?"

"No clue. Let's wait for the students to pass by and then stick to the original plan."

He gave her a stern look before finally relenting. "Fine. Activate your shield when... Actually, they are approaching us!"

"Got it." Irida slowed her breathing and touched Walter's hand. Then she let her Gift take effect. Initially, a fog enveloped their bodies, rendering them invisible. She completed the process just in time for the group of students to emerge from the corner. The young woman in the striking dress, the one Irida had noticed earlier, walked too close, and her elbow brushed against Irida's free hand.

The woman looked around, her big brown eyes widening in confusion. She extended her hand, touching the air.

*She can't see me*, Irida reminded herself as she stepped back, pulling Walter along with her. The woman didn't detect them, so she gave up checking and rejoined her group.

"Almost busted." Walter chuckled as they made their way to the stairs of the bank.

"Haha," she replied in a somber tone. "Quiet now. It's not *her* we should worry about."

"I hope so."

They halted at the first stair and stood still. Irida was relieved she couldn't see Walter's face at that moment. Without the sense of his touch, it was as if the guardian was not present. Unfortunately, this peace wouldn't last long. Maintaining an invisible shield for another person required a significant amount of energy. *Hopefully, the arrest would be swift.*

Two minutes passed, and the man emerged from the carriage, heading straight for the bank entrance. Another minute went by, and he exited the bank with a heavy bag in hand. After glancing around and smiling, he began descending the stairs.

"Now," Walter commanded, and Irida released his hand.

Walter materialized from thin air and sprinted up the stairs toward the man. He swiftly pulled him to the railing, causing the thief to drop the bag of stolen money. The bag tumbled down the stairs, but Walter was too preoccupied with handcuffing the man to pay it any mind.

Irida maintained her invisible shield, observing the scene. She had to remain undetected because if anyone from the gang discovered that she had exposed their plan to the guardians, she would be in serious trouble.

"With the authority of the King, you are under arrest!" Walter bellowed, raising his hand and compelling the thief to halt in his tracks. Walter possessed a Gift of Telekinesis, enabling him to immobilize individuals with the power of his mind.

Out of the corner of her eye, Irida noticed the carriage advancing toward her. She had to leap aside to avoid being struck by the vehicle. The money bag lay on the road, and if the coachman drew nearer, he could easily retrieve it, completing the robbery. Though she wasn't a guardian, Irida knew that without the bag, there would be no evidence to apprehend the culprits.

"Walter!" She shouted at the top of her lungs. "Watch the bag!"

Walter glanced down and extended one hand, attempting to reach the bag with his telekinetic power. Beads of sweat formed on his forehead as he concentrated, but he could only manage to shift it slightly. It seemed that all his energy was focused on immobilizing the thief.

Irida hugged herself, trying to steady her racing heart. She contemplated dropping her invisible shield to divert the coachman's attention, but it would expose her face to everyone. She couldn't take that risk.

Suddenly, a Light signal illuminated the sky above them. Irida gazed upward, witnessing beautiful yellow energy sparkles dispersing in the skies. Each person possessed a unique energy known as the Light, which sometimes was used to summon the guardians for assistance. *Who did it?*

The answer swiftly presented itself – the attractive woman who had led the group and nearly discovered Irida was now sprinting toward the carriage, clutching a shining silver ball in her hand – a Paralyzing spell.

The woman hurled the ball at the coachman. Although she missed him, the carriage jolted as he evaded the projectile and swerved to the side. He had to maneuver to prevent overturning, then hastily fled from the street, neglecting to retrieve the bag of money.

*What a bold move!* Irida exhaled, and her invisible shield dissipated.

# 4

# The Witness

Lana sat on the stairs of the porch, watching the final scene of the arrest. Captain Harrison arrived shortly after she had sent the signal made of her yellow Light. No wonder he came first – he had been nearby all this time. Together with the other guardian, a blond man named Walter Mills, they held the suspect until the other guardians arrived at the crime scene in a black carriage with a golden dragon embroidery on its side.

Now, Walter was placing the suspect in a carriage. Captain Harrison stood aside, talking to the woman who had her invisible shield removed. The woman had smooth olive skin and beautiful almond-shaped eyes of amber color. Lana didn't doubt it was her she had accidentally bumped into when their group was leaving this street. Interestingly, if Lana hadn't touched a mysterious invisible obstacle, she might never have considered turning back. As it often happened, her curiosity prevailed, and she ran back as soon as she heard the screams in the street. This is how she was able to witness the scene of the arrest.

Oliver neared her and sat nearby. "Hey, are you okay? You ran away from the group without any explanation. I got worried."

Lana gave him an apologetic look. "Sorry. I didn't mean to ruin this tour. Did all the students leave?"

"I had to dismiss the group," he said in a sad voice. "There was a robbery, after all, and I couldn't bring their attention back to the architecture topic."

Lana snickered. "I can't blame them for that."

Oliver shook his head. "Alright, maybe the history of the city isn't your favorite theme, but Lana, you can't flee like that."

She shrugged. "I just wanted to help –"

"This is the job for the guardians," he interjected, pointing to the black carriage. "Why did you get involved?"

Lana averted her eyes. Despite her promise to give up on her childish dream of becoming a detective, she still had that spark inside of her. The one that ignited her heart each time she learned about crimes and did her best to prevent them. It was exactly what happened, and she regretted it now. Oliver was right – there was no need for her interference. "I'm sorry. It was silly."

"Silly?! What you did today was reckless!" He took her hand in his, a deep concern crossing his face. "You put your life in danger too easily, Lana. I've already lost the person I loved because of it. I don't want to lose you."

She narrowed her eyes at him. It was hard to believe Oliver had a sweetheart before. "You were in love? Why haven't you ever told me about her?"

He exhaled a heavy sigh. "It's not a romantic love I'm talking about. She was my sister."

"Oh, no..." Lana's voice dropped. "What happened to her?"

"She was too rebellious, that's what happened," Oliver said. "She was a bright person, the smartest girl in her school. And unfortunately, she got the forbidden Gift."

Lana listened without interrupting. Every mage had a Gift that always manifested in adolescence. Men could have any Gift, but as for women, it was considered to be the 'wrong' one if it was a destructive power. Fortunately, some Gifts could be easily tamed, like the most popular magic – Telekinesis. A special facility called Mercy House took such girls to educate them on how to master their Gift not to hurt others. As for the less fortunate women who acquired the Gifts of Fire, Poisoning, and other deadly powers, they could voluntarily give their magic away and keep living their lives without that power.

"My sister, Mia, got a Lightning Gift," Oliver revealed. "It manifested itself when she was in her biology class. Mia was sent away right from the school doctor's office, and we never saw her again. We didn't even say goodbye to her."

"Why didn't you visit her in Mercy House?"

"Visit?!" Oliver shook his head, "They don't allow visits, Lana. The location of all the Mercy Houses, as I learned, is classified."

Lana nodded in understanding. "Did you at least learn what happened to her?"

He sighed before continuing his story. "Months passed, and I couldn't bear seeing my parents so upset. So, I sneaked into the school doctor's office and stole Mia's records. I managed to learn where they took her."

"Wait... How come they revealed the location of the secret facility in school records?"

"They didn't," Oliver explained. "The records indicated how much sleeping potion they gave her and for how long it would last. The doctor wrote, 'The dose will last for ten hours and might evaporate fully by the time of arrival.' This is how I determined the time of her transfer – ten hours. Knowing the average speed of the carriage traveling through the forest, I made a simple calculation and discovered the distance to the facility. I only had to get a map and check the places in the area where my sister could be taken.

"With Middle Lake's landscape, it wasn't too hard – we have the great lake in the South, so I headed North and started searching that area. When I eventually found the black castle, hidden among the hills, I was on the verge of despair. I stood at the gates, demanding to see Mia, and the elder Mercy Sister agreed to talk to me on one condition – that I would never tell anyone about that place and our conversation. No one except for the close family. This is how I learned that Mia attempted to escape. On her way out, she killed a guard and a Mercy Sister." Oliver dropped his head, his voice getting quieter. "Mia was a free spirit, and she was released from the prison of her body. It was the only way for her not to hurt anyone else."

*Did they kill Mia?!* Lana frowned, trying to cope with the shocking discovery. Oliver, after all, was right in one thing – with this accusation of murders supposedly committed by his sister, her own sins looked bleak. "So, this is the dark secret your family keeps."

"Exactly." He paused. "Do you hate me now? After everything I told you?"

She put her hand on his shoulder, consoling him. "Of course not. I feel ready to go there myself and investigate what really happened to Mia. I simply don't believe a teenage girl could kill two adult mages."

Oliver looked at her with disapproval. "This is what I was afraid of. You have the same spirit, Lana. And it can put you in grave danger." He pointed at the black guardian's carriage that was about to leave. "I was first shocked by what they said about Mia. I wanted to scream that it was all a lie. But I didn't. I forced myself to believe their words. After all, I was the only child my parents had left, the one who could still take care of them. I had to forget about the rest and keep living a normal life. Since Mia's death, I try to stay away from the guardians and not cause any trouble. Lana, you have no idea what they are capable of. So please, stay away from all this mess. I beg you."

"Fine," Lana said, only to calm him. She doubted she would 'forget' it so easily.

Meanwhile, the crime scene was heading to closure. Walter clapped a closed door of the black carriage, and it started moving. Because of her talk with Oliver, Lana missed the moment when Captain Harrison and the woman with the Gift of Invisibility had left. *Probably, they rode away together with the suspect*, Lana deduced.

Walter neared them and stood over Lana. "Thanks again for your help, Miss Morris. If not for you, we would have lost critical evidence."

She felt a blush warming her cheeks. "It's just my civilian duty. I'm glad I could help."

He chuckled. "A duty?! I've never seen such dedication among civilians. You were ready to shoot that criminal! Where did you learn to make Paralyzing spells?"

"One guardian taught me."

"Her father is a guardian," Oliver implied.

Lana nodded. It was actually her ex-boyfriend who taught her the basics of the Paralyzing spell, and she never mastered it to perfection – the spells she cast were usually too weak. But her past didn't matter now.

"That's great," Walter said, frowning at her hand with the ring on it. Then he pulled his hand out of his chest pocket and revealed a black name card. "Here. I'll have to ask you to come and give an official testimonial."

"No problem." Lana took the card. "When?"

"The sooner, the better."

"She needs some rest." Oliver placed his hand on her shoulder, his voice growing protective. "What about the other day?"

"It's okay, Olive," Lana said.

He frowned. "It's not. You could have been hurt today… or even killed!"

"Tomorrow is perfectly fine," Walter said, giving her a curious look. "You aren't planning to leave the city, right?"

"Of course not." She smiled at him. "I'll be at the dorms. As usual."

"In case you don't show up, I'll find you there," he promised before leaving.

When they were alone, Oliver gave her a worried look. "I didn't like the guy. Are you sure you want to meet him again?"

"Don't worry. It's just a regular robbery case, and I don't mind helping investigate it." Lana gave him a small smile. After everything she had learned about Oliver, she was hesitant. Apparently, he was capable of risking his own life and breaking the rules for people he loved. On the other hand, he gave up on his sister way too easily. *What if something happened to me?* She wondered. *Will he just close his eyes and keep living his life as usual?* Lana shook her head, trying to shake off the gloom. After all, Oliver shared about it, which meant he made a step towards building their trust. She had to acknowledge it. "By the way, I appreciate that you shared your secret. I won't tell anyone."

"Especially that guardian," he said, glancing in the direction where Walter had left.

"Especially to him," she assured. "I don't want any trouble for you."

"Thank you, Lana."

"Always." She took his hands, her heart racing with anxiety. Damn, she needed Oliver to do something to really consider him as a future husband. Perhaps, a little step towards sealing their new relationship status? Before the new doubts took over, Lana raised her tiptoes and planted a kiss on his lips.

Unexpectedly, Oliver stepped back, his face taking on a reddish color. "Lana... I've told you I can't."

"Come on, we're almost engaged. Can we at least share a kiss?"

He gasped. "No! Even when we are engaged, it's not appropriate to behave in that way."

She batted her eyes in confusion. "For real?!"

Oliver stared at her for two seconds, then shook his head. "It must be the stress you went through that affects you this way."

"As you said, when you love someone, you can't imagine your life without this person. And I want to be with you. I just need to be closer to you. To feel safe in your embrace. And this is an important part of my belief – this is how a normal relationship must work."

"What about *my* beliefs?"

Lana sighed. She could accept that she wouldn't try to interfere with his past and uncover the truth about his sister. However, it was just too sad to have a 'boyfriend' who couldn't even touch her without blushing. Such an attitude might ruin their romantic relationship before it even started! Perhaps, she had to try harder to break through this wall of prejudice. "There is only one true belief – love. I guess if you do things out of love, there is nothing wrong about it." Lana came closer but didn't risk touching him this time. He was too tense. "I see you are full of doubts, but at least give it a thought. As I gave our marriage a chance."

He breathed out. "Fine. I'll think about it."

"Whatever you decide, let's talk about it in a calm atmosphere. I'll be waiting for you in my room by five o'clock."

# 5

# A Final Touch

Lana smoothed out the folds on her creamy bed sheets and smiled. Her room, with candles placed on the nightstands and red roses in a crystal vase, created the right atmosphere for her evening with Oliver. But something was missing. Lana paused for a moment, then took a rose. Its delicate aroma sent shivers down her skin. She tore off the bud and scattered the petals over the bed, letting them fall chaotically on the sheet. *Now it's perfect!*

She walked over to her tall mirror. The young woman reflecting back at her was stunning, with shining brown eyes and long flaxen hair cascading freely over her shoulders. Today, she wore red-trimmed lingerie that she had purchased specifically for tonight.

It would be naive to expect Oliver to sleep with her, but it was a reliable tactic – to suggest something unacceptable, so the partner would agree to a lesser evil. Lana had no doubt that Oliver would be shocked as soon as he walked into her room. Lana's role was to act innocent and explain that she was simply 'preparing the attire and setting for their wedding night.' She could even pretend to be upset, hoping that Oliver would console her and agree to a long-anticipated kiss. That was all she needed.

There was only one final touch to complete her image. Lana retrieved a red lipstick from her drawer and carefully applied it. She puckered her lips, admiring her reflection. Due to the strict academic rules, she had refrained from wearing makeup throughout the whole year. Typically, she only wore a layer of good face cream and natural-colored lip balm. But not today.

She finished applying the lipstick when her ring shimmered, catching her attention. Lana moved her hand closer, her heart pounding in her chest. *Do I really want to marry him?* Lana didn't have any certainty on this matter. She wished she could be as confident as she was in the moment when she rushed to stop that damn robbery.

Unfortunately, as women were not allowed to be guardians, she had to choose from the limited options available to her. For Lana, it was a career in architecture and a life with Oliver. This was the path she must walk, and perhaps marrying him would help her forget about her foolish ambitions. Now, it was up to Oliver to make a move – if her plan worked, it would mean that he wasn't entirely hopeless. *Whatever happens next, it will be my destiny*, she decided.

A knock on her door made her flinch. Lana instinctively moved her hand, causing her ring to slip off her finger. It bounced on the wooden floor, then rolled somewhere under the bed. *Damn it!*

The knock repeated, and Lana had to respond before Oliver realized she wasn't there and left. "Open! Come on in!"

*If Oliver sees me without the ring, he might get upset, which will ruin my strategy.* It wasn't too late to rectify the situation. Cursing under her breath, Lana knelt down on the floor, searching for the spot where the ring had landed. Of course, the damn thing had rolled to the furthest corner under her bed, hidden in a layer of dust as if mocking her with a silent *Not in this life.*

Frustrated, Lana rose from her knees and blinked in surprise as her eyes met his. It wasn't Oliver standing before her. The person in front of her was Walter.

Lana was so taken aback that she couldn't muster a proper greeting. She simply stared at him in silence.

"You said it was open," Walter remarked, gesturing to the entrance door behind him. He stood on the opposite side of the bed, clad in his black uniform. The dragon embroidery on his shoulder gleamed attractively.

*He is so handsome!* Lana swallowed, trying to push away her improper thoughts. *I'm just too aroused to think clearly,* she scolded herself, *I must pull myself together.*

"Yes, it was open," she finally managed to utter. "I was waiting for my..." Lana hesitated, unsure if Oliver was truly her friend, boyfriend, or fiance. Technically, they were not engaged, however, they weren't dating either. The confusion made it difficult to continue speaking, so she fell silent.

"Your fiance," Walter said.

She offered him a small smile. "Uh-hum."

"He is one lucky man," Walter chuckled, his gaze lingering on her with a hint of greed.

It was only then that Lana realized she was clad in nothing but her red-trimmed lingerie. She hastily attempted to cover herself with her hands, her cheeks burning with embarrassment. She wished she could simply vanish into thin air, wishing she possessed an Invisibility Gift.

"Sorry," Walter said, delicately turning away to give her some privacy.

Lana breathed heavily, torn between feeling anger at him for staring at her and excitement that at least this man found her desirable. After Oliver's rejection to kiss her, it was a relief to know that she was still considered an attractive woman.

"What are you doing here?" she asked, stepping into the safety of her wardrobe. Now, with the solid wooden door separating them, she was able to resume speaking in her usual tone.

"It's about that robbery investigation," he explained. "And I'm really sorry for misreading your signals."

She became intrigued. "What signals?"

"When you said you were ready to help us immediately, your fiance looked a bit... overprotective. I thought you didn't want to upset him by arguing. And since you gave me your whereabouts, I thought you wanted me to find you later in the dorms."

Lana had to admit – she truly wanted him to find her and involve her in the investigation. Walter had correctly interpreted her signals, like a true detective. However, she didn't want to give him too much credit for it. "It was nice of you to respect my personal life. And since you came all the way here, I can try to help. What exactly do you need?"

"Your Gift."

"My... what?" Lana popped her head out from the door, only to see his back clad in a black shirt and his broad shoulders. Curious about where he was looking, she glanced at the wall mirror and their eyes met in the reflection. *Oh, man.* Suppressing a laugh, she raised her eyebrows, feigning offense. "Hey, aren't you supposed to turn away?"

He smiled slyly and averted his gaze to the ceiling. "You're a mind-reader, right?"

"That's correct," Lana confirmed. She had disclosed this information to another guardian, Captain Harrison, during a brief witness report.

"Very well." Walter smiled, his eyes sliding back to the mirror.

Lana shook her head and retreated behind the door. It seemed that he wasn't as reserved as Oliver, and his lingering gaze was beyond his control. Despite enjoying the flirtation, she knew she shouldn't toy with his interest. It wouldn't be fair to Oliver. "So, what about my Gift?"

"I need you to read one person. A criminal," Walter explained.

"Why me? Aren't there any mind-readers in your team?"

"Exactly."

Lana remained unconvinced. "I can't believe you couldn't find other mind-readers in such a large city!"

"It's not about finding people with this rare Gift. It's about finding someone I can trust. And I have a feeling that you are the right person to read the memories of that thief and provide me with all the necessary details. Am I right?"

"Well... I suppose so."

"Plus, I've heard about your father and your work in Triville. Did you really help them?"

"As a secretary, yeah," Lana replied, her heart fluttering with bittersweet memories. "Sometimes, it was useful to read the witnesses to assist the guardians with more detailed reports."

The floor squeaked as he turned towards her. Despite the door separating them, she could almost feel his intense gaze. "Then please, get dressed," he said before the floor squeaked again as he walked towards the door. "I'll wait in the corridor."

"Sure. I'll be there in five."

Lana ran her hand over the hangers holding her clothes – among pencil skirts and strict blouses, there was a set that she couldn't bring herself to discard. She selected a hanger with her black pants and a handmade black shirt with long sleeves. It resembled a guardian uniform, except for the absence of the dragon embroidery that she was never meant to wear in her life. Now, when she had the opportunity to help, she didn't care about this detail. Lana held her clothes close to her chest, inhaling their slightly dusty scent. *Gee... I had no idea how much I missed this.*

# 6

A Gulp of Air

Irida sat in a leather chair, her hands folded in her lap. The spacious room was adorned with black river stones on two walls. A large fireplace on one side remained unlit, its charred interior hinting at recent use. A massive oak desk and two visitor chairs completed the Captain's office furnishings. Now, Irida occupied one of them as she awaited the start of their meeting.

Growing weary of the silence, Irida lifted her gaze to Harrison, who stood by the expansive window, his silhouette nearly blending into the bright daylight. "Captain?" she ventured.

"I sense that you are hiding something," he remarked, causing her to flinch.

Irida moistened her dry lips. "We all harbor our secrets, don't we?"

"I suppose," he replied, his piercing blue eyes locking onto hers. "Your sole responsibility was to lead Walter to the bank robbers. I assured you that I would handle the rest. That was our agreement."

She nodded. "That's correct. I fulfilled my part, so you should release me."

"Release you?" He smirked. "It's not that simple. First, you must answer some questions."

Irida shot him a weary look. "Questions? This is already the second mission you've assigned me, and I've done as you requested. Do you ever honor your promises?"

"Speaking of the first assignment." He narrowed his eyes at her as if trying to decipher her thoughts. "I instructed you to infiltrate the group of thieves planning to rob the bank. Your task was to facilitate their arrest and imprisonment. Everything you did was mutually beneficial, except for the part where you deceived me."

A shiver ran down her spine. It was true; Irida had become somewhat carried away during her first mission. Now, it appeared that leaving this room wouldn't be as simple as she had hoped. Irida longed to vanish, a possibility within her grasp thanks to her Gift. However, Harrison's imposing presence left her with no opportunity for escape.

"I could handcuff you," he warned, "preventing you from using your Invisibility."

Irida gulped, feeling as though he had just plucked the thoughts from her mind. "Are you... reading me?"

He nodded. "In a way. I'm an empath."

"Like a mind-reader?"

"It's a variation of that Gift," he patiently explained. "I can't visualize your thoughts or memories, but I can perceive your current emotional state."

"Oh, a weaker version then," she retorted, scowling at him in an attempt to wound his pride. From her experience, men despised it when their vulnerabilities were exposed. "It's like being blind, isn't it?"

Despite her attempt to provoke him, he remained unfazed. "Some people think so. However, I view it as a significant advantage. I can discern emotions without physical contact, even from a distance."

"Not a considerable distance, I assume."

"Twenty steps. Occasionally more, depending on the intensity of one's emotions," he explained, fixing her with a penetrating gaze. "And you are currently quite frightened."

Irida drew in a deep breath, steadying her racing pulse. "Perhaps it's due to your threats?"

"Just cooperate with me, and you'll be free to leave."

Irida nodded, willing to comply if it meant securing her release. "Alright. What do you wish to know?"

He took a step back, creating a more comfortable space between them, which helped Irida feel slightly more at ease. "It's about a thief we apprehended this morning. According to our interrogation, you stole something from him a week ago."

Irida rolled her eyes. "You mean his sister's diary that you instructed me to steal from him?"

An anger flickered in his eyes. "I mentioned it occurred a week ago, Irida. Why did you only deliver it to me last night?"

She swallowed. "I became preoccupied with preparing for the mission with Walter. How does that detail matter now?"

He continued to glare at her. "It matters because you withheld classified information for an entire week, and I strongly suspect you read it. Did you?"

She shook her head, hoping to persuade him otherwise.

"I can sense you're lying," he declared, dashing her hopes of escaping the confines of the room. "Now, I want to know how much you learned. I urge you to be truthful this time. Otherwise, I'll be forced to silence you."

She exhaled. She had nothing left to lose, so there was no reason to pretend any longer. "Silence me? Like you do with all the women you dispatch to Mercy House?"

"Exactly," he retorted. "I see you've acquainted yourself with the concept. It means that I can't release you at this juncture."

Irida took a deep breath before posing a question. "Will you... kill me?"

Captain Harrison chuckled. "Why would I do that? You may have violated the rules, Irida, but as I see, you prioritize your own interests over justice. Even upon discovering this perilous information, you intended to use it to manipulate me."

"I would rather say for self-protection."

He grinned. "Call it what you will. Fortunately for you, this knowledge has rendered you a valuable asset for one mission at Mercy House."

*Here we go.* She regarded him wearily. "And what do I get by agreeing to it?"

He paused, contemplating. "You will attain what you desire most: freedom."

She scoffed. "You mean returning to my former life on the streets?"

"Of course not. I refer to financial independence," he clarified, piquing her interest. "If you accept and successfully complete this mission, I'll compensate you generously. It will be enough to start a new life elsewhere."

"You mean... I'll have to depart from Middle Lake?"

"As far as I know, you have no ties keeping you here. Frankly, this place is a dump. Why not return to the Southern Kingdom? You could have a lovely seaside home, and if you grow bored, you could start helping the poor."

Irida furrowed her brow. "How much money are we talking about?"

"Plenty," he affirmed with a grin. "Irida, I want you to trust me, so I'll talk openly."

She nodded, ready to embrace the new opportunity.

"That bank robbery was orchestrated by me," he revealed.

"What?!"

"My associates carried out my orders. The robbery scheme proved lucrative, securing my financial future. So, it's time to utilize my savings. That's why I need your services. The item I need you to steal will facilitate a shift in my career, so I won't need to involve myself in such risky activities any longer."

*How intriguing! He, too, desires to quit thievery*, Irida noted with a smirk. "Very well," she agreed readily. "What's my role at Mercy House?"

"Not so fast. Before we proceed, you must demonstrate your loyalty."

"What do you mean?"

"I need your assistance in resolving a particular task," he explained. "As you can imagine, I've planned to end the bank robberies for some time now. The involvement of numerous people has endangered my reputation. Consider the criminal we apprehended today. His possession of that accursed diary suggests he was up to something."

Irida concurred. "He did appear to have a plan."

"Exactly. I suspect he may have been a double-agent or something of the sort. That's why I opted to conduct the interrogation personally, sidelining Walter. However, it's only a matter of time before my top detective gains access to him. We must ensure our suspect remains silent about the robbery scheme and the diary."

Irida regarded him with uncertainty. "I'm not a killer."

Captain Harrison let out a weary sigh. "I know that. Your task is to keep a close eye on him. Ensure that no one interacts with him before I orchestrate his departure from this world."

Irida pondered his words. "If, as you suggest, someone takes his life, how will you justify it?"

He grinned. "Our 'daring gang' may be able to bribe our personnel to gain access to him."

Irida sighed inwardly. "Well... Alright. Where is he located?"

"He's currently locked in the dungeons."

It made sense. "How can I ensure my safety? Won't your hired killer eliminate me as a witness?"

"And here comes your Gift of Invisibility," he remarked with a sly smile. "Use it to conceal yourself as soon as you notice a threat. Allow them to carry out their task, then pull the signal rope to alert the team for assistance."

"A rope?"

He nodded. "Yes, the rope that hangs from the ceiling for easy access. It serves as a signal to indicate any incidents in the dungeons, prompting the on-duty guards to respond."

"And how long am I expected to remain there?"

"Just give me a couple of hours."

Irida shrugged and wrapped her arms around herself, seeking warmth. Seating against the frigid basement wall was far from an enjoyable experience. Clad in a simple summer dress, she shivered in the cold. Her task was simply to monitor the dungeons, yet thus far, there had been no activity. Her time crystal glowed turquoise, indicating it was nearly five in the evening. Perhaps, she could take a brief stroll to alleviate the chill and kill some time.

Rising to her feet, she enveloped herself in her invisible shield. The dungeon cells and doors were constructed of copper, a metal that effectively contained any energy within. This design prevented the prisoners from utilizing their destructive magic to harm the guardians. Even without her invisible shield, Irida was safe, however, it was better not to draw attention to herself. She moved along the prison cells, observing the incarcerated. The men within their cells appeared either bored or despondent, lacking the motivation to resist or strive for freedom. Perhaps they conserved their energy for interactions with the anticipated arrival of the guardians.

The sound of footsteps echoed from the stairs, breaking the silence. Irida pressed herself against the wall, observing the unfolding scene. The newcomer was a guardian, likely a young cadet. He carried a large tray filled with bowls containing a brown substance that resembled shit. *Perhaps this is the prison's version of a meal,* Irida surmised.

"Dinner!" The guardian announced, prompting a stir of activity among the prisoners. As he distributed the bowls, the clinking of metal against the bars resonated, accompanied by the lively chatter of the inmates. Irida's stomach rumbled in hunger. *Hopefully, this surveillance duty will conclude soon.*

The thief Irida was tasked with monitoring was situated in the farthest cell, and the guardian approached it last. Irida followed quietly, keeping a close watch on both men.

"First time here?" the guardian inquired, placing a bowl on the floor for the suspect to retrieve.

"None of your business," the thief grumbled in response.

Glancing over his shoulder, the guardian produced a loaf of garlic bread from his pocket. The enticing aroma caused Irida's stomach to growl, prompting her to step back discreetly to avoid detection.

"I can see you're hungry," the guardian remarked softly. "Please, take this."

"Nice try. I don't accept gifts from strangers. So, buzz off."

The guardian shrugged, taking a bite of the bread.

This action seemed to affect the thief, who then reached his hand through the cell bars. "Alright, hand that over to me."

The guardian shrugged again and passed the bread to the thief.

Irida smiled. It was rare to witness a moment of kindness amidst the darkness of the dungeon. It offered a glimmer of hope that humanity might not be entirely lost. However, her optimism was short-lived as the young guardian suddenly began choking.

His hands flailed in the air, clawing at his throat as he struggled to breathe. Irida swiftly dispelled her invisible shield and rushed to his aid. The guardian's complexion rapidly shifted to a bluish hue as he gasped for air, his desperate attempts to draw breath growing more frantic.

"No!" Irida cried out, shaking him in a desperate attempt to help. Regrettably, his eyelids began to droop, and the light in his eyes dimmed.

Irida's gaze shifted to the prison cell. The thief's face was swollen and flushed. He was clutching his chest as he perspired profusely. The realization dawned on her – both men had consumed the poisoned bread loaf they had shared. It was a grim confirmation that Captain Harrison had fulfilled his promise – the witness of his crimes had been eliminated. However, the thought of the innocent young guardian facing the same fate was unbearable.

Shaking the guardian once more, she let out a piercing scream at the top of her lungs. "Fuck no!"

# 7

# Afterlife

"Welcome to our amenities!" Walter smiled cheerfully as they neared the back door of the Guardian House. As he had explained, Lana was some sort of his secret weapon – Walter didn't trust anyone in his team, so he led Lana directly to the dungeons to read the suspect. The heavy metal door squeaked open, and the smell of mold reached them. Lana wrinkled her nose.

Walter chuckled. "Sorry, princess. These are our best chambers."

"In Triville, they are just the same."

"Then you are quite used to it, huh?" He raised his hand, casting a Light ball – the simplest form of energy that mages sometimes used to light up their way in the dark. His Light had a lovely aquamarine color and shimmered with blue sparkles.

She gave him a small smile and stepped into the darkness of the corridor. "And still, I don't understand this," Lana said as they walked down the stone stairs. "Why don't you just give him some truthful potion?"

"Too risky. It might damage his brain."

She gave Walter a curious look. "I'm surprised you care so much about some culprit."

"I don't. It's all the paperwork followed by official use of this potion. It might delay the interrogation, and we can't afford to wait."

Lana nodded in understanding. At least, Walter was honest.

"The Captain personally interrogated him," Walter kept explaining, "but that culprit is a tough rock."

Lana frowned. "Did you guys torture him?"

He hesitated. "No. I mean that we tried to make a deal. You know, sometimes we give the arrestants softer prison terms if they agree to name the person they work for."

"And if they say 'no,' you beat the crap out of them," she remarked. "I used to work in such a place, so I know the truth."

"Well, we can't really cross certain limits," he explained, choosing his words carefully. "Plus, I hate such a cruel approach. I'm a guardian, not a gang member. I always try to work it out with minimal harm."

"How exactly?"

He gave her a playful look. "If my memory serves, I called you to read his mind."

*Right.* Lana breathed out. Something inside, her gut probably, told her that it was better not to dig too deep. After all, Walter seemed to be a decent man, and he meant only good. Also, it was her decision to help him with this investigation, so she must trust him now, as if she would rely on her partner if she were a guardian.

*A partner*, she savored this word. It felt incredible to return to her passion of solving mysteries. Just one last time. It was a perfect way to say goodbye to her childish dreams before returning to reality where everything was simple and predictable. And Oliver would be a part of it. Before leaving, Lana jotted down a short note explaining her brief visit to the Guardian House. She stuck it into her door, so Oliver would read it and wouldn't have to worry. Even though Lana had to postpone her plan to unleash his passion, it still might work...

"Here we go," Walter said, pulling her out of her daze.

They walked down the last stair and appeared in the long corridor with black walls. The air was humid and unwelcoming. The dungeons were just around the corner, as Lana could see from the reflection of the burning torches. Then, a desperate cry pierced the air. Without a second thought, Walter rushed around the corner, dropping his Light. The energy ball fell on the stone floor and burst into shards, like if it was made of glass. Lana ran after him.

The woman sat on the floor, cradling a guardian in her embrace. Tears streamed down her caramel cheeks, dropping on his lifeless face.

"Shit!" Walter grumbled as he passed them and pulled the rope hanging from the ceiling.

Lana gave him a puzzled look.

"I just called for assistance," he explained before switching his attention to the woman. "Would you mind explaining what the heck is happening here?"

She raised her glossy eyes at him. "A poison. I was... I was watching the suspect as the captain asked... Then he came, serving food... It happened so fast..." She sobbed, unable to form any more words.

Walter threw his glance at the abandoned empty tray. Then he turned to the dungeon cell and covered his mouth. Lana followed his gaze. The incarcerated man was on the floor of the dungeon cell, writhing in agony. Walter rushed to the cell, taking a key from his belt with his shaking hands. He almost dropped it before he managed to open the lock.

Lana ran inside and kneeled to the floor. The man's eyes were unfocused but not completely frozen. *Still alive. But for how long?*

"Sorry for bringing you here," Walter said. "He's useless now. That gang got to him, and they killed the guardian, too."

Lana stroked the prisoner's head. "It's not too late. I can still read his memories. Even after our heart stops beating, our mind can still live for several more minutes."

The woman walked inside. "Don't do that!"

Lana raised her eyes at her. "And who are you, by the way?"

"Irida," she said, frowning. "And I don't advise you to connect your energy with his. He's a dead man, and he can pull you with him if you attempt –"

"I'll take my chances." Without any further delay, Lana closed her eyes and focused. The voices around her got muffled as her consciousness connected with his.


The man stood on a pier, admiring the sunset. In white clothes and with his black hair accurately brushed, he didn't look like a criminal anymore. Just a human, a pure soul, getting ready to leave this world behind. Lana stepped closer and stood by his side.

"I saw you there." The man turned to her. "In the dungeon where I was dying. Are you some sort of an angel?"

Lana smiled at him. "You can call me that if you want. But I'm just a human. As well as you. My name is Lana."

"Timothy," he introduced himself. "Shit. I never believed I would experience my own death in such an odd way." He gave her an apologetic look. "Sorry for swearing. Just a bad habit. I do it if I'm nervous."

"It's okay, Timothy." Lana touched his shoulder, attempting to comfort him. "I'm here to help. I'll be around before you... depart to another dimension."

He shifted his eyes back to the sunset sky. The sea below took on a golden shade and now looked like melted jewelry. "What do you think awaits us there, over the horizon?"

Lana shrugged. "I suppose you'll simply join Divine Light and be at peace."

"I doubt that."

Lana gave him a reassuring look. "Why not? Yes, you might be a thief. But who cares now? I don't believe in the existence of hell or paradise. As I learned, hell is located right here, on earth. And it's run by greedy people who make our lives miserable."

"Can't argue with that." He ran his fingers through his hair, his eyes filled with anxiety. "But it's not what I meant. Lately, my life has been dedicated to one purpose. How can I depart now, knowing that I left things in disarray?"

The shadow fell on his face, and Lana looked up. The clouds, almost black, were covering the skies now. Soon, they would be in the dark, and she would lose her chance to gather the information she needed. She had better hurry up.

"I hear you, Timothy. Why don't you tell me your truth? I promise – I'll fulfill your mission once you reveal who arranged that robbery."

"It's all connected," Timothy said, taking Lana's hand. Then he waved his other hand, and their surroundings had changed.

They found themselves in the dead end of the city street. Perhaps, the place was a backyard of some night club. The garbage cans stunk nearby, surrounded by empty boxes filled with trash.

"Sorry. It's a terrible place to bring a girl," he joked.

Lana chuckled. "Agreed. Fortunately, it's not a date."

"True." He nodded at the door of the club that squeaked open. "Watch."

Now Lana could see Timothy again. This time, it was another version of him – an image from his own memory. That Timothy was a bit younger, and he walked out with a woman who wore a black cloak and a big hood. By the light wrinkles around her eyes, Lana could say she was around forty.

"Why can't you stay with me?" The younger Timothy asked.

"Because I must go back to my duty," the woman explained in a plain tone.

"Denise, you might stop punishing yourself for the things that you can't change –"

"This is exactly why I must go. Because I can change it. Maybe not for my own daughter, but for the other girls who perished there." She touched her chest, her teeth clenching in pain.

He held her elbow. "Are you alright?"

"Yes," she replied in a weak voice. "I just said too much." Then she gave him a small road bag. "Here. Please, keep it with you in a safe place."

He weighed the bag in his hand. "What's that?"

"Timothy, please just do it. I need you to trust me now."

"How can I trust you if you don't tell me anything?"

"I will. I promise." She licked her dry lips. "Just give me some time."

The rain became heavier, and the street went completely dark, so Lana had to come closer to be able to catch their talk.

"What secret can't you tell your own brother?" Timothy's younger version asked. "Are you in trouble? Someone is threatening you? If so, I swear, I'll do everything to protect you. Whatever it is."

She gave him a small smile. "I love you, Timothy. Now, I need to go."

"Just like that?"

She nodded. "I risked a lot by getting back to the city. And I need to return before sunrise."

A thunder deafened her, and Lana turned to Timothy who was in a form of spirit. "What was that about?"

"You asked to show you my truth, so here it is. That woman, Denise, is my sister. I mean, she was my sister," Timothy corrected himself. "She died of heart failure last year. Which was suspicious – Denise had never had any heart problems in her life! Since she passed, I've been restless, looking for the answers. One day, I decided to check that bag with her personal belongings, the one she had given me that night. All the time I was keeping it in my attic, following her request. On the bottom of that bag, there was a diary that she had written. I read it and I figured everything out. She worked in a secret facility, and the diary she gave me... It contained all the truth they hid from everyone!"

"Okay, okay... slow down." Lana waved her hand, trying to grasp the information he poured on her. It was too much for processing it all at once. Also, they had no time to waste, so she must make him focus. "How is that connected to that robbery?"

"I got into that gang to be able to earn their leader's trust. As I learned from Denise, all the guards serving at her workplace came from his referral. He is working in the Guardian House."

"You mean... the guardian is organizing those robberies?"

Timothy nodded. "Exactly. This place is rotten, Lana. I won't be surprised if Irida works for him as well. She was the one I trusted. She became close to me, and I told her about that diary. She stole it and most likely passed it to him, so here we are." Timothy spread his hands aside, exposing his vanishing body. "As you can see, she let me down. Never trust that woman."

The rain poured, and it was like they were caught in a waterfall. Timothy's body was almost translucent, so Lana clung to his sleeve not to lose him. "The robbery. How do they organize it?"

"Oh, that... It's a simple money laundering scheme. The chief of the bank lets the guards go on a break, then we come and collect money. We erase all the traces and share our cut in the end. As for the crimes my sister witnessed, it's nothing compared to that. Lana, you must stop them. You must go there."

The water roared, making her shout into his face. "Where?"

He leaned closer before saying his last two words. "Mercy... House."

*Mercy House?!* The mention of the facility where Oliver's sister was killed made her stop breathing. Her hands trembled, and she released Timothy from her grasp. All of a sudden, the sounds around were muffled, and the lights dimmed. Timothy appeared in front of her, his translucent body emitting a soft glow. He didn't speak, only smiled at her.

"Thank you, Timothy," Lana said. Even though she got more answers than questions, she had to get out of his mind. Otherwise, it would be too hard to return to her consciousness. "You did the right thing by showing me that. You can be at peace now."

He nodded at her and disappeared.


Lana got back to the dungeon cell. However, she found herself in a form of spirit. She stood in the corner, watching her own body from the side. *Am I dead?* She thought with alarm.

Apparently, she had just passed as well as Timothy. Her motionless body lay on the floor near to his, her face and hands morbidly pale. Walter and Irida were looming over. Lana neared them, hoping they would figure something out and bring her back until it was too late. *There must be a spell for it*, she told herself. *Or not?!*

Lana raised her eyes to the ceiling, pleading Divine not to take her away. It would be too unfortunate to depart without fulfilling her promise to Timothy. *I don't wanna die... Please, not today!*

"And why didn't you listen to me, silly?" Irida asked her dead body in a shaky voice. It was even cute that she was so worried about her. Not helpful, though.

Walter touched Lana's pale neck, probably looking for a pulse. Then he shook his head, tears welling in his eyes. "Damn it. She was so eager to help. I can't believe she couldn't make it..."

"Get off!" Irida yelled, pushing him away. She leaned to her body, and her mouth covered hers. Puzzled, Lana watched her blowing air into her lungs. Then, Irida pulled back and raised her clenched fist. Her hand landed on her chest, pulling Lana's spirit back to her body.

# 8

❦

# Unspoken Truth

Irida was in the kitchen, preparing hot drinks. It felt strange to be in Captain Harrison's house, but as he had explained after the incident in the dungeons, it was the only safe place for her and Lana. Irida wasn't sure if she wanted to spend any more time with this man; however, she now felt attached to that reckless blondie. After all, she could have died tonight!

The night had been stressful for both of them, which is why Irida volunteered to make some soothing tea. She opened a cabinet door to find some herbs. The Captain had a good collection for making various teas and potions – there was lavender, melissa, chamomile, and at least five more glass jars with dried leaves. She smiled and took some of them to prepare a calming tea. Then she placed the herbs in the kettle and put it on the stove.

The door to the living room was ajar, and Irida stepped closer, eavesdropping. Captain Harrison asked questions about the gang members, and Lana readily answered. Surprisingly, she was aware of the money laundering scheme behind the bank robbery. *She had managed to learn so much from Timothy's consciousness, Irida acknowl-*

edged. Then, another worrying thought crossed her mind – *what if Lana knows about Denise's diary and the secrets of Mercy House?*

The kettle's whistle pierced the air, making Irida flinch. She shivered and rushed to find a tray she could use to serve the tea. It was better to hurry up before Lana spilled the dangerous information. Knowing how easily the Captain got rid of any witnesses, it was better to watch Lana closely and not let her speak too much.

Irida walked into the spacious living room, carrying a tray with two steaming teacups. A fireplace crackled in the corner, making the air stuffy. Captain Harrison sat in a spacious chair near the fireplace, with Walter beside him. Lana was on the sofa, wrapping herself in a comforter. She had just finished talking about the mystery behind the bank robbery.

"How unfortunate," Captain Harrison said, shaking his head. "I can't believe someone from that gang works in our team! I swear, I'll do everything possible to find the rat and shut down these activities."

Irida gave him a dirty look. *What a cunning man!* If she hadn't heard Harrison's plan to close the robbery scheme, she would have believed his words.

"I'll do my best to help you, sir," Walter assured, looking at the Captain with admiration.

Irida shook her head and placed the tray on a coffee table before sitting in a corner of the sofa. Seeing that Lana didn't show any interest in the hot drinks, she handed her a cup of tea. "Here. Chamomile and lavender. It will help you feel better."

Lana took the cup and gave her a nervous smile. "Anything will taste better than death."

"Experiencing death is quite a unique journey," Irida remarked.

"True," Lana replied, lowering her voice. "I saw you kissing me, then hitting my chest. Then I awoke in my body. Is it some sort of magic ritual you performed on me?"

"It's called first aid," Walter said with a grin. "And watching it was fascinating."

Irida let out a weary sigh. She remembered how Walter had almost been in tears when he couldn't find Lana's pulse. He was like a child whose toy had been taken away!

Captain Harrison gave Walter an annoyed look. "Hold your horses. It's not the proper time or place to joke about it."

"Exactly," Irida agreed. "By the way, Captain, how is that guardian who was poisoned?"

"He survived," he grinned, making Irida shrink under his gaze. "All because of you. The doctors who arrived were surprised you stuck a tube into his airway. How did you know what to do?"

Irida shrugged. It was all a blur when the poisoning had occurred, but when Lana walked in and rushed to risk her life for the sake of finding the truth, it made her think clearly. Her gut instincts kicked in, and Irida remembered that potions like that caused severe throat spasms, preventing breathing. So, she took a feather pen from her pocket, broke it to make a tube, and inserted it into the guardian's neck. It wasn't too difficult. It felt natural, as it always did when she was practicing it in medical school. "Didn't I mention I was studying to become a doctor?" Irida asked.

All three shook their heads.

"What a drastic career change," Walter remarked in a sarcastic tone. "From a doctor to a thief."

"It wasn't my choice," Irida explained. "When I was taking my final exams, one of the professors flunk me intentionally. When I returned to reschedule the exam, he suggested that I please him so he would allow me to continue studying."

Lana gave her a worried look. "Did you file a complaint?"

"I did. Guess who they chose to keep – me or an experienced tutor?"

Lana said nothing, just shook her head in disappointment.

"My parents were upset, too," Irida continued. "They thought I was too stubborn. They said, 'It wouldn't have hurt to do what he asked, but now all the money we paid for your education is wasted.'"

Lana gave her a compassionate look. "I'm so sorry it happened to you."

Irida sighed. "In the beginning, when my parents disowned me, I had to live on the streets and survive. Thanks to my Gift, I managed to evade capture for so long."

Captain Harrison shifted in his chair, appearing uncomfortable with the conversation topic, though Irida seriously doubted it. "You did the right thing, Irida. You don't have to please anyone. But if it ended so badly for you, why weren't you more insistent on seeking justice for that professor?"

"Back then, I was too scared of his threats," Irida explained. "And now it's too late for that."

"Unfortunately, this is the world we live in," Lana said, giving the captain a sad look. "Often, there is no way for a woman to get what she wants unless through someone's bed."

"And how do you cope with that?" Captain Harrison asked.

"I got used to it. I learned to lower my expectations, so I don't aim high, and everyone is happy."

"Are you happy?"

Lana shrugged. "I'm fine. After all, I don't need much in life. I came to terms with being an architect designer and even settled for marriage."

Irida frowned. Something seemed off about Lana tonight. Before the mind-reading session, she had been full of energy, but now she appeared to have given up on life. Maybe it was just tiredness?

Lana turned to her. "Today you saved me. And that young guardian. Thank you for that."

"You're welcome," Irida replied with a smile.

"Yes, Irida is the hero of the day," Captain Harrison chimed in. "The guardian is still weak and doesn't remember where he got that poisoned bread loaf, but tomorrow I'll talk to him again."

Irida nodded. She could only hope that it was true and that the guardian had indeed forgotten where he got the poisoned bread. Otherwise, he was as good as dead. The same fate awaited Lana if she mentioned knowing more than she should. Irida did her best to change the topic and distract them with her life story, but now it was time to send Lana away.

"Speaking of tomorrow," Irida said, twisting her empty tea cup in her hands. "I guess we all have a lot of important things to do. Why don't we call it a day?"

"I'm fine with that," Captain Harrison said. "But Irida, you need to stay here tonight."

She frowned. "Is it really necessary?"

"Yes. I asked my maid to prepare a guest room for you," he replied in a possessive tone. "In case you've forgotten, you are departing to Mercy House tomorrow."

"Where?!" Lana asked. It came out a bit loudly, causing everyone to turn to her.

"Mercy House. Is there any problem?" Captain Harrison asked, his eyes piercing her.

Irida shifted her eyes to Lana and subtly shook her head, silently pleading with her. *Please, don't tell him anything. Please.* The heat from the fireplace had become almost unbearable, and Irida could feel her cheeks burning.

Lana glanced at her with worry and slowly turned to the captain. "Nothing to worry about. I just heard that there are nuns serving in that facility. And Irida looks too..."

"Too what?" Irida asked, feigning offense. It was better to play this card and cause a scene. Yes, she might appear as an overreacting woman, but it was better than allowing Lana to say something suspicious and potentially become another victim who 'knew too much.' "Are you suggesting that I look like a whore?" Irida challenged. "Just because I was almost assaulted by my professor?"

"No, you've got it all wrong," Lana said, pressing her hands to her chest. "I didn't mean that! I was trying to say that you're too pretty to be a nun."

"A liar!" Irida stood up and stomped her foot, leaving the men speechless. "Fine, you all can stay here and continue to belittle me because I shared something deeply personal! I didn't expect any better from you." With that, she pressed her palms to her burning cheeks and rushed out of the living room. In the kitchen, she stopped, pressing her back against the wall.

The fireplace crackled, blending with their voices.

"What the hell was that?" Walter asked in a hushed tone.

"Just let her be," Lana said. "We all have our traumas, and I guess hers just started bleeding."

"Then why did she share it in the first place?" Walter continued to question. "If she was still so emotional about it?"

"Who the hell knows," Captain Harrison said with annoyance in his voice. "I swear, I'll never understand women." The chair squeaked, indicating he had stood up. "Anyhow, this day is taking its toll on us. Mills, please, escort Miss Morris to her quarters."

"Yes, sir," Walter affirmed.

"And as for you, Miss Morris," the captain continued, "sorry again about that incident in the dungeons. None of us expected you would jump into his memories like that. I hope you'll have a good rest and forget about what happened."

"And what if I can't forget?" Lana asked.

"Then, if you have anything to discuss, you can always find me here. Or in the Guardian House," the captain said in a syrupy voice, which made Irida cringe.

As the guests walked towards the exit doors, Irida exhaled a sigh of relief. Today, Lana was safe. Of course, it would be tomorrow... but tomorrow Irida would be away, which meant Lana's safety must stop being her concern.

# 9

# A Leverage

"I hope you'll feel comfortable," the maid said, smoothing the bedsheets. She was a nice woman with nicely pinned gray hair and a snow-white apron.

"As comfortable as I can," Irida replied, shuffling her feet at the threshold. Her guest bedroom was spacious but there was nothing cozy about it – just a simple bed, a nightstand, and a small window with dark-gray blinds. "Do you live here, in this house?"

"No, I live across the street," the maid said with a nonchalant smile.

*Shit.* Irida was about to stay alone with Captain Harrison. It didn't bode well. "How many people live in this house?"

"The captain, his wife, and their son," she revealed. "They are away now, but they must be back next week."

"Harrison has a son?!"

The maid nodded. "Howard. He is thirteen years old, and he dreams of becoming a guardian. Just like his father."

*Hopefully, he won't become such a monster,* Irida thought.

"Don't worry, we have guards," the maid added, seeing her uneasiness. She pointed somewhere in the corner, "This man will be here, protecting you."

Irida turned her head and flinched as she realized there was a man standing in the corner. Apparently, he was there the whole time of their small talk. No wonder she never noticed him – he was like a silent statue, all in black, a hat shading his face. She swallowed. "Excuse me, will you stay here all night?"

Without giving any reply, he turned and walked to the other door, making his exit. *What a creep!*

The maid snickered. "They have orders not to talk to any guests, so don't take it personally. But I can assure you – he got it. He will be just out of the door."

"Great," Irida remarked sarcastically.

When the maid left, Irida sat on the bed and hugged herself. Only the glow of a red time crystal on the side table illuminated the space. It was midnight, but despite her tiredness, Irida couldn't make herself undress and get to bed.

*I must find leverage against the captain*, Irida thought. As Irida had learned from the maid, the captain's son dreamed of following his father's steps. *If he wants to have a guardian career, his father's sins might ruin his life*, Irida thought, rubbing her hands together. Well, it was something she could work with in case things go awry.

The door squeaked open, and Captain Harrison walked in. "I see you are in a cheerful mood. How fast everything changes!"

Irida gave him a weary look. "In case you didn't get it, I'm not sleeping my way through. If you want to keep working with me, keep your pants on."

His expression turned hesitant. "I'm not here for this!"

She exhaled a sigh of relief. "Okay, then. What's up?"

"It's about that girl. Lana."

*She definitely knows more than she told you*, Irida thought with worry. "What about her?"

He grinned and started pacing the room, like a shark circling its prey. "I first believed it when you pulled that drama and left. But then I thought, what the heck? You knew I was trying to make her speak in case she learned something from that dead thief. You also knew I could sense her lying. So, right after she almost started speaking, you hit my senses with a whirlpool of emotions, blinding me."

Irida swallowed. Captain Harrison was definitely a rotten person, but he had extraordinary detective skills. There was no reason to play games and lie to him. "I just hate that you kill everyone who crosses you."

"You're still alive," he pointed out.

*Yes, but for how long?* "I'm still alive because you need me for another mission. I'm pretty sure you'll get rid of me as soon as you're done with my services."

He gave her an offended look. If Irida didn't know him so well, she would probably buy it. "What makes you think so? I always keep my word."

*Yeah, except for the Guardian Oath when you swore to protect people from evil.* She looked him in the eye. "I'm pretty sure Lana didn't see much. After all, she wasn't in the suspect's mind for too long. And even if she caught a glimpse of something, will you kill her? The same way you almost killed that young guardian?"

He exhaled an irritated sigh. "I didn't want to kill him."

"Ah, that's why he is in the hospital now. Oh, wait... it was me who saved his life. Otherwise, he would be dead."

He raised his hand protectively. "Stop this farce! Here is what happened – I was at the dungeon entrance, waiting for the guy who was about to serve dinner. We had a small talk, and I took a bread loaf from my inner pocket. I advised him to give this bread to the new prisoner to cheer him up a bit. That guardian was new, naive, and he was supposed to see it as an act of kindness! Who knew he would bite it himself?!"

"*You* knew! As you said, he was naive, and he really wanted to do a good thing. If you warned him about the deadly poison, he would never eat it!"

The captain scratched his chin, a mischievous smile playing on his face. "True. On the other hand, I was going to issue a reprimand because he gave the prisoner unchecked food. He was supposed to be scared of firing and never raise questions."

"What if Walter talks to him and learns it was your deed?" Irida questioned. "As I'm aware of, he has no idea what you pull behind his back."

The captain waved his hand dismissively. "Don't worry about that. That young guardian was given a forgetful potion, and he really doesn't remember what happened."

Irida nodded somberly. The fact that the captain shared so much about his crimes only meant that he never intended to leave her alive. By speaking so frankly, he claimed his dominance, pointing out that Irida was only a pawn in his perverted game. Well, then... she could let him think so. At least, for now. "Let's get to our business already. What do you want me to do next?"

"I like your professionalism," he said with a grin. Then he walked to the side table and ran his finger along the time crystal. "You know what people say? Time is money."

"Yes, I know," Irida replied. "And honestly, I feel exhausted, so let's wrap it up."

"Fine. Tomorrow, you'll head to Mercy House and pretend to be one of the aspiring Sisters. Your experience in medical school will look good along with my recommendation letter, so the Sorority will welcome you."

"I got that part already."

"Good. So, when you blend in, I'll need you to find *The Book of Life*."

"The book of what?"

He smiled at her. "It's the name of the classified manuscript. That's all you need to know to accomplish your mission."

She nodded. Well, stealing a book shouldn't be a problem. After all, she was quite skilled after so many years of practice. "Anything else I must know?"

"You have two weeks. Then I'll get you out of there."

She frowned. "I don't need that much time –"

"It's better to be safe than sorry. So, you have two weeks to do it on your own. After that, I'll send my person to meet you. Also, in case you fail, he will push things."

Irida looked at his face attentively, but he didn't crack a smile. "Are you serious? Who else can get there except for women like me?"

He smiled mysteriously. "Don't worry, I have my ways. And as I said, time is money, Irida. I recommend you to focus on your task, and don't waste it."

**10**

# Unwalked Path

They were walking along the night alley, the tree trunks around glowing mint-green. Lana's thoughts were far away from admiring the nature. Tonight, when she had spoken to Captain Harrison, Lana said that she had come to terms with her profession and her upcoming marriage. It was a lie. Frankly speaking, after everything she had gone through, including her own death experience, it was unimaginable to go back to her previous life.

*How could I be so oblivious?* Lana thought. All these little observations about Mercy Houses that she had been ignoring until now popped up, making it clear that something creepy was happening there. Starting from her childhood, when all the school girls had been taught to be obedient and shamed for having 'the wrong Gift,' to the suspicious death of Mia, Oliver's sister.

It wasn't too often for a young woman to receive a destructive Gift, though. As Lana could remember, in Triville, it had only happened three times during her life there. However, none of those girls had returned home.

There were multiple 'happy cases,' of course – sometimes, the girls had difficulty controlling their Telekinesis power, which was one of the most common Gifts among all the mages and wasn't considered as 'destructive.' According to the protocol, those girls were sent to Mercy Houses. Usually, they returned in a few weeks, but none of them liked talking about it. Lana considered their experience to be something deeply personal, so she never asked or questioned the order of things. Not until now.

Now, she was ready to head to the nearest Mercy House and dig for the truth. However, there was one problem – how to get there? Lana doubted there was a standard job application for prospective Mercy Sisters. Although, she might try to get there using Oliver's knowledge of the location. After all, he had managed to get in somehow, which meant there was a chance of breaking through those walls.

"I'm glad you stayed alive," Walter said, breaking her train of thought.

Lana gave him a small smile. "Me too. Thanks to your girlfriend."

"Irida?" He chuckled. "She isn't my girlfriend."

She gave him a curious look. "Who the hell is she, then?"

He chuckled. "Now you sound jealous."

Lana turned away, her cheeks blushing. Honestly, she was jealous, but it wasn't about Walter. Irida was heading to Mercy House tomorrow, as the Captain had mentioned. And Lana only had a weak hope to get there.

"Lana?" Walter's voice pulled her back to reality. "Please say something. Otherwise, I'll keep thinking you are jealous."

"Why would I? In case you forgot, I have a fiancé." Technically, Oliver wasn't her fiancé, but this word sounded more persuasive than 'a guy who gave me the diamond ring, so I promised not to cheat on him.'

"Yeah, that guy. The one who... never mind."

She frowned. "Please, finish your thought. What did you want to say?"

He gave her an apologetic look. "You just seem to be a bit neglected in this relationship."

"That's about right," she agreed, thinking of Oliver, who had pushed her away after their kiss. "But it's none of your business."

"I just wanted to say that you deserve a man who can treat you better."

Lana smiled at him. Walter was a handsome guy, and she truly enjoyed his flirtations. However, it was possible that his affections were only an attempt to make her speak about her findings in late Timothy's head.

Lana had never mentioned anything besides the robbery during her talk with Captain Harrison. Even though she sympathized with that man, she simply couldn't speak openly when Irida was in the same room, watching her every move. As late Timothy had warned her, Lana couldn't trust that woman. And as far as she knew, Walter worked with Irida at the time of the arrest, so they both might be in cahoots with the criminals.

Lana shook her head. No, it wasn't likely that both Irida and Walter were working with that gang. Walter worked too hard to resolve that robbery case. He even risked his career by bringing Lana to the Guardian House dungeons and letting her read the man who knew way too many secrets. Did it mean that Lana could trust Walter? She didn't know for sure, but fortunately, she could use her Mind-Reading Gift to check it.

Lana moved closer and playfully touched his shoulder, trying to look nonchalant. If Walter was a criminal, she would learn everything right now. She focused and pulled her energy to connect with his consciousness. However, her attempt wasn't successful – her head hurt, and a wave of dizziness washed over her. Lana had to pull her hand away before she fainted.

"What?" Walter looked at her inquisitively.

Her heart pounded. Perhaps, after today's events, her ability to read minds was impaired. And now, she was about to be caught in an attempt to read him. "I...I just wanted to thank you," she managed to say. "For trusting me and taking me on this mission."

To her relief, Walter wasn't suspicious about her awkward behavior; he simply misread her gesture as an invitation to make a move. He leaned closer and kissed her lips.

Kissing him was pleasant, more than Lana might have expected. His touch spread goosebumps over her skin, making her blood boil. Being without a man's touch for so long, she realized how much she craved it – to be wanted. Her hands gripped his neck as the passion grew deeper. As Lana bit his lower lip, he placed his hands on her shoulders and stepped away.

His breath was ragged. "It was... the best way... to say 'thank you.'"

Lana gave him a mischievous smile. "Sorry. Just got carried away a bit."

He ran his fingers through his messy hair, his eyes attractively gleaming in the moonlight. "I think I shall go now."

Lana glanced back at the dorm building. Walter had a point – it was time to get back to her room and brainstorm her idea about breaking into Mercy House. Also, she had to sort things out with Oliver. If he reconsidered his views on their relationship, it meant they might have a chance as a couple. It would be great to have his support while she was on her dangerous mission. And as for the kiss with Walter, it clearly was a mistake. Lana was just too wound up to think clearly once his lips crushed on hers.

"Unless you want me to come with you," Walter suggested out of the blue.

Lana gave him a sad look. "I wish I could do that. But I can't."

"Right. Engagement and everything."

She nodded.

He sighed. "Good night, then."

"Good night, Walter."

She watched him disappear among the glowing trees, then turned and walked back to her room.

The letter she had written to Oliver was still stuck in her doorway, just as Lana had left it before departing with Walter. She pulled it out and crumpled the paper in her hand, gritting her teeth. All her efforts were in vain because Oliver had never even shown up at her doorstep. Apparently, her hopes were foolish.

Lana walked inside her dark room and slid to the floor, hugging her shoulders. *Who am I kidding?* Deep inside, she always knew Oliver would never become the man she could love. Yes, he was a nice, supportive friend. His honesty was a rare trait among all the people she had ever met, and Lana truly appreciated it, especially after being in a relationship built on a lie.

On the other hand, Oliver was never too decisive, and he would never be as passionate as Walter, the guardian she had just met. Apparently, Lana wasn't too lucky in her personal life, and she could do nothing to change it. Again, she was on her own, in complete darkness, and she had no idea how she might carry out her reckless plan on her own.

The door to her room flew open, and someone rushed inside. The steps of heavy boots echoed in her ears. Lana lurked against the wall, afraid to make any sound.

"Lana?" Walter called out. Probably, he had difficulty seeing her in the dark after the brightness of the well-lit corridor. "Are you here?"

She raised her eyes to him. His face, lit up with moonlight, was anxious. It was the second time she had seen his despair. The first was in the dungeons when he thought she had died. Lana rose to her feet so he could see her. "What happened, Walter?"

He breathed out. "I thought they got you."

"Who?" she asked, completely puzzled.

"The gang," he explained. "In the street, I saw a suspicious carriage heading to the dorms."

Lana revealed a smile, trying to calm him. "Please, don't be paranoid. Why would anyone want to get to me?"

"Because those people saw your face. It just occurred to me – they might try to find you and question you in case you learned something from that dead suspect."

"That coachman who escaped only saw me throwing a Paralysing spell. No one knew I was going to read that man, Timothy. Unless you told anyone."

He shook his head.

"See? Nothing to worry about," she reassured him.

He visibly relaxed. "Fine."

Lana breathed out. It was heartwarming that Walter was worrying about her so much. Perhaps it was all the worries she had experienced that day, or maybe her state of upset about Oliver, but her tongue moved faster than her mind. "If you are that concerned, you can stay in my room tonight. To make sure I'm safe."

He looked hesitant. "Thanks, but no. I don't want to tempt my-self."

"Why not?"

He gave her a sad look. "You're engaged."

She shook her head. "Not anymore."

He knitted his eyebrows. "Just like that?"

"Technically, it wasn't even engagement. Just a fancy proposi-tion of dating that never worked. He pushed me away after I at-tempted to kiss him, and he clearly doesn't want me. You were right – I can't be with a man who treats me so coldly." Lana brought her lips to his ear, her voice lowering to a whisper. "Just one-night stay. You won't regret it."

His eyes gleamed. Then, his hands wrapped her waist, making her forget about everything else. The flame of forbidden desire, like a wildfire, enveloped them both. Kissing her neck, Walter rushed to open her shirt, tearing the buttons off. Like pieces of charcoal, they fell on the floor with a muffled sound.

"Sweet," he whispered under his breath, as he discovered she wore the same red bra that he had already seen on her.

Lana laughed and pushed him on the bed. Surrounded by the torn rose petals, Walter looked enjoyable. She opened his belt and pulled his pants off. She took a moment, enjoying his heat, and his strength. Then she climbed on top of him.

His kisses were wild, and his movements confident. Like a de-stroying force of nature, he was inescapable, and she submitted to his power. All she wanted was to burn into the night together with him. Not to see the sunrise and not to get back into the gloomy reality.

**11**

# Betrayal

Lana opened her eyes to the room lit up by the bright daylight. She blinked. Someone was knocking on her door with the dedication of a woodpecker. *What the hell do they want?* She thought, placing a pillow on her head. *Whatever. They won't be knocking forever.*

Lana closed her eyes, trying to pull herself back into her dream. As her foggy mind could recollect, she was dreaming of something exciting. Lana turned on her side, and her hand landed on a man's body. *Walter.* She sat up, rubbing her temples. *Then, it wasn't a dream,* she finally realized. *We really spent the night together.*

The knock on the door repeated, and Lana moved her gaze to her nightstand. The time crystal glowed pale pink, indicating it was ten in the morning. *Crap.*

Oliver's voice from behind the door made her heart skip a beat. "Lana, I know you are here. Wake up!"

She held her breath, hoping he would leave them alone. Half asleep, Walter turned on his back. "Who the heck is that?"

Her voice went to a whisper. "Hush. There is no one. Just sleep."

Walter obediently closed his eyes.

Oliver, on the contrary, wasn't going to give up without an effort. "Oh, right," he said, "there is a key under the doormat."

Her heart raced. Not that Lana had lied about breaking up with him. Last night, this decision seemed clear and logical. However, if she was supposed to break Oliver's heart, the last thing she wanted was to traumatize him like that. Lana grabbed a bedsheet and rushed to the door, wrapping it around herself and stumbling on her way. She was just in time when the key turned in the door lock. She placed her hand on the door, catching it before it opened too widely and revealed a naked man in her room.

Oliver gave her a puzzled look. "What's going on?"

Lana did her best to speak nonchalantly. "Nothing. You just woke me up."

"I mean..." He swallowed. "Did you see yourself?"

Lana took a step back and glanced in the tall wall mirror. The woman reflecting in it was wrapped in a wrinkled creamy bedsheet, with traces of red rose petals all over it. Her face was puffy, and her hair messy. *It won't be easy to explain myself*, she concluded. Fortunately, Lana knew one tactic that might work. The best defense was an offense.

Lana stepped into the corridor and closed the door behind her. "You didn't come to my room last night! And I was waiting for you. Like a fool."

"What are you talking about?" He frowned. "I came, but you were gone. So I left you a message."

Lana shook her head. "No. It was me who left a letter stuck in the door frame. You never even opened it."

"I did. Underneath your message about your departure to the Guardian House, I wrote that I would come in the morning, so you could have a good rest after your mission."

Lana stopped breathing, wishing only one thing – to disappear. Or to open her eyes and realize it was just a bad dream. She blinked forcefully, but she was still experiencing a harsh reality.

"Don't get so upset," Oliver reassured her in his usual calming tone. "It's just a little misunderstanding. I put the letter back in the same way, so you probably thought I never opened it."

Her voice seemed to belong to someone else. "That's exactly what I thought."

He laughed. "That's alright, just a little misunderstanding. Let's go check our final marks. They must be posted in the hallroom."

"I'll need... A minute."

"Of course. I'll wait here."

Lana bit her lip hard. *Oliver wasn't that cold to me. He just needed a bit more time.* If Lana were more patient last night, she would have read that damn letter. Unfortunately, she chose to give up on him and welcomed Walter into her bed. The night with that guardian was a terrible mistake that she must erase.

Lana gave him a sheepish smile. "There is no need to wait for me. Just go down to the hall and grab us some coffee. I'll meet you there in ten."

"Do you hide anything from me?" He was likely joking, but it made her heart sink.

"No."

Then the metal clunked behind the closed door, making them both flinch.

"What's that?" Oliver asked.

"Erm... A wind?" she suggested.

"I thought you're alone." Not giving Lana any chance to find a reasonable explanation, he pushed the door and stepped into her bedroom. As the door opened widely, Lana could see Walter. Shamelessly stunning with his naked torso, he was pulling his pants on. It was his handcuffs that fell off on the floor. Now they rested by his bare feet, shining in the bright sun rays. Seeing Oliver, Walter gave him a smile. "Morning."

Speechless, Oliver turned to Lana, his face pale.

"I can explain," she mumbled.

"There is no need. I got it." Oliver turned and rushed to the stairs.

Lana hurried to her closet. Her shaking hands shifted the hangers with her blouses. Finally, she found a dress that didn't have any stupid laces and buttons. She pulled it on and turned to Walter.

He sat on the bed, buttoning his shirt. "You could tell him you feel uncomfortable talking to him undressed. He wouldn't ask too many questions, then."

*And why do all the epiphanies occur to people after the tragedy?* She gave him a weary look. "Please, go home."

Walter put his right boot on and grinned. "So, you just took advantage of me last night and now ask me to get out?"

Lana pulled on her ballerina shoes and opened the door. She didn't have time to argue with him. "Seriously, disappear." Without any further delay, she ran outside.

Oliver was in the street, standing in the shade of a willow tree. Lana stepped nearby in silence. *Are there any words to make him forgive me?* She doubted it. After everything Oliver had seen in her room, it broke his heart. If only Lana knew how to help him heal after it. In her previous relationship, she couldn't forgive a man who betrayed her, but in fact, she wasn't any better. Maybe she was even worse, and she hated it.

Oliver turned to Lana, tears welling in his hazel eyes. "Unbelievable. It's been a few days since you started wearing the promise ring, and you brought a stranger into your bed."

Her heart beat in her stomach. "I'm so sorry..."

"By the way, where is the ring?"

Lana averted her eyes, unable to come up with a proper reply. The ring was where she left it yesterday – under the bed. The same bed where she and Walter.... *Shit.* She wished the ground would swallow her now.

He shook his head. "I have only one question. Why?"

Lana shrugged. "I don't know. I thought you abandoned me, and I was mad at you. Honestly, I was seriously thinking of breaking up when Walter showed up on my doorstep. It was just a mistake." She took a step towards him, and he stepped back.

"Just a mistake?" He narrowed his eyes. "Am I supposed to forgive you now? Especially after you were 'seriously thinking of breaking up' with me?"

She gave him a pleading look. Oliver was religious, and she could try approaching from this side. "Isn't it what *The Book of Wisdom* teaches us? To be merciful to the ones who made mistakes?"

"You must be kidding me. Even if you read that book, Lana, you learned nothing from it." He gave her a despising look. "How didn't I see it before?"

She winced. "What do you mean?"

"I thought you were different, Lana. But you are just like others – selfish and miserable. You always complain about your life, but you are the one who ruins it."

"Why don't you try to understand me? To see my perspective?"

He shook his head. "It's you who doesn't want to see another perspective. And probably you never will."

The tears welled in her eyes. "What about our connection?"

He shook his head. "If you cheat on a person, you break the connection. And let's be honest, you never loved me."

"Maybe I could fall in love with you. I just needed more time –"

"There is no time." He cut her off. "It's all over now."

"Oliver, please. Don't do that!"

"You can keep your ring," he said coldly. "Maybe it would give you some sanity when you're about to make another mistake like that." Then he turned and walked away.

Lana watched his blurred silhouette through the wall of tears until he disappeared into the dorm building. She kneeled on the grass and dropped her face into her palms. *Is it really over?*

Her shoulders shivered as she cried. Lana couldn't believe she was so stupid to screw up like that. During this year, she managed to build a real connection with this man, and it took her just one night to ruin it. She had nothing left but that ring, which would be a silent reminder of her stupidity. And she had no idea how to fix it.

# 12

# Burning the Bridges

When Lana had cried all her tears, she stood up. Walter stood by the tree, looking at her with pity. He held a paper cup of steaming coffee with the local cafeteria logo on it. He handed her a paper napkin, and Lana wiped her nose.

Her voice was weak. "Why are you still here?"

"Listen, I'm sorry you lost your boyfriend –"

"Fiancé-to-be," she corrected him.

He gave her a weary look. "What difference does it make now? Anyways, you two broke up."

She crumpled her napkin, ready to break into tears again.

"Listen, I'm very sorry." Walter handed her a cup of coffee, and Lana took it with both hands. The warm drink calmed her, and the caffeine helped her stop shivering.

"I didn't mean to hurt you," he added quietly.

"And I didn't mean to hurt Oliver. I was mad at him last night and had to read that letter instead of..." she sobbed. She had no idea if Oliver would ever forgive her.

"I know. It was hard for both of you." He hugged her, letting her moisten his shirt before calming down in his embrace. "I probably shouldn't have come to see you last night."

She raised her eyes at him. "You just came to check on me."

"Not only. I mean... I was supposed to refuse your proposition of a one-night stay because I knew that you were in a serious relationship. But I didn't do that."

"It was all my fault," Lana exhaled a sigh. "Last night was a mistake. I hope we can leave it behind."

"Of course." He nodded. "Are we good now?"

"Yes." She gave him a small smile. "Just out of curiosity, why do you care so much about me? We barely know each other."

"Because I can't just leave knowing that I ruined something important. If you want, I can help fix that. I can talk to Oliver and say I slept on the floor –"

"There is no need. He already knows the truth."

"Are you sure there is nothing I can do for you?"

Her heartbeat quickened. There was one thing she couldn't stop thinking about – how to help late Timothy find justice for his sister and to stop whatever was happening in Mercy House. Since her original plan with Oliver went awry, Walter had become her last chance to get there. Last night, Lana was too exhausted to read him to find the answers, but now she could give it a try.

Lana closed her eyes, focusing on their touch. Fortunately, he still held her elbow. The images flashed before her sight. It seemed like Walter was a fine guardian with no connection to those criminals who robbed the banks. Lana tried to find any significant memories about Mercy House, and she caught the one where Walter was talking to the Captain last evening. It was just before Lana and Irida had arrived at his house. Walter questioned the purpose of sending Irida to Mercy House, and the Captain had a good reply. Now, Lana got an idea of how she could arrange her departure to that place.

She opened her eyes and smiled at him. "I want to ask you about one thing, if you don't mind."

"I'm listening."

"I want to be sent to Mercy House. As a member of the Sorority."

He gave her a puzzled look. "Why there? It's the worst place to spend your summer break."

Lana paused. She wasn't a good liar, but she hoped Walter would be convinced. "When I walked outside after Oliver, I saw a suspicious black carriage. It's not just a coincidence that you saw a carriage last night. I'm afraid someone is really spying on me."

"Are you sure?" He looked at the dorm's entrance, probably trying to spot the carriage Lana was talking about. The yard was empty of any transport.

"They were gone as soon as they saw me," Lana said, mustering a frightened look. "I'm afraid they could come back at any moment."

He sighed. "I believe you. Actually, it makes sense. Last night we learned that there is a rat in the Guardian House. They might figure out that you read that guy and that you are a student. They might abduct you to interrogate. Or even kill you."

A cold shiver ran down her spine. The way he described things made her believe in her own lie.

Walter placed his hand on her shoulder. "You're a witness in this investigation, and it's my job to protect you now. I'll talk to the captain as he's running a witness protection program. Tonight, you'll go to a safe place."

*A safe place?* This was not what she had aimed for. "Please, Walter. I know why you're sending Irida to Mercy House. This *is* your witness protection program."

He narrowed his eyes at her. "How do you know that?"

Lana shrugged. The truth was that this is what Captain Harrison had told Walter, and she had read about it in his memories. "Irida told me," she lied.

"Honestly, we sent Irida there because of her criminal past. It's like a prison, with strict discipline and terrible food. You'll hate it there."

*A prison with multiple secrets.* "I want it. With my Gift, I can help all those girls to tame their powers. Wouldn't it be nice?"

"What about your classes? You're in the middle of your study program."

Lana gave him a reassuring look. "It's not a problem. I'll take a summer break, then return to my studies when the dust settles. In the fall. It will be alright, I promise."

He frowned and glanced at his time crystal. Its shade turned dark-pink as they were talking, indicating it was already eleven in the morning. "In that case, we can't delay your departure for too long. The carriage will be at the dorm's entrance by noon. I'll quickly visit Harrison to arrange that, then get back right away. I'll watch the entrance doors and make sure you're safe."

"Like a scarecrow?" She joked.

His face remained serious. "Exactly."

Lana nodded. If she had an hour, she must use this time wisely.

How much can one person accomplish within one hour? As it turned out, quite a lot. Firstly, Lana walked back into her room and washed her face to remove the salty tears. Then, she brushed her hair. After that, she retrieved Oliver's ring from the dusty corner and cleaned it. The memory of their breakup made her heart ache. *Will he ever forgive me?*

Even though Lana hated the idea of leaving him in such a terrible state, it seemed she had no choice. She was embarking on a dangerous mission, which meant she might inadvertently put Oliver at risk if the gang members showed up in the dorms. The least she could do for Oliver was to return his ring. Perhaps, she could leave it with the curator along with the application for her academic leave.

Lana gathered her favorite clothes, all of which fit into her small road bag. Then she left her room. Uncertain of how long she would be gone, or if she would ever return, her heart filled with sorrow. It was even more difficult than leaving her hometown. Despite all the mistakes she had made the previous year, Lana had been striving to build her life as an adult. Sadly, she had failed at that too.

The hall was empty – most students had already left for summer break, and Lana had to pretend she was doing the same. She approached the board to glance at her final marks. She only wanted to ensure that Oliver had achieved enough scores to receive his desired scholarship. However, once her eyes landed on *The List of The Best Students*, she froze.

Lana had never been a diligent student, nor had she ever been among the top performers, but somehow her name was third on the list. *Third.* It meant she had secured a guaranteed scholarship to study for free the following year. Her gaze slid down, and she saw Oliver's name just below hers. "No fucking way!"

Someone chuckled nearby. "I know, right? Who knew you would beat Oliver!"

She turned to the student from her math class. It was a tall guy with long raven hair, his hands always marked with charcoal from the pencils he used for sketches. Seeing her serious expression, he stopped smiling. "Oh, it's probably not good for your relationship. But it's impressive!"

Lana rubbed her forehead. "It's not fair!"

"Why? You wanted to be the first?" He grinned. "Nope. That's my spot."

She pointed at the board. "I mean that Oliver won't get the scholarship he deserved. Damn, he worked his butt off to get a good mark! What the heck is wrong with this world?"

He shrugged. "Nothing's wrong. The scholarship always goes to the top three students."

"How could this even happen? I couldn't beat Oliver on any of the exams. It must be a mistake!"

"There is no mistake, Lana. Your assignment for recruiting the students was a huge success. Yesterday, we received ten letters from the students who attended your tour. They were all inspired by your courage when you helped catch a thief." He fixed his hair lock. "They all named you, not Oliver. Our curator was utterly impressed, and he gave you a hundred points. Ten for each student you helped recruit."

Lana glanced back at the board. It seemed that the students had seen her stop the thieves, and this had left a lasting impression on them. She had no idea it would have such an impact. "I was just helping."

He chuckled. "Listen, I don't know exactly what you did, and you might not realize it, but if people show you this appreciation, it means you were born for it."

Lana's head spun, and she had to lean over the windowsill. All this time, she had been so upset with herself because she couldn't enjoy building a 'normal life,' but now she saw everything crystal clear. *My life purpose isn't to 'fit in.' It's always been about helping others.*

After all, this was all she wanted to do – to protect others from injustice. Each time she helped someone, her heart fluttered in her chest, which meant that her groupmate was right – it was her calling. Lana could only embrace it and keep doing what's right. It was all she wanted. And she could do it right now.

Lana hugged him. "Thank you. It means a lot."

"Always." He glanced at her road bag. "Are you going away for the summer?"

"Yes. Actually, it might take a while." She handed him a key. "Here. You can take my room."

"The best view in this building? Thank you!" He took the key and pressed it to his chest. "Did you say goodbye to Oliver, too?"

Lana glanced at the end of the corridor, where their curator's office was. "Not yet. I need to do something first."

The door to Oliver's room was slightly open, and Lana peeked inside. He was packing, tossing his belongings into his suitcase. *He's still upset with me,* Lana concluded. Maybe it wasn't a good idea to see him in person. However, after learning about his scholarship, she knew she had to talk to him, no matter how difficult it might be.

Lana pushed the door open and stood in the doorway. "Are you leaving?"

Oliver shot her a sharp look. "What do you think? Stupid people have to pay for their mistakes. I'm leaving the program."

"You're not stupid, Oliver."

He paused in his packing and sat on the edge of his bed. "Then how else would you describe someone who squandered all his education funds to buy jewelry for the girl who ended up cheating on him?"

His words still stung. On the bright side, Lana hadn't come to his room empty-handed. She could at least try to make things right. She sat beside him and placed the promise ring in his hand. The diamond sparkled in his palm. "Please, give it to the woman who deserves you. One day, you'll meet someone who will love you as much as you love her."

He sighed. "It's a kind gesture, but I can't keep it."

"You can."

He shook his head. "I mean, I need to return it to help pay for my education. But thank you for returning it to me."

She smiled. "It's the least I can do before saying goodbye. I'll never forget you, Oliver."

He looked at her with concern. "Why are you talking like that? If you're thinking of leaving because of that... unpleasant morning incident... you don't have to go."

"I've already submitted my resignation notice."

He widened his eyes. "Are you in your right mind?! You could study for free!"

"Just listen," Lana said in a quiet voice. "According to the academic policy, if one of the students from the A-list drops the program, the next student takes their place and receives a scholarship."

He paused. "You turned down your scholarship... for me?"

Lana nodded. Besides that, her return date was uncertain, as was her future. Lana couldn't tell him about the Mercy House, as it was the only way to keep him safe. "It's okay. You worked hard, and it was your idea with that city tour. You deserved it."

He shook his head. "I know you made a mistake, but Lana, you shouldn't give up on your future. You can't just throw away a year of studying."

"It was a good year, and I learned a lot. I met you, and you taught me how to listen to the quiet voice of my heart among the millions of other voices."

"What's gotten into you?"

"I just want to challenge myself, to understand who I truly am. And I'll do what I must, no matter what. I could be a mediocre architect if I wanted to, and a passable wife. But it would never bring me true happiness. I've always had a desire to help people. You were right, I used to complain about my life often. So, it's time to take control and make things right."

He took her hands. "I like this new version of you."

"Thank you."

His eyes gleamed. "I'm so proud of you, Lana. I want you to pursue your true passion and trust your instincts. Remember – your heart doesn't deceive you."

"I'll remember." Lana smiled and kissed his unshaven cheek. "Take care, Olive."

<h1 style="text-align:center">13</h1>

⚬⚬⚬

# Mercy House

The wheels squeaked as the carriage stopped by the dorm's entrance. Irida moved the curtain on the window, activating her Invisible shield. This morning, Captain Harrison had informed her that Lana would join her on this trip. Moreover, he gave Irida another task – to watch this blondie closely and report to him. It meant only one thing – Lana knew more than she said, and considering that Captain Harrison was suspicious, Lana had just signed her own death sentence.

*What a pity!* Irida thought as she watched Lana walking to the carriage. *Such a pretty young woman, and so foolish.*

The door opened, and Lana walked inside. Today she wore a simple blue dress which suited her much less than her improvised 'guardian uniform.'

Lana looked straight at her and knitted her eyebrow. "You can drop your shield. I know you're here."

Irida eased her focus on her magic, and her body appeared from the air. She laughed. "What a sharp eye. Is it another side of your Mind-Reading Gift?"

"Not really. I knew that you were going to keep me company. Walter placed me in the same witness protection program as you," Lana said, giving Irida a cunning smile. "Hopefully, we can provide each other with some support. After all, we'll soon become sisters."

The carriage shook, and they started moving.

*She's definitely joking with me*, Irida concluded. *She even used Walter to get here. Maybe Lana isn't as foolish as she seems.*

"Just out of curiosity," Irida said, "what did you say to Walter to convince him?"

Lana shrugged. "Nothing. He suggested it after we both saw someone spying on me starting last night."

"And you agreed to go to that prison voluntarily?"

"You might call it 'a prison,' but all I want is to help those hapless girls tame their magic. Does this answer satisfy you?"

*I must not underestimate this woman*, Irida decided. "It's a good deed. I only asked because last night you said that you got in terms with being an architect designer and even settled for marriage."

Lana exhaled a sigh. "Things change, I guess. My fiancé-to-be broke up with me, and I quit the architecture profession."

Irida widened her eyes. "Are you serious? I don't believe all of that could happen so quickly."

They stared at each other, not saying a word. In heavy silence, Irida could distinguish the sound of the rolling wheels and horses puffing.

"Okay, let's make a deal," Lana finally suggested. "I don't ask you questions or attempt to read you. In return, you don't question me about my life or my motives. When we arrive, we just let each other be."

Irida gave it a thought. Basically, it was one of her tasks – to spy on Lana. However, Captain Harrison had given her way too many assignments, so she could always do it at a later time, once she finished with her main job. After all, whatever Lana was up to, she couldn't care less. "Okay. I won't question you, Lana. And you never read me."

"Deal." Lana extended her hand, but Irida refrained from shaking it.

"What? You think I'm going to read you right now?"

Irida frowned. It was exactly what she thought, because their verbal agreement had no power. Fortunately, she had a way to fix that. She took her purse and extracted a small notebook and a pen. Putting together a simple confidentiality agreement wasn't a big deal, so she started jotting it down. "Our deal will last for two weeks," Irida explained as she was writing. "If you break it, you might get seriously sick."

"Gee, do you ever trust anyone?"

"I just try to be proactive," Irida said, taking her hairpin. She pinched her index finger, so a tiny drop of blood formed on her fingertip. She pressed it to the paper, completing her oath. Then, she passed the notebook to Lana.

A drizzle and wind greeted them when they arrived at their destination. The crystal of time on Irida's bracelet glowed pink, indicating it was ten in the evening. Their trip took around ten hours, and all her body hurt from lack of moving. Moreover, Lana was the worst trip companion she had ever met – after they had made a deal, Lana took a book from her road bag and didn't pay any attention to her.

Irida climbed out of the carriage after Lana and shivered. They were surrounded by hills and forests. The tree barks were glowing green, illuminating the gloomy night. Among them stood a monstrous castle made of black stones. Its narrow windows were completely dark, as if it had swallowed all its inhabitants and was now awaiting new victims. Only a lonely candlelight shimmered on the porch.

"Charming," Lana said with a hint of sarcasm in her voice. "I bet our stay will be fun."

Irida chuckled. "Can't argue with that."

The path paving the front yard was made of rough stones, and Irida stumbled twice on her way to the porch. By the doors, there was a woman in a long dark cloak. Her face was hard to distinguish under the hood she was wearing, however, the candlelight lit up the wrinkles surrounding her pale, dry lips.

"Welcome," the woman nodded in greeting. "I'm Edwina, the senior member of the Sorority. From now on, you'll respond to me."

They beamed in response. As Irida had been instructed by Captain Harrison, they had to be silent in the presence of senior Sisters, unless they were asked a question directly. Probably, Lana was told the same as she didn't utter a word.

Edwina's lips widened in an insincere smile, and she waved her hand, inviting them in.


The corridors seemed too big for ordinary human beings. Their steps echoed over the tall ceiling as they walked to their chambers. Edwina was instructing them on their way. "We all wake up at six in the morning and pray together in the hall room. Then we eat and get to work. As you two have just arrived, you'll have to shadow other Sisters for the first two weeks. This is how you'll learn. Also, they will watch all your moves carefully."

Irida gritted her teeth. The only thing she hated more than early wake-up calls was when someone watched her. *I have an important mission,* she reminded herself. *It might be challenging, but after I finish, I'll finally be free.*

They stopped at the massive door at the end of the corridor, and Edwina turned to them. Her hood fell off, revealing her grey hair tied in a knot and a round face with narrow eyes. "You will share this room."

Lana waved her hands, her voice filled with disappointment. "Isn't there enough rooms in this castle to accommodate each of us?"

Edwina frowned in response.

*Oh, you must hate it when people question your orders,* Irida remarked inwardly. She took Lana by the elbow and gave Edwina an apologetic smile. "Please, forgive my sister's boldness. She is young and a bit spoiled."

Lana attempted to take her hand off, but Irida held her firmly. "I'm not –"

"Hush, dear," Irida said through clenched teeth, silencing Lana. "I guess it's better if we stay in the same room with each other than with anyone else. Don't you think so?"

"That's... true," Lana agreed. "Fine. Let's settle in."

Edwina gave her a sharp look. "I assume you two are tired after the long road. But if this misbehavior repeats tomorrow, I'll have to reconsider your placement in our facility."

Lana swallowed and muttered her apology. "You're right. I'm really sorry. I swear, I'll pull myself together by the morning."

"She learns fast," Irida remarked.

"I hope so," Edwina said, raising her hand. She held a metal ring with multiple keys on it, and they gleamed in the candlelight. "We lock the doors for the night to prevent the guards from walking in," she explained, unlocking their door. "Sometimes, they become too tired and mix up the floor where their chambers are. All the men here must sleep on the first floor."

Irida suppressed a laugh. *Men mixing up the rooms? Sounds like the good old days of my studenthood.* She extended her hand, assuming she would receive the key. She was wrong. Edwina pushed their door open and kept a key to herself. With a weary sigh, Irida walked inside, and Lana followed her.

The room was big enough to fit two narrow beds and one nightstand with a glowing crystal of time. Two sets of white sheets were folded and placed by the naked pillows, suggesting they had to make the beds themselves. *What else will they make us do here?*

"Now, your road bags," Edwina said.

"What's wrong with them?" Lana asked, pressing her bag to her chest.

Edwina knitted her gray eyebrows. "You're too talkative. Next time you feel the urge to open your mouth, just bite your tongue and wait for three seconds. It's usually the time I explain the rest."

Lana rolled her eyes but kept silent.

"You must pull all the contents out," Edwina instructed them. "So I can see you don't have anything forbidden in your room."

Irida scoffed but followed her request. Edwina ran her wrinkled hand through her folded sweaters and skirts. She frowned at the white trimmed nightgown. "This is unnecessary here." She placed it around her arm and moved to Lana.

Her bag, to Irida's surprise, contained mostly summer dresses and lingerie of all shades. Edwina's cheeks took on a red shade as she extracted a small bottle with brownish liquid from the pile of clothes. "What's that?"

"My... medication," Lana said in a hushed voice.

*Gee, she looks just like a schoolgirl caught stealing supplies.* This thought made Irida smile, and she covered her mouth with her palm, not to irritate Edwina with her cheerful mood.

"In your referral letter, there is no mention of any diseases." Edwina narrowed her eyes on Lana. "Is it a potion for wanton women? Don't lie, because I'll confiscate it anyway and check it."

Lana's face took on a puzzled expression. "Wanton?!"

"Whores," Edwina clarified. Her expression was plain, making Irida think that the smile she had given them at their arrival was the kindest emotion she was capable of showing. "Are you drinking it to sleep with men and satisfy your lust? If so, we can't keep you here."

Lana opened her mouth and closed it.

"Sister Edwina, please allow me to explain," Irida said to break the heavy silence.

Edwina nodded silently in response, her lips pressed together.

Irida mustered her best apologetic look. "You're absolutely right – it's a contraceptive potion. My sister keeps it only because she experienced harsh times with her fiancé. You see, that man wanted to take her innocence before marriage. She only tried to protect herself from having a baby out of wedlock. To be honest, her trouble made both of us think of moving here and leaving that world behind."

Lana widened her eyes in surprise, and Irida winked at her.

Edwina's cold eyes pierced Lana. "Is that true? Were you engaged?"

Lana nodded. "Yes. I had a fiancé, and we broke up just recently. You can check it."

"I will," Edwina promised, placing the potion in her pocket. Then she took the bag that belonged to Lana and moved to the door. "Sweet dreams," Edwina said before she closed the door after them. Her key moved in the lock, sealing them inside.

They exchanged glances.

"Freaking grump," Lana said, obviously referring to Edwina. Then she sat on her bed corner, embracing her shoulders. "Thank you for saving me, though. Now I owe you two."

"You don't owe me anything," Irida said with a smile. "Just be careful next time. Bringing that potion here was a huge risk."

"I just didn't expect someone would check my personal belongings." Lana gave her a scared look. "Shit! I must drink it tonight."

"Why? Are you planning a date?"

"No. I had a date... last night," Lana explained, her voice trembling. "And I'm in the middle of my moon cycle. I can't believe she freaking took it away! What shall I do now? Wait and pray that I don't carry the baby of the man who I barely know?"

Irida gave her an attentive look. There was no way Lana barely knew her ex-fiancé, so it wasn't him she talked about. The other man Lana could likely sleep with was... Walter. It made perfect sense – he was the one escorting her home last night. Also, as Irida had learned in the morning, Walter personally talked to Captain Harrison, insisting on sending Lana to Mercy House. *Shit, Lana just used him to get here!* What was at stake, so she had to do that? Even though the question bugged her, Irida restrained from asking. Since they were bound by their deal, there was only one way to make Lana speak about it – to win her trust, so with time Lana would reveal everything herself.

"Okay, don't panic," Irida said in a calming voice.

Lana stood up and started pacing the room. "It's easier to say than to do. I swear, I'm about to jump from this damn window now."

"It's the third floor," Irida reminded her. Then she pulled her hand under the lace of her bra and extracted a small bottle with the potion. "Plus, I have some spare drops of what you need."

Lana eyed her with numb excitement.

"As I figured, it might be in demand in places full of lonely women," Irida explained. "So I thought I could sell it for a reasonable price."

Lana came closer and extended her hand to the gleaming liquid in anticipation.

Irida moved her hand back, teasing her.

Lana gave her a dirty look. "Alright, I got it. How much do you want for it?"

"When I said 'a price,' I didn't mean money. I meant a favor. If you take this bottle, I'll ask you one question. And you must answer honestly."

"What?! You promised not to ask me anything. We even made a deal!"

Irida grinned. "Don't worry. It's not about your reasons for being here."

Lana relaxed a bit. "Then what?"

"I'm curious why you risk sleeping with men when there are so many other ways of relaxing."

"Well... I don't do drugs if that's what you mean. They aren't good for my Gift as well as alcohol and other doubtful potions –"

"I mean sex."

Lana's eyes gleamed in the moonlight. "Well, I like being with myself. But sometimes it's good to be with other people, too. To connect, to feel someone's warmth and the way our hearts race together, obeying the same desire."

Her words sent tickles to Irida's skin. "Have you ever been with a woman?"

Lana winced. "No!"

Irida laughed. "Relax. There is a difference between being with a man and with a woman – in the latter case, you don't have to explain yourself or rush things. Just think about it, okay? Then let me know if you want to try. Whenever you're ready." With that, she gave Lana a bottle.

# 14

## The Oath

The first gray light crept into the room, casting a dull glow on the ugly, cracked ceiling. Lana let out a sigh. The wake-up call was imminent and she wasn't able to sleep until sunrise. Indeed, she would be exhausted all day.

Lana's gaze shifted to the portrait hanging on the wall. It wasn't particularly large, but the woman depicted in it captured Lana's attention – it was as if she was watching her. Her brows were knitted, and her gray eyes seemed to look at her with suspicion. *How haven't I noticed it before?* Perhaps she had been too preoccupied with losing her potion and her conversation with Irida. Now, Lana was unsure of what to do about her. As Timothy had warned, she wasn't supposed to ever trust this woman. However, so far Irida had only helped her – first by saving her life in the dungeon, then by explaining herself to Edwina, and finally by providing the potion Lana so desperately needed.

So, the questions lingered – was Irida working diligently only to gain Lana's trust and exploit her later? Or was she truly trustworthy? Lana rolled onto her side, observing Irida. Unlike Lana, this woman appeared to be impervious to stress. Her chest rose and fell rhythmically as she peacefully rested her head on the pillow, her parted lips releasing calm breaths. Lana started feeling a twinge of jealousy when an unexpected event unfolded – Irida's body became almost translucent and vanished into thin air. All that remained was an empty bed with a bare mattress. The bedsheets had disappeared as well.

Lana blinked repeatedly, utterly perplexed. Was this a figment of her imagination or was she dreaming? Intrigued, Lana rose to her feet and tiptoed towards the bed. Carefully, she reached out and touched the 'empty air,' her fingers encountering the softness of the woman's bare shoulder.

The air quivered, and Irida materialized out of nowhere. Her amber eyes bore into Lana. "What the hell? Are you trying to read me?"

"No!" Lana withdrew her hand. "I've never seen anything like that before... you just completely disappeared."

Irida sat up, her expression softening. "Oh, that... Yes, it happens with my Gift. When I'm in a certain stage of sleep, my shield can activate itself. It usually occurs close to awakening."

"That's so fascinating!"

Irida shrugged. "Not really. The first time my Gift manifested, my parents panicked. They thought I was abducted or something..." A hint of sadness crossed her face as she mentioned the past.

Lana recalled that these were the same parents who had disowned Irida after she was expelled from medical school. She still struggled to comprehend how parents could abandon their own child like that. At least she was here now, able to offer some comfort to Irida. "Well, at least your parents witnessed your Gift manifesting. My mother left me and my father before it happened."

"Oh... I assumed you were one of those happy girls."

Lana gave Irida a puzzled look. "'Happy girls'? What does that even mean?"

"It's when you have a healthy relationship with your folks," Irida clarified. "Such girls often believe they deserve it and look down on others with arrogance. I despise it."

"Me too," Lana said. "I had a classmate like that. She taunted me, claiming I didn't deserve my mother's love and that no one would ever love me."

"Did you manage to forgive her?" Irida teased.

"Not right away. I punched her in the face first."

"Ouch... I had no idea you were capable of such things!"

"I'm capable of many things," Lana declared proudly. "You'll see."

Irida opened her mouth to respond, but at that moment, a loud bell rang out, piercing the air. They both clapped their hands over their ears. *Is it a fire?* Lana wondered in alarm. The fact that the door was locked meant they were trapped. She leaped to her feet as the deafening sound abruptly ceased.

Lana stood in the center of the room, her heart racing. Then the door lock clicked, and it swung open, revealing a middle-aged woman in a shapeless gray robe. Her fiery red hair was neatly braided. In her hand, she held a scroll. *Another Mercy Sister*, Lana presumed.

This woman appeared to be more animated than the stern Sister Grump Lana had encountered the previous night. She greeted them with a cheerful smile. "Good morning, Sisters!"

As Lana pondered a response, Irida stood up, approached the woman, and smiled warmly. Lana followed suit, tilting her head slightly, prepared to listen to the woman's instructions.

"Ah, I see you're more alert today," she remarked with a chuckle. "I'm Sister Amanda, and I'll be your instructor. I'll lead you through our training sessions, which will commence right after breakfast."

Lana nodded in understanding, suppressing the urge to pose one of the numerous questions swirling in her mind.

"But first, I need you to promise that everything you learn here will stay within these walls." With that, Amanda handed the roll of paper to Lana.

Lana unrolled the paper, her eyes scanning the elegant handwriting in ink.

"It's their standard oath," Irida whispered in her ear.

Lana furrowed her brow. "I believe you mean a 'confidentiality agreement.'"

"No, your friend is correct," Amanda interjected, her gaze fixed on Irida. "It is indeed an oath rooted in magic. Violating it carries severe consequences."

Lana's heart skipped a beat. "What kind of consequences?"

Amanda sighed, clearly displeased with Lana's inquiries. "Death."

Lana stared at her, feeling numb. The agreement with Irida had already put her health in jeopardy, but she had agreed to it under the assumption that it would protect them both. Now, she was being asked to essentially sign her own death warrant.

"Alright, let me explain how it works," Amanda said, noticing Lana's unease. "Your words will be bound to your bloodstream. If you disclose anything about Mercy House to someone outside of our Sorority, you will suffer a heart attack."

*This is exactly how Denise died*, Lana realized. During her time in Timothy's memories, he had mentioned that his sister, Denise, had passed away unexpectedly due to a 'heart failure.' Now, at least one mystery was solved – the consequences for sharing information, whether verbally or in writing, were dire. Could Lana afford to take such a risk?

Irida took the roll from Lana's hands. "I'll go first, then."

"Very well," Amanda said, smiling approvingly as she handed Irida a pin.

Irida nodded obediently and pricked her index finger. A ruby droplet glistened on her fingertip, and she pressed it to the bottom of the paper. Her fingerprint glowed red, as did Irida's chest. The glow lasted only a few seconds before fading, and Irida let out a relaxed breath.

She handed Lana a pin. "Now, it's your turn to demonstrate what you're truly capable of."

As Lana accepted the pin, her hand remained steady. She had come to Mercy House with a mission – to uncover the secret that had cost Denise her life. There was no room for hesitation now. With determination, she moved the pin, piercing her skin.

# 15

## A Training

"This is why we must do our best to persuade these girls to abandon their magic," Sister Amanda, a coach who had met them in the morning, explained. As Irida had learned during their briefing, Amanda had spent half of her life in Mercy House, training new Sisters. Now, she was walking back and forth along the blackboard, giving detailed instructions on how to work with the 'patients,' teenage girls who were sent here because of their destructive Gifts.

Irida stifled a yawn and slightly lifted the sleeve of her robe to glance at her bracelet. The crystal of time shone lilac. *Gee, it's already nine in the morning!* Sitting through these boring classes and pretending to be an exemplary student was a waste of time. Especially when she already had all the answers in her pocket – thanks to the diary that she had acquired from the late Timothy. Well, from his sister Denise, to be precise.

According to Denise's diary, the theoretical part wasn't that tricky – just some techniques they had to know by heart. The most important thing was to do everything the Mercy Sisters asked and never dare to improvise. The latter wasn't too hard for Irida. After all, she was used to being flexible to reach her goals. She wasn't so sure about Lana, though.

Suppressing another yawn, Irida looked around. There were just a few people in the classroom, including three other newly arrived Sisters in the back seats. Like stormy clouds, they all wore equally ugly gray robes that hid most of their bodies. Lana was at her right side, blinking slowly as she rested her cheek on her hand. Her obvious boredom caused Sister Amanda to frown.

"Miss Morris?" Amanda called out to her.

Lana batted her eyes. "Yes?"

"Would you care to repeat three persuasive techniques we've just discussed?"

"Erm..." Lana helplessly looked around. When her eyes locked with Irida's, she exhaled a sigh.

"Miss Morris?" Amanda came closer. "Is there something wrong with your ability to speak?"

"I'm sorry. I can't recall them."

Amanda gave her a disappointed look. "If your memory isn't good, you must take notes. Where are your writing supplies?"

*I bet she forgot them in that prison that you call 'our room.'* Irida bit her tongue not to say it out loud and not to make this woman even more dissatisfied. Irida couldn't behave so arrogantly; otherwise, she risked being kicked out of this place. She couldn't afford that, not before her mission was accomplished.

Amanda knitted her brow. "Miss Morris, I'm afraid you are not quite ready for the role of a Mercy Sister."

"I am fully ready," Lana objected. "I just learn better through practice. Theory isn't my thing."

"Without passing through the theory, you aren't allowed to work with people."

Lana exhaled loudly. "I apologize. I'll listen better from now on."

Amanda shook her head, then turned her attention to Irida. "Now, you. What can you recall from our lesson, Miss Hashemi?"

*Now, it's my chance to shine.* In contrast with Lana's sloppiness, she would resemble an exemplary student. Irida revealed a charming smile before giving a detailed reply. "I remember everything you said. This castle was built two centuries ago, and its purpose is to help women with strong Gifts. As women aren't suitable to have destructive magic, they have difficulties learning to control it. Here, our educated Mercy Sisters train them to tame their power. Sometimes, the Gift is too strong for female nature, and not to cause harm to people around or themselves, we make them give up their magic."

A genuine smile tugged at the corners of her lips. "Almost correct. But as I said, we can't take anyone's magic by force."

Irida nodded. "Exactly. This is why our job is to persuade them to give it voluntarily. For that, we use three techniques. Firstly, sympathy. We always listen carefully and support the patients to make them believe that we aren't judging them. Secondly, authority. We share multiple examples of successful treatment on similar Gifts, so they rely on our experience and trust us. And lastly, compassion. We do multiple small gestures of care to help them feel better in this place, like bringing a comforter or a cup of calming tea."

*Actually, those techniques are quite handy,* Irida thought. Last night, she used all of them on Lana – as soon as she needed help with the Preventive potion, Irida didn't judge her. On the contrary, she listened carefully and supported her. Then, Irida shared why she brought this potion here in the first place. She didn't lie about her idea to sell it. Lastly, Irida gave her the potion bottle and never asked for anything serious in return. She only asked Lana a little intimate question to get to know her better. Now, Irida was confident Lana was reconsidering whether to trust her or not.

"Excellent." Amanda's face brightened. "Miss Hashemi, I bet you'll have success here."

"Thank you." Irida pressed her palm to her chest in appraisal. Then she shifted her sly look at Lana. "I'll do my best to help my Sister be more attentive."

Amanda nodded approvingly. "That would be really nice of you."

After the lecture was over, everyone started rising from their chairs and rushing outside. No wonder – all the women were eager to leave the stale room to finally enjoy an afternoon break.

Irida was collecting her writing supplies when a shadow loomed over her. She raised her eyes to meet Sister Amanda's concerned face. Irida looked around, realizing the room was empty. There were only two of them now, and it didn't bode well.

Irida mustered her best innocent look. "Do you have any questions for me, Sister?"

"I just wonder... How did you learn so much about us?"

Irida shrugged, trying to look nonchalant. "I'm just a good listener."

"Perhaps. However, I never told you when Mercy House was built." Amanda narrowed her eyes, her gaze piercing her to the core of her soul. "So, how do you know that?"

*Perfect.* The last thing she needed to do was to expose her source of information. "Why is that such a big deal?" Irida asked, rising to her feet. "Maybe I heard it somewhere. I don't remember exactly."

"Just asking," Amanda said, softening. "Because we do our best to guard our secrets. And if you can name the person who told you this, you can even be rewarded."

Irida gave her an intrigued look. "Rewarded? How?"

"We provide an opportunity to work here permanently. And the benefits are exciting."

*There is nothing more exciting than finishing my work and getting out of here.* Although, considering Amanda's persistence, rejection might offend her. After all, Amanda was her coach. So, it was better not to rush into dismissing her. "What kind of benefits are you talking about?" Irida asked.

"You can become a senior Sister and work with us, not afraid of being judged by society any longer."

Irida knitted her eyebrow. "Judged? What do you –"

Before she could finish, Amanda stepped closer and kissed her lips. It was brief but it left Irida awestruck. Gee, this reckless act explained why Amanda chose this place, away from the society that was judgmental and full of forbidden temptations. Ironically, in this prison, she was free to be herself.

Amanda smiled at her. "I see you quite liked it."

Maybe it was her blurred mind, but Irida got interested. How would it be – to seduce a Mercy Sister? She shook this thought away. No, it can't be that easy. *Maybe it's some sort of a test?* Then, Irida must set a boundary not to screw everything up on day one. "I can't believe you think I'm gay."

A smile played on her lips. "Are you saying you are not? Because I don't believe it."

Irida shrugged, trying to maintain her composure. "Honestly, I have nothing against a romance between two women, but ... you and I ... it isn't right."

"Why not?"

"We are a student and a teacher," Irida reminded her. "So, there must be a boundary between us. I don't want to let it affect my study performance. No offense."

Amanda exhaled a sigh of regret. "Fine. And you are right – we must first think of the patients."

"Exactly."

"In two weeks, we won't be tied by this obligation," Amanda said seductively. "I hope, by then you'll have enough time to decide what you want."

*All I want is to find the Book of Life and get out of this damned place before the training is over.* Irida mustered a smile. "Agreed. Let's take our time."

# 16

## A Pick

Close to the afternoon, Lana sat on a bench in the distant corner of the garden. The food had not been served yet, so most of the Mercy Sisters gathered outside, enjoying the warmth of another spring day and chatting. It wasn't raining like last night; today, the mist enveloped the trees and trails, blurring their silhouettes. It conveniently hid Lana from their curious glances, allowing her to postpone putting on a polite face and acquainting herself with her new colleagues. Instead, she busied herself thinking about Irida and how this sneaky woman managed to impress the annoying Sister Amanda.

"Freaking walking encyclopedia," Lana muttered under her breath. Apparently, Irida had come well-prepared, and it meant that she was a real professional in her field. Lana could only guess what she was up to.

The sound of quiet steps pulled her out of her thoughts. Irida sat on the bench beside her, her face shining. "Hey, what's the matter?"

Lana shrugged. "I just hate long lectures."

Irida gave her an encouraging smile. "It's just for a couple of weeks, then you'll get to practice. The way you love learning."

"Aww... You remember what I said during the class," Lana said with a weary look. Apparently, Irida was very proud of herself right now. As annoying as it was, it deserved some teasing remark. "As a mind reader, I'm impressed. You have an excellent memory."

Irida grinned. "Let's say I came prepared."

*Then I was right about her.* "Cheating, then?"

Irida lowered her voice. "I happened to acquire a diary that belonged to one of the Sisters who used to work here. Her name was Denise. Believe it or not, she had a summary of the study lectures, and she described her experience with the patients in detail."

Lana widened her eyes. It wasn't a secret for her that Irida had stolen that diary from late Timothy. But why was she so open about it? There was only one way to find out – to play this game, whatever it was. "How interesting. So, you read it after you stole it?"

"Stole?! Because I'm a thief?" Irida laughed. "No, I'm not doing it anymore."

Lana mustered an intrigued look. "No? Then how did you get it?"

"From her brother. After Denise died of a heart attack, he found a road bag with her possessions that included her diary."

"Timothy," Lana said, finishing the farce.

Irida's eyes gleamed with intrigue. "How do you know?"

"I read his mind in case you forgot. Just before he died."

"Ah, this is how you learned about this place."

Lana went silent, unable to believe she had foolishly given away the origins of her secret mission. *What the heck?* Apparently, Irida was too skilled. She knew how to get what she wanted. Lana needed to be careful before revealing another truth that could jeopardize her plans. Especially the fact that she had come here specifically to uncover the secrets buried in this place.

"No, I didn't see anything about Mercy House in his memory," Lana lied, trying to rectify her mistake. "Only his sorrow about the death of a sister. He called her by name, so when you mentioned 'Denise,' I simply put two and two together."

To her relief, Irida accepted this explanation. "Yes, what are the odds of hearing it twice within two days?"

"I can't believe it's only been two days since I almost died," Lana said, changing the subject.

Irida gave her a sympathetic look. "I'm glad you're still alive."

"But for how long?"

Irida furrowed her brow. "What do you mean?"

"This blood oath that we took this morning... It's creepy. I'm constantly afraid of saying something wrong and ending up like Denise."

"Don't worry. It doesn't kill you quickly," Irida reassured her in an encouraging tone.

Lana frowned. "Is that supposed to cheer me up?"

"I'm just saying that you'll feel it if you start talking about something you shouldn't. You'll notice it's getting too hard to breathe and your chest hurts. Once you have these symptoms, simply change the subject."

*That's exactly how Denise handled a similar situation with her brother,* Lana recalled. "Thanks. It's good to know that."

"Plus, you're absolutely safe here in the Sorority. You can freely share with all the Sisters who are bound by the same oath."

"How did Denise manage to share it? As far as I know, she didn't drop dead right after passing the diary to her brother."

"I guess the deadly spell works slower with the written word. Denise might have started feeling unwell once she gave her diary away. As Timothy said, she died a few hours after their last meeting."

Lana exhaled a heavy sigh. *What a horrible price to pay! And for what?* Denise had entrusted her secrets to the only person who could help, but Timothy was killed. Another troubling thing was that Irida showed no compassion about it. On the contrary, she revealed a smug grin, perhaps happy about solving a piece of the riddle.

"So, here is the question," Lana said, intending to spoil Irida's mood. "If she died, then will we, too?"

"I prefer to forget about this place as soon as I leave," Irida replied, her expression turning serious. "Plus, the oath is effective for only three years, as it's the limit the spell could last."

"Why didn't Denise just quit after three years, then?"

"Hmm... That's a good question to ponder," Irida mused, raising her eyes to the misty sky as she formulated a theory. "I guess she was quite a reckless woman. Unable to wait for her oath expiration date, she spilled some secrets on paper and gave it to her brother."

"It doesn't make sense," Lana countered. *Unless... They forced Denise to extend the contract after three years.* As Lana knew, In the criminal world, people allowed a certain level of secrecy could never simply walk away. Moreover, if Denise was willing to put her life at stake to share her secrets, then she must have known something truly horrifying. Lana couldn't wait to uncover what it was.

"What?" Irida asked, interrupting Lana's train of thought.

Lana gave her an attentive look. "You've been so honest with me since we arrived. Why?"

"I just want you to trust me."

"Persuasion technique number two, then. Want to impress me by sharing the truth about your link to the late Mercy Sister?"

Irida shrugged. "Put it as you wish. Honestly, I can't rely on anyone here but you. And you seem to be up to something, too. So if you want, you can tell me –"

"I'm not up to anything," Lana interjected, raising her hand in defense. "And by the way, when we sealed our deal, you promised not to question me. I'm here for the protection program, as you remember, just like you."

Irida exhaled a sigh. "Fair enough. Actually, I only need one thing from you."

"Which one?"

Irida looked around, then moved closer, her breath reaching Lana's face. "Promise not to tell anyone."

Lana lowered her voice. "Okay. I'll be silent, I swear."

"You and I are locked in that damn room all night like some lawbreakers. But I can find a way to open the door so we can take night walks after curfew. What do you think?"

Lana gave Irida an intrigued look. Maybe Irida wasn't a good person, but having her as an ally could be very beneficial. If Lana could get out after curfew, she might be able to explore the libraries, archives, and other places that were off-limits during the daytime. This could help her learn more about the place. "I think it's a great idea. I would love to get out of there."

Irida smiled. "Awesome."

"When do you think you can get the key?"

Irida gave her a sly smile and then lifted her hand. Lana stared at her bracelet – a thin silver chain with a time crystal attached to it. There was also a small metal object – a pick.

"No fucking way," Lana muttered. "Will it open our door?"

"This pick will open any door here just fine," Irida replied, concealing her wrist with a sleeve of her robe. "If you keep your word, we can use it together. We can explore the building at nighttime."

"Can I have a spare copy?"

"You don't have the skill to use it. But I'll gladly open the door for you when it's your turn to get out."

"You mean when we *both* get out."

Irida shook her head. "One of us must be in the room in case someone decides to check on us."

*How convenient.* This way, Irida could conduct her mysterious business while Lana was on watch in their bedroom. She kept this thought to herself. Whatever this woman was up to, Lana could continue her investigation after curfew, and it was a good starting point. Additionally, if she needed more answers, she could spy on Irida. After all, their deal didn't mention that Lana couldn't do it.

# 17

## A Spy

2 weeks later

Irida opened the door to the dark room of a secret archive. The space was located in the basement and lacked windows, leaving her to stare into the black void. However, the darkness couldn't erase the smile on her face. Unlike most people she knew, she didn't harbor a foolish fear of uncertainty. On the contrary, she couldn't wait to step into the darkness and uncover what was hidden there. Hopefully, she would finally acquire *The Book of Life*.

Taking a deep breath of anticipation, she moved forward. Unexpectedly, her body bounced back as if it had encountered an invisible obstacle. Confused, Irida extended her hand and touched an invisible wall. It appeared that the room was under a protective spell. But which one?

As Irida knew, guardians sometimes set such traps to catch criminals. A special spell placed on the floor or ceiling could allow someone to enter but prevent them from leaving, creating an invisible dome. In this case, it appeared that the entire room was secured from intruders.

"Fuck!" Irida gasped, clenching her fists. It had been two weeks since her arrival, and she had spent most of her evenings researching this monstrous castle, only to discover this invisible barrier.

Irida took a deep breath, trying to push aside the anxious thoughts about running out of time. However, despite her efforts, the memory of her last conversation with Captain Harrison resurfaced in her mind. *"You have two weeks to do it on your own. After that, I'll send my person to meet you. Also, in case you fail, he will push things."* Those were his words when Irida had been assigned to this mission. Now, she couldn't shake the feeling that someone was watching her, waiting for the right moment to 'push' her. She could only guess whether it would be a verbal threat or a physical one.

The sound of footsteps in the corridor made her flinch. Irida turned her head, catching a glimpse of a shadow moving along the far wall. Without wasting another second, she stopped breathing and activated her invisible shield. If it wasn't the person sent by Captain Harrison, then she risked encountering one of the Mercy Sisters. The last thing she needed was to deal with any of them.

Closing the heavy door would have created too much noise, so Irida simply stepped aside, patiently waiting for the intruder to pass by so she could leave unnoticed and retreat to her room. As expected, the shadow drew closer. The rustling of her clothes sounded like crunchy fall leaves under the wind, giving the impression of the clumsiest spy ever. Among all the Mercy Sisters, Irida had only met one person who possessed such a trait. She froze against the wall, waiting for her suspicion to be confirmed.

In a minute, the person approached, a shining yellow sphere in her hand casting light on her big brown eyes and blond hair tied in a plait.

"What's up, Lana?" Irida called out from her hiding spot, causing the spy to shiver and drop her Light, which crashed to the floor, plunging them into darkness.

Before Lana could escape, Irida reached out and revealed her own turquoise-colored Light. She dropped her shield to confront her.

Lana stepped back, visibly uncomfortable. "Sorry. I just..."

"Just spied on me?" Irida narrowed her eyes at her. "Did Amanda send you?"

"What?" Lana looked utterly puzzled. "No... Why would she?"

"I don't know. Perhaps to see if I'm worthy of her trust."

Lana shook her head. "No need to pretend, Irida. I know that you work for them."

Now it was Irida's turn to be puzzled. "Work for whom?"

"For the Sorority, who else?"

Irida stared at her for several long seconds, then burst into laughter. The suggestion alone was so ridiculous that it left no room for further discussion. The shadows cast by her Light ball danced around, adding to Lana's confusion.

"What's funny?" Lana asked, frowning.

"It's just..." Irida waved her hands, laughing. "Just so freaking odd! This whole thing with all these secrets... Just look at us!"

Lana didn't share her joy. "Well, I guess you aren't working for them, then. You're just a regular thief sneaking around in search of some treasure."

The mention of her mission brought Irida back to her senses. "You better watch yourself. By the way, did you leave the door to our bedroom open?"

Lana shrugged. "I assumed you wouldn't be punished anyway."

"Because you thought I was one of them, right?"

"Exactly."

"Great job. Now we are both in trouble!"

Lana glanced at the open door to the archive. "Well, then I'll leave you alone so you can figure out how to enter this secret archive. I would help you, though, but... it would spoil all the thrill."

She turned to leave, but Irida caught her by the sleeve of her robe. "Wait!"

Lana gave her a cunning look. "I'm listening."

"How do I open this thing?" Irida nodded towards the archive she was trying to access.

"Well, it wouldn't be fair if you got it without a deal. Don't you think so?"

Irida exhaled a weary sigh. She had already given too much – from saving Lana's life to providing the opportunity to unlock their door and assisting with her mysterious business, whatever it was. It seemed Lana was too greedy to acknowledge that. Unfortunately, Irida had no time to waste on bargaining. "Okay. What do you want in exchange?"

Lana frowned, pondering. "Let me see... On the night of our arrival, we made a deal – I never question your mission here, and you never ask me about anything, so we just let each other be."

"Exactly."

"That deal expired this afternoon."

Irida gave her an annoyed look. *Why did I make that damn agreement so short?* Perhaps it was Harrison's warning about the two-week arrangement that had influenced her. Irida hadn't anticipated it would take that long. How frustrating! Now, after all the trouble, she also had this nosy blonde to deal with.

"I'll talk openly," Lana continued. "Since you told me about Denise's diary, I can't help but wonder... what the hell Denise tried to tell her brother? What could she possibly know that she agreed to die voluntarily just to reveal the truth?"

Irida gave her an attentive look. She had read many things in that diary, but the question remained – why did Lana need to know it? As Irida recalled, Lana often brought up the diary in their conversations, as if its secrets held incredible value for her. Perhaps, uncovering those secrets was her reason for being there. Well, then she might use it as leverage.

"So?" Lana pressed. "In case you forgot, now I can read you."

"Try, and I'll tell Edwina that you came here to snoop around," she cautioned.

Lana widened her eyes, speechless.

"What?!" Irida stepped closer. "It's clear that you lied about your desire to help those hapless patients. Otherwise, you wouldn't be so sleepy in classes. You only want to learn the secrets of the Sorority! I don't know where you sell those secrets, and I couldn't care less, but I bet the senior Sisters will have many questions for you."

Lana shook her head, her tone apologetic. "I'm so sorry if my words sounded like a threat. I didn't mean that. I only wanted to give you an opportunity to tell the truth in exchange for the knowledge of how to access that archive. After all, you don't really care much about their secrets, and you want to get out of this place as much as I do. Let's help each other out."

Irida exhaled a weary sigh. She had to admit she had missed her mission deadline, just as Captain Harrison had expected. Damn, it was annoying! Another bothersome issue was that their first day of practice with real patients was scheduled to start tomorrow.

Irida hated the mere thought of dealing with all that mess. Perhaps, dealing with Lana would at least speed things up. "Fair enough. But how do I know you won't trick me? What if you get what you want, then rat me out?"

Lana gave it some thought. "You're right. You have no reason to trust me."

"Exactly."

"Then I'll give you one. I'll just tell you how to open it, and after it works, you do your part of the deal."

Irida smiled at her. "That will work."

"Alright. Here's my theory – my father is the Guardian Captain, and we have a secret archive, too. To be able to get inside, all the guardians must bring an oath, similar to the one we bring here."

"We already did it, didn't we?"

"Yes, but there are more layers to it."

"That's exactly what I thought. What are they?"

"The secret room might only let certain people in. Like one of the senior Sisters who can be trusted."

"You mean, someone like Amanda?"

Lana shrugged. "Maybe. Also, Edwina has all the keys, so she can certainly access this room. I suppose any of them will do because usually, access is granted to at least two people. You know, in case something happens to one of them, the access won't be lost."

"That makes sense," Irida agreed. "So, what's your suggestion? To tie Sister Grump and drag her to the threshold?"

"It would be too much hassle." Lana chuckled. "Fortunately, there is an easy way – access to that room is linked to Light, a person's unique energy print. You simply need to steal a piece of energy from her. Then place it into a glass object so it won't dissipate too quickly. With that, you can enter any room."

Irida breathed out. "That's helpful. Thank you."

"You're welcome." Lana exhaled a sigh, visibly satisfied. "I hope it will work."

# 18

# A Hopeless Case

Lana followed Edwina down the narrow, windowless basement corridor, illuminated only by the bright yellow and foggy white Lights they carried. She made a conscious effort to maintain a slow pace and avoid stepping on Edwina's heels. It was the first day of her guided practice, and Lana was eager to finally start helping someone.

The previous night, Lana had been taken aback when Irida accused her of only caring about the secrets of the Sorority. Well, it was true that Lana's initial goal had been to uncover the truth. However, her ultimate purpose was to help all the girls in any way possible, even if it meant being their guide. Now, it was time for Lana to prove her worth. *This is what I'm meant to do*, Lana encouraged herself. *Good luck will be on my side.*

As the corridor turned, Edwina gave her a stern look. "These are the chambers for our new patients."

Lana nodded, silently acknowledging her understanding. Since her first days in this place, she had learned to behave and rarely opened her mouth in the presence of senior Sisters.

"Your assignment for the day will be to meet the new girl and explain that you will be the one to help her tame her magic," Edwina instructed. "She's an easy case – Telekinesis Gift."

Lana gave her a small smile. Telekinesis was one of the most popular Gifts, and there were many women she knew who had this magic. *Hopefully, I'll manage to help her quickly*, she thought to herself.

Edwina caught her look and frowned. "Sometimes this Gift is too hard to control. Here, we teach them how to do it. If you manage to teach her not to ruin everything she looks at, then she can keep her magic channels intact. Is that clear?"

Lana cleared her throat before replying, "Yes, Sister."

"Also, kill your Light," Edwina added. "You should never remind them of the magic they can't use."

Complying with Edwina's instructions, Lana clapped her palms together, extinguishing her Light. Now, the space was only illuminated by Edwina's white sphere. In its pale glow, they appeared like two ghosts trapped in this dark labyrinth.

"Good," Edwina remarked, taking her key chain and inserting one of the keys into the door lock. Somehow, Edwina always managed to remember which key went where with so many of them. Lana held her breath, expecting her to make a mistake and mix them up. However, as usual, the key turned smoothly without any issues, and the lock clicked open.

The cramped room had a small basement window near the ceiling. Almost indiscernible against the black walls, there was a narrow bed and a wooden stool, likely for the Sister conducting the session. The bed was unoccupied.

Lana had to wait for her eyes to adjust to the dim lighting before she could make out a skinny girl sitting on the floor in the corner, hugging her bony knees to her chest. Barefoot and clad in a beige robe, the girl's greasy dark hair cascaded over her shoulders.

Lana took a deep breath and knelt beside her, placing a cup of herbal tea on the floor. She had prepared the hot drink for the girl in advance as a gesture of care.

"Hi, I'm Lana," she introduced herself in a soft voice.

The girl met her gaze with bloodshot eyes but remained silent.

Resisting the urge to question Edwina about the inhumane conditions in which their 'patients' were kept, Lana offered the girl a compassionate look. "I'm here to help you. I'll do everything I can to guide you through this. Just tell me what you need."

The girl averted her eyes, her voice barely above a whisper. "I want to go home."

"You'll go home. I promise. We just need to ensure that you can control your magic."

"Can you take these off?" The girl raised her hands, revealing the copper bracelets encircling her thin wrists. Her pale skin, where the bracelets rested, was marred with bruises and bleeding wounds. Lana's heart sank. The guardians typically used copper handcuffs to block the magic channels of criminals. This poor creature was not a lawbreaker; she was simply a frightened and lost girl.

"I... I can't..." Lana mumbled, her voice barely above a whisper. She closed her eyes and took a deep breath, trying to compose herself. Throughout her educational sessions, she had been informed that the girls had their magic temporarily blocked by copper bracelets, but witnessing it firsthand was a shock. This was why she despised excessive theory; it often bore no resemblance to real-life experiences. Lana could only recite the phrases she had learned from Sister Amanda. "This is a temporary measure to prevent you from harming yourself or others."

"But it hurts!"

"I know. I'm truly sorry this happened to you. It shouldn't be this way," Lana empathized. She gently took the girl's hand, being careful not to startle her. Placing her handkerchief between the girl's skin and the metal, she created a protective barrier. "It should feel better now."

The girl's eyes filled with hope. "Will you really help me?"

"Of course," Lana promised. "What's your name?"

"Dorothy."

Lana refrained from saying, 'It's nice to meet you.' Now, she was grateful for her lesson on thinking before speaking. "We'll go through this together, Dorothy. Okay?" she offered instead.

The girl nodded silently.

Lana glanced back at Edwina. Sister Grump was observing them with a stoic expression. Her lack of reaction indicated she was likely content with Lana's performance. She turned back to Dorothy. "Okay. I'll return tomorrow and bring you something. What would you like?"

"I want to see my mom."

"You'll be reunited with your family soon. For now, let's take care of you. I can bring you a softer blanket and a book. Do you enjoy reading?"

Dorothy nodded.

"You've had a long journey here. Please, drink this." Lana handed her the teacup, and Dorothy accepted it. "It will help calm you."

As Dorothy began sipping her drink, Lana stood up. "I'll return soon. Try to get some rest now."

"Firstly, the establishment of trust was well-done, and now the patient trusts you," Edwina praised with a stern expression as they walked down the corridor. "Secondly," Edwina continued, "you successfully calmed her with the tea. Patients often refuse to drink, fearing we might have added a potion."

Lana nodded, quietly acknowledging the feedback.

"What could be improved is not promising too much," Edwina added.

Lana gave her a puzzled look.

"Sometimes, the process of Gift taming can be challenging," Edwina explained. "It may occur when they become overly reliant on their guides. They must trust you, Lana, but not more than they trust themselves. Your assurance wasn't entirely accurate, so I rate today's practice as three out of five stars."

Lana clenched her teeth, forcing a smile and remaining silent like a well-trained soldier. It was frustrating to get a low mark. However, her score didn't matter. After all, the challenging feedback from Sister Grump made perfect sense – Dorothy had to believe in herself and use her own will to tame her magic successfully. The thought of helping Dorothy get out of this place ignited a spark in Lana's heart.

Suddenly, a desperate scream echoed through the corridor, jolting Lana out of her thoughts. She flinched and turned her head to see two guards clad in black emerging from the corner. They were dragging a girl by her elbows. Though Lana couldn't see the girl's face clearly from that distance, it was evident she was fighting for her freedom.

"Poor creature," Edwina remarked, her expression remaining indifferent. "She's from the most challenging group. A Gift of Fire. She's beyond help and will have to undergo the magic removal procedure."

Lana's heart raced as she observed the unfolding scene with wide eyes. The guardians drew closer, prompting Lana to press her back against the wall to give them room. As the girl turned towards her, their eyes met. *It couldn't be. Rebecca?!*

Cold shivers ran down Lana's spine as she struggled to comprehend the sight before her. The girl she once knew stood before her, now in a dire situation within these walls. The shock of seeing her again was overwhelming.

Rebecca blinked in surprise at the sight of Lana, then directed her attention to the guards restraining her. "Do you know who my father is?! When he finds out what you've done to me, he'll raze this place to the ground!"

One of the guards chuckled dismissively. "Not if you burn him first."

Gritting her teeth, Rebecca retorted, "We'll see."

As the silhouettes of Rebecca and the guards faded into the distance, Lana remained rooted to the spot.

*"Beyond help,"* Edwina repeated as she moved on towards the stairs, leaving Lana alone in the darkened corridor.

From that moment on, Lana's focus shifted to a singular mission – to confront Irida after curfew and find out everything she could use to rescue Becca.

# 19

# The Flames

Becca was pushed into the cell. She landed on the stone floor, and the metal door closed shut, locking her inside. She breathed heavily, watching the guards walking away down the corridor. When they turned the corner, she was left in complete darkness.

Becca dropped her face into her palms, her body shaking. Since waking up in the carriage, she had used all her rage to fight the people in black. Now, there was no one around, and a wave of exhaustion washed over her. She didn't cry, though. Becca was simply too confused. She was most likely delusional – in that corridor, as she was being drugged to her prison, it seemed to her that she saw Lana, her best friend from Triville.

"No, it can't be," Becca said out loud to reassure herself. "Lana has nothing to do with those executors!"

"Who is Lana?" a voice asked from the darkness.

Becca held her breath, trying to understand if it was another trick of her imagination or if someone was really talking to her.

"Hey, are you still there?" the same voice asked.

*It must be another prisoner*, Becca realized. "Of course I'm here. There is no way out, as I understand."

A soft chuckle reached her ears, bringing a little relief. "I'm glad you didn't lose your sense of humor. You'll need it not to break apart."

Becca hugged herself, the bracelets on her wrists rubbing against each other, causing her skin to tingle. "So, there is no escape from this place?"

"Not until you agree to give your power away. Then, you'll be allowed to get out of here. That is what they say."

Becca exhaled a heavy sigh. She had heard a lot about unfortunate women with destructive Gifts, but she could never imagine she would become one of them. Now, it was her turn to rely on the mages who invented all these rules and agree to a complex surgery that could kill her. If it was Divine's will, then it was the worst challenge she ever faced in her entire life.

"So, what's your Gift?" the voice asked.

Becca paused. Usually, when people met, they would first ask, '*What's your name?*' Perhaps here, everything was different. "Fire," she replied in a gloomy voice. "And you?"

"The same." A long pause followed before the voice spoke again. "I set my house on fire when I was asleep, and it burned to ashes."

Becca's heart sank. "Shit."

"I know... My parents and little sister managed to escape, so they didn't suffer."

"It's a relief."

"Not really. Sometimes, I wish they would burn. It was them who ratted me out."

Becca's heart pounded. She was mad, too, despite common sense. The law clearly stated that all girls who noticed signs of the destructive Gift in them must immediately go to the nearest doctor's office or guardian station. The same applied to their families – it was a serious violation if they tried to hide girls with forbidden magic. However, it was too upsetting when people she knew so well got rid of her so quickly.

Becca's 'violation' wasn't as serious – she had just caused a small fire in their chemistry class. It was quickly extinguished thanks to their teacher, Mr. Burke, who used a bucket of sand. After that, the teacher guided Becca to the school doctor's office, and she agreed to take a 'Calming Potion.' Of course, it was a strong sedative that knocked her out. It explained why Becca woke up shortly before their arrival at Mercy House. *How could they do that to me?*

"Are you still mad at them?" Becca asked, trying not to burst into tears.

"I am," the voice responded. "Even though I know they didn't have any choice. It would be too hard to explain why the house was burnt and I stayed alive when they extracted me from under the ashes."

"Did they at least say 'goodbye' to you?"

"No." The voice exhaled a sigh. "They rushed to send me away as soon as they learned it was me who started that fire... I'll never forget their eyes – it was like I wasn't their daughter anymore. Like I had become a monster."

*A Monster.* This word resonated in her chest, causing tears to well up in Becca's eyes. All her life, she had done her best to be an exemplary person. She was a good daughter, a friend, and she volunteered in church, helping the less fortunate. It was so unfair!

"Right, cry it out," the voice said, causing Becca to sob louder. "At least, you can express your feelings freely now."

"Why did it happen to me?" Becca shouted to the ceiling, addressing the power she foolishly believed was meant to protect her. "What have I done wrong?"

"Someone's coming," the voice said. "I guess it's Sisters."

"What the hell do they want from us?"

"What do you think? To give up, of course, so they can wipe us out."

Becca was speechless. *Does it mean we will be killed?* She couldn't risk asking this question – someone's turquoise and purple Lights were already shimmering in the corridor, indicating they were no longer alone.

Then the turquoise Light went off, and the door to her cell opened. Becca could see two women – one of them stayed in the corridor, watching, and the other woman walked in. She had pretty amber eyes and olive skin. If not for the ugly robe she was clad in, Becca would never have taken her for a Mercy Sister. She was simply too pretty for this place, and it seemed that she was here by mistake.

"Hey, I'm Irida," the woman said, revealing a charming smile.

Becca gave her a despised look. "Is that true? Will you kill us?"

"Who told you this nonsense?"

Becca swallowed hard. Perfect, she was about to rat out the only person who might understand her – that prisoner whose name she never learned. "There are rumors I heard in school," Becca said. She didn't lie – there were rumors like that flying in the corridors of high school. It was forbidden to talk about Mercy House; however, every girl on the verge of receiving her Gift knew the creepy tale that nobody with destructive magic made it out alive.

Irida frowned at her. "Oh, those rumors! I have no idea who might believe such absurdity!"

"Then prove it. Show me the ones who went through the surgery and stayed alive."

Irida's eyes gleamed with disappointment. "You are so smart, aren't you?"

"No one complained so far," Becca responded. "So?"

Irida paused before coming back with a reply. "As you might understand, we don't keep the patients who went through the procedure. They became free to go, so they left this place. I promise, after you go through the surgery, you can meet women like you. I can even help arrange that."

Becca narrowed her eyes at her. It seemed that Irida was sincere, but she didn't trust her. "How many girls died during the surgery?"

Irida glanced back at the other woman who stood in the corridor like a silent statue.

"None of them," the other woman said. "I swear by the name of Divine."

"See?" Irida smiled at Becca, as if it was supposed to convince her. "It's all just silly rumors."

"So, you ask me to go through a very risky procedure without giving any actual proof. How fair is that?"

Irida exhaled nervously. "Fine, I'll try to find something that might change your mind. As for now, I really want you to start feeling better. What can I do to make you more comfortable?"

Becca gave it a thought. As far as she knew, they couldn't take her magic by force, so she could at least use this strange woman to find some answers. Becca could start by making sure she wasn't losing her mind. "Can I ask you something?"

"Of course," Irida replied in a quiet voice. "My purpose is to help you. Do you want a soft comforter? A herbal drink? Or a –"

"No," Becca interjected. "Tell me, how well do you know the other Mercy Sisters?"

"Well, I'm pretty familiar with most of them. Why?"

Becca ignored her question. "Do you know a blonde one, petite, with big brown eyes?"

"You mean Lana?"

She stopped breathing. So, she wasn't delusional, and Lana really was here.

Irida leaned closer, her voice dropping to a whisper. "How do you know her?"

Becca paused before replying. It was better to be careful; otherwise, someone might use their acquaintance to ruin Lana's plans. Becca didn't doubt her best friend was up to something. "Can you bring her in? I want to talk to her."

"Just like that, huh?" Irida grew suspicious but continued speaking in whispers. "And why do you think I'm going to help you?"

"Because you want to gain my trust. It's your main goal, isn't it?"

Irida gave her a weary look. "If I arrange that, will you agree to the procedure?"

"I promise I'll start considering the procedure after you prove it's safe," Becca said. "But on one condition."

"Which one?"

"Nobody must know about my request regarding Lana."

Irida glanced at the other woman, then turned back to Becca and grinned. "Deal."

# 20

# A Stolen Light

"Proof. What proof does she want from us?" Sister Amanda questioned as they walked back through the dungeon corridors.

Irida followed closely behind, her eyes fixed on the purple Light Amanda carried. Like a cat hunting for a mouse, she waited for the right moment to make a move. Irida slipped her hand under her robe, feeling a small glass jar.

That morning, she had emptied one of the jam jars she found in the kitchen. Her intention was to use the glass vessel to scoop some Light belonging to senior Sister Amanda, just as Lana had advised her. With that Light, she would finally be able to access the secret archive and steal *The Book of Life*. Then, she would get her payment and start anew. Yes, she always dreamed of having a nice beach house, so she could always hear the whisper of the ocean...

"Alright, I must give you my feedback after today's session," Amanda reminded her, glancing back.

Irida quickly withdrew her hand from the jar. "Feedback?"

"Yes. I'm supposed to evaluate your progress with your very first patient and give you a score. Please listen quietly, and we can discuss your questions at the end. And for the sake of the Divine, can you walk by my side so I can see you?"

Irida nodded silently and moved closer to Amanda. Perhaps it wasn't the best moment to attempt stealing her Light, but they would soon reach the narrow stairs, and then...

"So, firstly, your introduction," Amanda said, interrupting her train of thought. "You introduced yourself, but you never learned that girl's name."

*I never cared to know it.* That strange patient could only bring trouble. Somehow, the girl knew Lana, which meant that senior Sisters would soon learn about it and start asking inconvenient questions. Considering how much Lana knew about her secrets, it was better to get out of this place as soon as possible. If everything went smoothly with her plan, Irida would be free in a matter of hours.

"For the future, her name is Rebecca," Amanda said. "Also, you made a strange promise to bring proof without consulting me first."

Irida nodded, trying to appear apologetic. Meanwhile, the long corridor was coming to an end – Irida could see the dim torchlight from the stairs.

"And lastly," Amanda said, stopping by the stairs and forcing Irida to follow suit. "What was all that whispering about? When you were discussing something at the end?"

*And here everything gets fucked.* Irida gave Amanda an attentive look. Amanda's expression didn't bode well, but Irida could try to persuade her to be more lenient using her charms.

"You're so beautiful tonight," Irida said in a sugary voice, gently tucking a strand of her red hair behind her ear.

Sister Amanda frowned. "Seriously?! You're going to play that card now? Just when I ask you difficult questions?"

Irida shrugged nonchalantly. "I'm sorry. The truth is, during these two weeks of training, I couldn't stop thinking about our kiss. Maybe it affected my performance with the patient, and I messed up. I'm truly sorry about that."

Amanda's expression softened. "You need to be more attentive from now on. If you want to become a senior Sister, you can't afford to make mistakes."

"Agreed," Irida said, locking eyes with her. "Luckily, I have some ideas on how to rectify the mistakes I've made."

"I'm listening."

Irida gave Amanda a small smile. "Firstly, about those whispers at the end of our session. That patient, Rebecca, had an intimate issue. She was too shy to speak loudly about it."

"What was it?"

Irida let out a weary sigh. "She's about to get her period, so she asked me to bring her a napkin."

Amanda nodded in understanding, accepting her explanation. "I see. It can be difficult for some girls to talk about it. It's good that she trusted you."

"Which means my tactic worked," Irida said proudly. "I didn't ask for her name because I didn't want to push her. Rebecca was already distressed, and I wanted to hear about her problems first to gain her trust."

"Good job," Amanda praised. "However, you promised to bring her proof that she would be safe, and that may be challenging to arrange."

Irida shrugged. "'Challenging' doesn't mean 'impossible.' I believe I can help convince her to say 'yes,' and I'm prepared to work hard on it."

Sister Amanda narrowed her eyes at Irida. "And what's your plan? As you mentioned, we don't keep the patients who have undergone the procedure."

Irida pondered for a moment. "Agreed. But they might write gratitude letters to the sisters. The ones who helped them through the darkest times of their lives."

Amanda scoffed. "You're joking, right?"

Irida remained serious. "I know. We both know what we do to them, so it's clear that no one in their right mind would write a gratitude letter. But what if we forge several letters? Then I can pretend I sneaked them from your desk. It might change her mind."

Amanda bit her lip, contemplating. "Wouldn't that contradict our initial tactic? They must believe they entrust their lives to the Divine and feel blessed for surviving the surgery. To make it work, they must believe they really can die."

"To make it work, they must say 'yes,'" Irida pointed out. "The letter might help expedite the process. And I can add some fuel by suggesting that disbelief is a sign of weakness. Trust me, nobody likes being accused of being weak. What do you think?"

"I think we can try it and see how it works," Amanda said, a smile gracing her lips. "I love how you turn failures into victories. I'll give you the best score for this session."

Irida smiled. She couldn't care less about her scores, but it was nice to have calmed Amanda.

Amanda's eyes gleamed, reflecting her purple Light. "Also, you were mentioning something about our kiss?"

"It's impossible to forget."

"Then we shall repeat it sometime."

Irida grinned. Their little game was going smoothly. Perhaps she could take advantage of the time she had to spend within these walls? It would be a nice treat for all her troubles here. "My schedule says I'm free tonight," she whispered.

"Unfortunately, I'm on duty tonight," Amanda said, her voice tinged with regret. "And it's almost curfew hour, so I must escort you to your room."

Irida sighed. The last thing she wanted was to talk to her roommate. She had no doubt Lana would try to push her to get some information about the Sorority secrets, fearing that Irida would disappear right after acquiring *The Book of Life*. Which wasn't entirely untrue. However, engaging in conversation with Lana would only delay things.

"What?" Amanda inquired, noticing her uneasiness. "Is there a problem with your roommate?"

Irida shrugged. "No, she's perfectly fine. I just want to start preparing the letter we discussed, and it would be too risky if Lana notices I'm working on it. She might start asking questions."

"You're right," Amanda agreed. "I see you really want to help your patient as soon as possible, and you rarely have time alone."

"Exactly."

"In that case, I think you should work in the library tonight after curfew."

"Will Edwina approve?"

Amanda grinned. "I'll handle it. How much time do you think you need to write the letter?"

Irida paused, thinking. How much time did she need to explore that secret archive without knowing its size? She had no idea. "I want everything to look perfect, so I would say give me three hours."

"Fine. I'll check on you after midnight, then escort you to your room. Or maybe to my room, so we can have some fun?" Amanda suggested.

Irida smiled, feeling a tingling sensation on her skin. "Sounds great to me."

Amanda smiled back and headed towards the stairs.

Irida followed, but this time, she slowed her breathing and activated her invisible shield. As they reached a wider area where the stairs turned, Irida swiftly extracted the glass vessel and scooped some purple Light. *Perfect!* If she found the book quickly, she could hide it somewhere. Luckily, she would be in the library, so it would be easy to conceal the stolen manuscript behind the rows of other books. Then, she could spend the rest of the night in the bed of a senior Sister and vanish before sunrise.

# 21

# What Future Holds

Irida climbed the ladder to reach the top shelf where the thickest books in leather covers were stored, covered with a solid layer of dust. She ran her fingertips along their spines, reading the titles. They were all ancient encyclopedias, including *The Book of World Creation*, *The Book of Divine*, and even *The Book of Magic Origins*. However, the manuscript she had been searching for so long, *The Book of Life*, was nowhere to be found.

Irida let out a disappointed moan. Her mission was turning into a nightmare. She had spent three hours meticulously checking all the books in this secret archive, but her search had been fruitless so far.

Taking a deep breath, she tried to come up with any idea of where else the manuscript might be hidden. The dust she inhaled made her sneeze, causing her to lose her balance. Her toes slipped, and unable to maintain her grip on the ladder, she fell backward.

Time seemed to come to a standstill as Irida helplessly extended her hands towards the shelves, staring at the dusty books. Her mind struggled to comprehend that this might be the last thing she ever saw. In that moment, her entire life began to flash before her eyes.

Bright memories of her childhood days were quickly replaced by the bittersweet recollection of her first kiss with a girl from her class. The joy of that moment was overshadowed by the heartbreak of losing the girl she loved to pneumonia. It was this tragic event that had sparked Irida's determination to become a doctor. The memories then shifted to her time in medical school, where she encountered a professor who harassed her. Irida vividly remembered his foul smell and the disgust she felt when she stood up to him, telling him to go to hell.

The recollection of these events was followed by dark days of unsuccessful job searches and hunger, leading to her involvement in her first robbery, and eventually, her last. All these experiences had culminated in bringing her to this final day.

Irida closed her eyes, silently praying for a swift and painless transition out of this world. As her back made contact with something bony, she instinctively halted her movements. *That was smooth.*

It took several moments for Irida to realize that she was still breathing. Slowly, she opened her eyes, only to find herself not on the floor and miraculously still alive. Instead, she was being held by a man with a hat and a short black beard.

Blinking in surprise, Irida managed to stammer, "What the...?!"

The man, with emerald-green eyes that seemed to smile at her, introduced himself, "Hey there. I'm David."

Irida gasped, slowly coming back to reality as David gently placed her back on the ground. She found herself clinging to his arm for support, her feet feeling too weak to bear her weight.

"Thank you," she managed to say in a shaky voice. "You saved my life."

He chuckled. "Actually, you wouldn't have died today. You would've just broken your leg. It would have hurt a lot, though. Then you would have needed six months to fully recover. And the worst part – you would've been caught tonight by one of the Sisters, resulting in your expulsion from this place with a huge scandal."

Irida furrowed her brow at his words. The man seemed to have a vivid imagination or perhaps he was simply unhinged. Dealing with him was the last thing she needed at that moment. "Who the hell are you?"

"I'm an Oracle," he explained calmly. "I can see the future."

Irida shook her head in disbelief. "No way. Oracles are born only once every twenty-five years, and there is only one in the entire world."

He nodded, a mischievous grin spreading across his face. "That sounds about right."

"Thank you, then, Mr. Oracle," Irida said with irritation in her voice. Throughout her life, she had encountered many men who had tried to hit on her. Some had pretended to know her future and 'predicted' that she would say 'yes.' None of them had realized that she wasn't interested in men, rendering their entire strategy pointless.

"Relax, I know you prefer women," David said.

Irida's heart raced at his words. She almost believed he could read her mind, or perhaps he had somehow learned about her. "Are you working here? Did Amanda send you?"

"No, I work on Harrison," he clarified. "And before you ask, I didn't lie about my Gift."

Her frown deepened. "So, now I'm supposed to believe that the one and only man like you works for some greedy bastard? Sorry, but it sounds ridiculous."

"It certainly does," David agreed, removing his hat and taking a seat in the only chair in the small room. Irida remained standing, leaning against the wall. "So, how is your search going so far? Do you have any leads on *The Book of Life*?"

Irida let out a sigh. Whoever this man was, he seemed to be well-informed about her mission. Harrison had warned her that his associate would check on her after two weeks, and it seemed that this was the appointed time for his arrival. With nothing to hide, Irida decided to be forthcoming. "As you can see, I've had no luck. I've searched all possible places, including the shelves in the senior Sisters' rooms. There is no sign of such a manuscript."

He gave her a sympathetic look. "Well, it's clear that you've put in a lot of effort and done all you could."

"Exactly," she affirmed. "I've given it my all. Perhaps Harrison was mistaken, and the book isn't actually here?"

"The book is here, Irida," he insisted. "As an Oracle, and I can see that there is a chance you can find it."

"If you're an Oracle, why don't you just retrieve it yourself?" Irida asked, her patience wearing thin. "I mean, you can foresee where each step leads, including your own. You managed to gain access to the Mercy House secret archive without any issues!"

"Yes, I did manage to get here using my Gift. However, there is a limitation to my abilities that not many are aware of – I cannot see the future of people I've never met. I arrived here because I can only see my future and yours, and I followed the most straightforward path to meet you without encountering any guards or Mercy Sisters."

Irida regarded him with confusion. "But you've only just met me. How were you able to see my future?"

"I saw you when you were at Harrison's house. Do you recall when the maid brought you clean sheets?"

Irida nodded, remembering the moment. At the time, she had been too exhausted to pay much attention to the guard whose face had been concealed by a hat – the same hat he was wearing now.

"I was standing near you," David continued to explain. "That's how I could sense your energy and establish a connection with it. And as you might understand, I don't need to reveal myself to read a person." He glanced at his watch. The time crystal glowed a rusty-red color, indicating that it was past midnight. "Alright, I hope that answers all your questions. We only have fifteen minutes left before someone checks this place and discovers us."

Irida's heart raced at the thought of being caught. Who would be visiting the archive at such a late hour? Perhaps it was Amanda, who had failed to locate her in the library room. She sighed. "Okay, I understand. But I still can't comprehend one thing – why can't you foresee the safest way to retrieve the manuscript yourself?"

"*The Book of Life* is protected by a special ancient spell that shields it from Oracles," he explained patiently. "I'm unable to see the book or sense its location unless someone willingly gives it to me."

"Then how do you know that it's within this building?"

"It was a hell of a research journey, including piquing Harrison's interest in this manuscript. It took me nearly five years to discover its whereabouts, so let's get back to searching already!"

"Wait," Irida interjected, raising her hand to silence him. "Are you saying... Harrison is just a pawn in your game? You're using him to obtain that book?"

He met her gaze unwaveringly. "Aren't we all pawns in someone's game?"

Irida gave him a weary look. "Enough with the philosophical bullshit."

"Alright. You want the truth? Here it is – *The Book of Life* contains the fundamental principles governing our world's order. Harrison knows that possessing this knowledge will open numerous doors for him."

"So, you won't keep it for yourself?"

David shook his head. "There's no need to keep it. I seek this knowledge solely to solve my own problem."

"What problem?"

He grinned. "We only have twelve minutes left now. If you want to accomplish your mission, you need to focus. Otherwise, you'll fail and end up back to your life as a small-time thief until you get caught –"

"Okay, fine!" Irida interrupted, rolling her eyes. She couldn't bear to hear any more of his predictions. David did have a valid point – she had a task to complete, and his personal plans regarding the book were not her concern. "What do I need to do to find it?"

"Firstly, I would appreciate it if you put in more effort," David said, giving her a sharp look. "I may not be able to sense the book's location, but I can see it through the perspectives of others. If there's a chance for you to find it, then you must keep searching."

"Then tell me how to obtain it."

"I wish I could. Unfortunately, that's not how my Gift works. I can only predict several possible scenarios of your immediate future, Irida," David explained. He gestured towards the ladder from which she had fallen, leading her right into his arms. "The likelihood of you falling from that ladder was high if you were exhausted and stressed. I also foresaw that you would feel stressed due to the prolonged duration of your search. I even saw which bone you would break and how long it would take to heal. However, you also had the choice not to climb so high because of your fatigue. In that case, I would have met you at the door, and we would be having this same conversation, albeit a much shorter one."

"I see," Irida said. She briefly considered leaving the room and continuing her search the next day. However, her impatience prevailed over common sense. "What choices should I make to find the book?"

"I just described one event. The next day will be full of multiple new choices," David remarked as he rose from his seat and picked up a piece of charcoal from the floor. He began drawing a straight line on the wall. "This is how most people envision their day. But our lives are not linear. Each day is shaped by numerous choices. For instance, would you opt for cereal or toast for breakfast?"

He split the line into two branches. "Some choices may seem insignificant, like your breakfast, but others can lead to entirely different paths you might take. For example, you could make a friend or gain an enemy based on how you treat someone." He divided each line into further forks. "Then you have even more choices – how you spend time with your friend or how you handle conflicts with your enemy. Each subsequent day unfolds with new potential scenarios."

The visual representation made Irida think of Lana. Since her arrival, Irida had made continuous efforts to earn Lana's trust, although she had not succeeded in doing so. Nevertheless, their interactions had prevented them from becoming enemies, which was a positive outcome. "I think I understand the concept," Irida remarked. "But what about the manuscript I'm supposed to find?"

"That possibility does exist, but there are too many choices you need to navigate to reach it, creating numerous diverging paths that I can't clearly see. It's all jumbled into a vast kaleidoscope of events, and everything appears blurry," David explained. His eyes began to shine brighter, resembling two emeralds in the daylight.

In response to his mystical appearance, the bracelet on Irida's wrist vibrated, her time crystal turning white. Feeling the crystal grow warm, Irida shook her wrist in surprise. "Whoa, what's happening?"

David rubbed his eyelids, causing her time crystal to shift to a copper hue. "Time crystals always react when someone nearby uses the Gift of Time."

"Ah, that's interesting."

"Anyhow," David continued, "you've clearly reached your limits for now. You have searched all the possible places and hit a dead end. But here's the good news – someone in this very building knows exactly where the manuscript is, perhaps one of the senior Sisters. You just need to find a way to get this person to talk. You must choose the right approach to engage with them."

Irida furrowed her brow. She had no doubt that Edwina knew the manuscript's location, but she was certain the woman would not willingly share that information with her. *Unless...*

"Keep thinking," David encouraged. "I see the window of possibilities opening wider."

"Lana, the woman I share my room with. She's a mind reader and could potentially access Sister Grump's memories," Irida suggested.

David's smile widened. "Bingo! Is Lana reliable?"

Irida shrugged. "I've tried to earn her trust, but she's quite tough."

David gave her a mischievous look. "Have you exhausted all other methods of persuasion?"

The memory of her intimate conversation with Lana on the night of their arrival flooded back to Irida. "I tried to pique her interest to seduce her later," she admitted.

"How did it go?"

Irida shook her head. "She is as straight as an arrow! She can't be swayed in that way."

"Hmm..." David tossed the piece of charcoal to the floor and dusted off his hands. "Alright, we're running out of time. We have two minutes to leave the corridor without being noticed, and I can't risk staying any longer."

Irida's eyes widened. "Aren't you staying to help?"

He shook his head. "I've provided the assistance needed, Irida. You now have the clarity to proceed. From this point on, it's your responsibility to do everything in your power to persuade Lana to collaborate with you. I can't see her future as I haven't met her, but I'm certain she holds the key to finding the manuscript."

"Okay."

"I'll meet you once you've completed that task," David assured her.

"And when will that be?" she inquired, hoping for any hint or guidance.

He grinned. "On the day when a hundred fires blaze in the skies."

"Must you always speak in riddles?"

"Of course not. I simply find straightforward explanations dull. Riddles are far more engaging." He glanced towards the entrance door. "Alright, we need to leave now. I see you're on the verge of encountering a very irate Sister."

Irida let out a sigh and followed David out into the corridor.

# 22

# Busted

Lana crept along the corridor wall, her woolen socks muffling her footsteps. These socks were the only useful part of her wardrobe now that Edwina had confiscated her pretty dresses and even her lingerie. Instead, she was forced to wear the dull robes and itchy tops provided by the Sorority, along with panties made of flax that were too large and prone to slipping off her frame. Lana had resorted to using pins to secure them in place.

As she reached the next turn, Lana paused to scratch her itching belly and pondered the situation. Irida had missed curfew that night, yet Edwina hadn't questioned her absence. It seemed that Irida had found a way to bend the rules and had possibly broken into the secret archive. There was a strong possibility that Irida had already located the book and was planning to escape.

Lana was determined to prevent that from happening, which is why she persisted in using Irida's pick to unlock her door until she succeeded. Now, she faced another dilemma – where to find Irida? She must be hiding somewhere in the building. But where?

After some contemplation, Lana remembered that all the guards at Mercy House were recruited by the same person who had organized the bank robberies. It was possible that one of these guards was aiding Irida. After all, she would need assistance to escape unnoticed. The thought of apprehending Irida and her accomplice made Lana's heart race. If she could catch them in the act, Irida would likely divulge all her secrets to avoid trouble. With a determined smile, Lana hurried towards the stairs.

On the first floor, in the wing where the guards and rare visitors usually slept, Lana began to approach the closed doors one by one, listening for any suspicious sounds. At one door, she pressed her ear to the keyhole and froze. She could hear a man speaking quietly to someone inside. The voice sounded familiar. Too familiar. *Walter?!*

Lana retrieved her pick and inserted it into the lock, relying on her newfound skills as a burglar. With a twist, the lock clicked open, and Lana burst into the room.

There was only one person inside, and she fixed him with a steely glare. "Where is she?"

Walter appeared utterly bewildered. "Who?"

Lana advanced towards him. Walter stood there, half-naked in only his cotton pants, but Lana paid no mind to his appearance. "I know you lied to me, so don't waste my time pretending."

"Fine." Walter raised his hands in surrender. "I may have lied to you. But only once."

She narrowed her eyes, waiting for him to continue.

"That night when I slept with you, I lied about the carriage I saw," Walter confessed, swallowing nervously as he met Lana's gaze. "I only came to see you again. I hoped you were vulnerable and... I took advantage."

Lana stared at him in disbelief. "You lied about the carriage?!"

Walter shrugged, his expression apologetic. "Sorry. You tempted me too badly, I guess."

"What the hell?" Lana almost screamed. "You ruined the life I had!"

"That night, it didn't seem like you regretted it. Not at all," Walter countered, crossing his arms defensively.

"I thought my relationship was over," Lana retorted.

"As did I."

Lana fell silent. It was true – Walter wasn't solely responsible for the breakdown of her relationship with Oliver. It was her own fault for being full of doubts when Walter had visited her room.

Despite this, Walter was still hiding something. Lana regretted not reading his mind deeper when she had a chance. Just before her departure to Mercy House, she had only briefly explored his connection to Irida. There must be more to it.

"What are you doing at Mercy House?" Lana inquired. "Have you come to offer belated apologies?"

"Hush." Walter's expression turned alarmed, causing Lana to clench her teeth. In the ensuing silence, they could hear footsteps echoing in the corridor.

"Ah, here she is." Lana pointed towards the corridor. "Let's see what else you two are hiding from me."

"I'm hiding nothing!" Walter protested, rushing towards the door and attempting to shut it.

Lana reacted swiftly, leaping towards the door and gripping the doorknob to prevent Walter from locking it.

"Holy Divine!" A voice from the other side of the door startled them both.

Lana stepped back. That the voice did not belong to Irida. It had a monotonous tone that reminded her of the training sessions that often put her to sleep.

Sister Amanda pushed the door open and entered, holding a purple ball of Light that trembled in her hand. "Just look at you two!"

Lana and Walter exchanged glances. Walter spoke first. "Please, Sister, allow me to explain."

Amanda scrutinized Walter from head to toe, her expression remaining neutral. *Interesting, when was the last time Amanda saw a half-naked man? And why is she so stoic?* Lana considered two possible explanations: Amanda was either deeply devoted to her Divine service or... she simply wasn't interested in men.

This theory would certainly explain her close relationship with Irida. Lana dismissed her musings because it was irrelevant at the moment. The crucial point was that Amanda was not Edwina. At least, this Sister could be reasoned with.

Sister Amanda escorted them to the reception room on the first floor, a place where she often performed night duty.

Seated on visitor chairs, Lana stole a glance at Walter. He had donned a shirt, likely to appear more presentable in front of Sister Amanda. Despite his efforts, he appeared uneasy. *Maybe I was mistaken and Walter truly has no involvement with Irida?* In that case, it meant Lana had caused unnecessary trouble for both of them.

Amanda settled behind the desk and interlocked her fingers. "Miss Morris, please clarify two things for me – how did you gain access to this man's room, and what prompted you to raise your voice at him so loudly?"

Lana adopted her most apologetic expression. "I'm very sorry. Walter and I have a complicated history. We were discussing an unresolved issue when you arrived."

"Um-hum." Amanda nodded, her disappointment evident in her expression. "That may account for the screams. Now, how did you manage to leave your room and gain access to his?"

Lana glanced at Walter, silently urging him to provide an explanation. After all, he had nothing to lose, and he could at least try to protect Lana. Especially, after everything he had done to her. However, Walter merely grinned back at her.

"Miss Morris?" Amanda prompted. "Do you have anything to say?"

*Fuck it. I don't need this man's help.* Lana cleared her throat before speaking. "Yes, of course. It's quite an interesting tale. One day, while strolling in the garden, I stumbled upon a pick. It appeared to be an antique trinket, so I kept it. To my astonishment, I later discovered that it could unlock the door to my room, and more!"

Amanda regarded her wearily. "Consider the consequences when I relay this clearly fabricated story to Sister Edwina."

Lana swallowed hard. Sister Edwina would likely dismiss her from Mercy House without hesitation, jeopardizing her ability to help Rebecca, Dorothy, and the other girls. The thought brought tears to her eyes.

"Okay, I can see that you genuinely regret your actions," Amanda said, offering Lana a handkerchief. Lana accepted it with a quiet sob. "I understand that you're young and emotional, and that you truly want to assist our patients."

Lana wiped away a tear. "That's all I want."

Amanda's tone softened. "Then why do you jeopardize your opportunities so recklessly?" She gestured towards Walter. "Is it truly worth it?"

Lana shook her head. The truth was that she had put herself in significant danger while searching for Irida. She must be more cautious moving forward. "I'm truly sorry. I've been under a lot of stress here, as you may know. Walter was one of the few people who supported me. He helped me get here. I simply wanted to see him again."

"Really?" Amanda's voice held a hint of skepticism.

"Yes," Lana affirmed. She took Walter's hand and squeezed it tightly, which only elicited a chuckle from him.

"I understand," Walter said, playing along with Lana's deception. "I missed you as well. But you could have waited until morning."

"I couldn't," Lana insisted.

Amanda cleared her throat, drawing their attention. "It seems like you two have some serious matters to discuss. However, your relationship isn't healthy. Lana claims she couldn't wait to see you, Walter, yet she ended up yelling at you. What was the cause of that?"

Lana reiterated her previous explanation. "It was an unresolved conflict. But I have forgiven him for it. We're on good terms now." She spoke sincerely this time. Meeting with Amanda had reminded her that, had it not been for Walter's deceit regarding the carriage, Lana would never have arrived at Mercy House and learned about Rebecca. Perhaps it was all part of a greater plan, orchestrated by Divine. Now, saving Rebecca was her primary objective.

"I'm glad to hear you've found the strength to forgive this man," Amanda remarked.

"Me too," Walter chimed in.

Amanda gave him a weary look. "Mr. Mills, you may leave now."

Walter rose from his seat and cast a parting glance at Lana. "See you tomorrow."

Lana nodded silently. She couldn't wait to meet Walter the following day. It seemed like an opportunity to catch a glimpse of the outside world beyond the confines of the facility's walls. She hoped that their talk would alleviate some of her worries.

"Now, about the pick." Amanda extended her hand, palm up. "Hand it over to me, and I'll keep it. Consider this a final warning."

Lana let out a heavy sigh and gazed at the pick in her hand. It represented a slender thread leading to freedom. If Irida truly intended to escape, Lana could use it to leave her room and rescue Rebecca from the dungeons.

"Hand it over to me," Amanda repeated.

Lana placed the pick on her palm and closed her eyes, acknowledging her defeat.

Amanda took the pick and placed it in her drawer, the sound of it clanking before she shut it. "I've heard you've started working with your first patient."

"Yes," Lana confirmed, giving Amanda her full attention. Sister Amanda wasn't as harsh as Sister Grump. She was a mentor and the only person Lana could converse with without needing special permission. Perhaps Amanda could offer assistance. "Today, I learned about one challenging patient who was just admitted. Can I also work with her?"

"Which one? The Gift of Fire?"

"Yes. I believe I can help her."

"Because she's from Triville?" Amanda's suspicion was evident in her narrowed eyes. "Just like you?"

Before Lana could respond, Amanda issued a warning. "Sisters are not permitted to work with patients they know personally."

Lana exhaled, relieved that she hadn't disclosed her connection to Rebecca. "I had no knowledge of that."

"So, have you two met before?"

"No," Lana lied, shaking her head. "She's a teenager, so there's a significant age difference between us. That probably explains why we've never crossed paths."

"Understood. Let me check." Amanda opened a registration journal containing all the patient records. "Rebecca Turner. She's a recent arrival, and her Gift falls under the third category. She's slated for surgery."

"She must provide her consent first," Lana reminded her. "And now that we know we're from the same town, it might help me establish trust with her more quickly."

"Well, in that case, it shouldn't pose much of an issue," Amanda agreed, her words instilling hope in Lana. "To gain permission to work with her, you simply need to pass your test successfully. Starting with your first patient."

"I'll give it my best shot," Lana promised.

"During your last assessment, you only scored three points," Amanda said, furrowing her brow. "It's not particularly impressive, but there's still a chance. You must pass your first three sessions with an average score of no less than 3.5 points."

Lana smiled confidently. "Then I'll do my best."

# 23

## The Force Within

Lana walked down the dark basement corridor, following Edwina. Somewhere deep in the dungeons, Becca, her best friend, was being held captive because of her Gift. The thought of Becca being alone in a windowless cave, cuffed and abandoned, made Lana's heart ache.

*Is there any hope for her?* As Lana had learned from Amanda the night before, there was a chance she would be allowed to see her friend. Being able to speak to Becca would make it easier to help her. Becca was brave and smart, and together they could find a way out of this darkness.

In order to see Becca, today Lana had to pass a test and teach Dorothy to control her magic. Lana had to give one hundred percent of her efforts to this session to get a good mark.

As they came to a stop, Lana nodded at Edwina and entered the cell. Dorothy sat on her bed, her feet in woolen socks barely reaching the stone floor. The night before, Lana had brought her a soft blanket and warm clothes to provide some comfort while sleeping.

"How do you feel?" Lana asked, approaching her.

"Still sore."

Lana sat nearby and took Dorothy's hands. Her thin fingers were as cold as icicles. While her wrists had healed somewhat since the previous evening, Dorothy still needed more time to fully recover.

"I'll take your bracelets off as soon as you learn to redirect your power," Lana said.

"How can I do that?"

"First, we need to understand what causes spontaneous energy boosts. Do you remember what happened the last time you used your Gift?"

"I was in class. One girl I don't like was teasing me, and I wanted her to stop talking. Her voice was annoying," Dorothy explained.

Lana waited patiently for her to continue.

"Then... that girl started choking. I just stared at her, firstly glad she finally shut up, then worried. I knew it might be my power doing it, but I couldn't stop it."

"What happened to her?" Lana asked, trying not to sound judgmental. "Did she survive?"

Dorothy nodded. "Yes. Someone in the classroom had figured it was my doing. That other girl pushed me, and I fell to the floor. I got scared, and my Gift stopped working."

"It's good that you let go of your power," Lana encouraged her. "See, no tragedy happened."

Dorothy didn't share Lana's optimism. "Those girls started yelling that I was going to kill them all! Our teacher brought me directly to the principal, and that very day, the guardians took me and sent me away." She sobbed. "I might never see my parents again. And everyone in my school thinks I'm a creep."

"Anger," Lana said.

Dorothy blinked, visibly confused.

Lana gave her a compassionate look before explaining, "Anger is a normal human reaction when someone attacks you. It's our base instinct, and there's nothing wrong about *feeling* it. But we can always choose how to *express* it. In your case, you unconsciously used your Gift to protect yourself."

"Maybe. Honestly, I had no idea I had this magic. It had just manifested."

"Now, you're aware of it. You only need to learn how to deal with your anger."

"How?"

"I'll give you something you can practice on," Lana said, standing up. She picked up the teacup she had brought with her the night before. The cup was now empty, so Lana placed it against the far wall and returned to Dorothy. "Okay. See that cup?"

"Yes."

"Now, when I take your bracelets off, you'll extend your hand towards it and focus. I need you to concentrate fully on this object and not wave your hands. Can you do it?"

"I'll try. Then what?"

"Then, you must destroy it."

Dorothy glanced at the cell door, then at Sister Grump. "Are you sure it's okay if I break the cup?"

"It's better if you break a cup than someone's neck," Lana reassured her as she began detaching the first bracelet using a tiny key. Lana then removed the second bracelet. "How do you feel?"

"Much better," Dorothy said, rubbing her palms together. Then, she extended her hands to the cup and squinted her eyes. "My power doesn't work," she concluded after a minute of puffing. "I try but nothing comes out."

"It's because you need to get used to it. Also, remember that anger is your trigger. Probably, right now, you aren't angry enough."

"Then how will I destroy it?"

Lana leaned in close to her ear. "Just remember that mean girl from your class, all the offensive words she said to you. How she looked at you when she said you might kill them all."

Dorothy's breath quickened, and her hands started shaking.

"Good," Lana encouraged her. "Now, focus and channel this anger into your hands."

Dorothy clenched her teeth, and then the cup exploded with a deafening sound. She breathed out. "Wow!"

"I know, right?" Lana smiled, taking the girl's hand. Her palm was warm now. "See? This is how you can release the remnants of your magic if you need to."

"Okay," Dorothy said, looking at her hands in amazement. "What if I feel angry but can't express it? Like in the classroom, when everyone is watching me?"

Lana gave her a sad look. "Unfortunately, women in our society are expected to embody patience and kindness. It's not always possible, and I explained why."

"The instinct to protect myself," Dorothy concluded.

"Exactly. With time, you'll have other people in your life whom you want to protect – your partner, your family. And you might not be able to do that with your Gift, for example, if someone attacks you verbally."

Dorothy fidgeted in her bed. "What should I do, then?"

"You will often need to remind yourself that there is no point in being angry with others. You see, all the abusers are usually deeply wounded people, and they are unkind to you because they don't know any other way to cope with their pain."

Her expression turned concerned. "So, they're all hurt?"

"Mostly, yes. And the deeper their wounds, the worse they treat you."

"Is there a way to help them?"

Lana smiled at her. This girl was so kind. With the proper guidance, she could have a bright future. "You can't help people unless they ask for help. Unfortunately, the wounded ones are often too scared to show their weaknesses. It's an instinct, too. That's why you must try not to be judgmental, even if they are very rude. Please understand that it's always their pain talking, not their common sense."

Dorothy nodded. "You're right. That mean girl has a bunch of issues. Her parents are constantly arguing."

"Then it might be the case," Lana said with a sigh.

"Gee, now I see," Dorothy exclaimed, widening her eyes. "There is no reason to be angry at her. It's *them*. Her destructive family."

"They are most likely wounded, too," Lana reminded her. "As well as their parents used to be. It is called 'generational trauma.'"

"Why can't they heal it?"

"They might if someone from their family breaks that cycle," Lana mused. "It might be that girl. She only needs guidance and support to do it."

"Can I help her?"

"You can try to be kind and supportive when she is around. This is how you can win her trust. But as for guidance, it's better if she sees a specialist who can help her deal with her issues and heal. Healing takes time, so you need to be patient."

"And if not, I can just blow up another teacup," Dorothy joked.

"Exactly."

"Two out of five," Edwina's words were like a knife piercing Lana's heart.

Lana widened her eyes in disbelief. She had worked so hard, and with these disappointing marks, her chances of ever seeing Rebecca seemed to plummet to zero.

"You can't teach the patients to channel their energy and release it. They must be able to bottle up their feelings." Edwina's voice was full of disappointment. "And that talk about generational trauma you gave her is complete nonsense! Where did you get it from?"

"From my therapist," Lana explained, seizing a rare chance to speak. "She helped me a lot with understanding my emotions and dealing with my Gift. Her scientific project on humanistic psychology yielded so many positive results –"

"I'll stop you right here," Edwina interrupted. "Science is evil, and we're completely against it. We're all creatures of Divine, and there are sacred rules we must obey."

*This place is evil.* Lana didn't regret her session with Dorothy, not at all. At least now, that girl had hope and enough confidence to control her Gift, regardless of what the other Sisters might try to convince her of. Lana doubted they had ever read any books on psychology. It was clear they preferred their outdated scripts and senseless rules.

Edwina gave her a despicable look. "I'll assign her to the other Sister, a more competent one."

Lana nodded in silence. As her chances of passing the test successfully sank to the bottom of the abyss, she knew she must think of another way to get to Rebecca. *I must find Irida before it's too late.*

# 24

# A Dying Spring

Lana couldn't find Irida in their room or outside. The late morning was foggy, and the humid air crept under her ugly robe as she wandered around the garden, but the cold was the least of her concerns. After searching behind all the trees, Lana settled onto the stiff bench and gazed at the azalea bush. It wasn't in bloom yet, but the tiny buds were a bright shade of pink, ready to blossom. *Unlike those girls who would have their power taken away*, her inner voice added in a grim tone.

"Hey there," Walter said as he sat nearby. "What's with the gloom and doom?"

His smile made her cringe. Lana had almost forgotten about his presence at Mercy House, and now she was expected to engage in conversation.

Lana spoke, but her voice sounded indifferent. "It's nice to see you."

He frowned. "Well, I warned you, this place isn't a resort."

"I know," she agreed.

"Is it that bad?"

She let out a sigh. "I'm going to miss the spring ball this year. It's so unfortunate."

"What?! Is that the only thing bothering you?"

Lana nodded. What else could she say to avoid breaking the oath of secrecy and dropping dead?

"Okay. Maybe my news will cheer you up." Walter's smile revealed his excitement. "There's no one tailing you. Since the day you mentioned seeing the carriage, we've been monitoring the dorms constantly. We even reached out to your curator and a few students you're close to. It's been over two weeks now, and no one has made any attempts to contact them. We also haven't noticed any suspicious activity in the area. So, I believe they've given up on you. You can safely return to Middle Lake and resume your studies."

His report didn't surprise Lana, considering they had both fabricated the story about the carriage and people spying on her. Only Walter was unaware of her deception.

"That's great news," Lana responded with sadness in her voice.

"Aren't you happy? You can leave this place now."

"Not until I see my friend," she spat, thinking of Rebecca locked in the dungeon. Her words caused her heart to squeeze in pain, making it difficult to breathe. Lana pressed her hand to her chest, gasping for air.

"Lana?" Walter shook her shoulder. "What's happening?"

*Damn oath.* Lana clenched her teeth as the pain enveloped her ribcage. *This is how inaccurate words might cause a heart attack.* Lana had to correct it before the spell tying her to the Mercy Sorority killed her. "I meant... Irida is my friend.... I need to see her before I go." The spasm began to ease, allowing her to breathe normally.

Walter looked concerned. "Okay. There's no need to be so worried. Talk to Irida, then I'll come get you."

"No. I'm not going anywhere."

He frowned. "Okay. I think I know what this is about."

"I doubt that."

"It's about our argument last night. You're still upset with me."

*Gee... Among all my problems, this is the last thing I worry about. And I can't even tell you about it.* Lana bit her tongue before she could reveal another truth. It was excruciating not to be able to open her mouth and ask for help. Walter seemed to be sincerely worrying about her, unaware of the dark secrets unfolding in this place. Lana had no doubt that if Walter learned about Becca, he would want to help. *If only there was a way to speak to him openly!*

His hand gently landed on her shoulder. "Please, don't be mad."

"I'm not angry with you, Walter."

"Then what's happening?"

She sighed. "I wish I could tell you."

He narrowed his eyes, deep in thought. "Okay, I think I get it. When we enter the Guardian House, we take an oath –"

Her palm covered his lips. "Please, stop talking. This is all new to me, and I'm afraid of making a mistake."

He nodded and gently removed her hand. "Then let's drop the subject and do something you would enjoy. Just tell me what else you missed here."

*I missed freedom.* Lana craned her head, gazing at his neck. His shirt was slightly unbuttoned, revealing his upper torso. Her hand traveled to his chest, seeking solace in his warmth. After enduring so much stress, her body felt as stiff as a dry fruit. What if she could allow herself to relax and forget about all her worries, at least for an hour? The idea of engaging in something forbidden behind Sister Grump's back seemed exhilarating. If she could ease the bitterness of her failure by inviting a man into her bedroom, then so be it.

Walter caught her hand. "Did I ever tell you how much you tempt me?"

"As much as you tempt me." She gave him a mischievous smile. "What do you say if you wait for me in my bed?"

He licked his lips, clearly intrigued by her proposition. "That sounds thrilling. But I don't know where your room is."

"Third floor, the last room to the left." She leaned in closer and whispered, "it's unlocked. Go in there and take your pants off."

After Walter left, Lana remained seated on the bench for another ten minutes to avoid arousing suspicion. This brief romantic interlude had provided a welcome distraction from her main concerns. Perhaps she should wait here in case Irida appeared, but Lana was too weary from waiting.

Standing up, Lana smoothed out the hem of her unattractive gray robe, pretending it was a beautiful ball gown. She then strolled along the yard, seeking the shade of the orchard trees. At this time of year, the trees had ceased blooming, and the tiny white petals lay wilted and brittle on the grass beneath her feet.

Upon reaching the castle entrance, Lana halted and gazed up at the narrow windows. In that moment, the clouds dispersed, allowing a beam of sunlight to reflect off the glass, momentarily blinding her.

Lana shielded her eyes, attempting to discern if the stairs were clear to pass without encountering another bothersome Sister who always sought to keep everyone occupied. Then, she spotted Irida. Irida stood on the other side of the window, pressing her forehead against the glass. A smile spread across her face as their eyes met.

"Miss Morris?" The voice behind her belonged to Amanda.

*Damn it.* Lana forced a polite smile and turned to face her. "Good morning, Sister Amanda."

Amanda's expression was filled with concern. "I just reviewed your records and noticed that your patient was reassigned to another Sister. What happened in your session today?"

*Edwina happened, with her ridiculous, outdated rules.* Instead of voicing her frustration aloud, Lana opted for a brief response. "Nothing."

Unsatisfied with her answer, Amanda continued to gaze at her inquisitively.

Lana glanced back at the window. Irida flashed her a teasing smile and began ascending to the third floor, likely to relax in their bedroom before lunch. *Bedroom.* Lana's eyes widened as she realized Walter was waiting for her there. And if her memory served her right, she had instructed him to undress. *Crap!*

"I know," Amanda said, pushing Lana's nerves to the edge. "It's unfortunate you couldn't assist her."

Lana shot her an exhausted look. "Me too. But I have to go now."

"Where to?"

*To prevent Irida from bumping into Walter. And to finally read her mind!* Lana swallowed, trying to maintain her composure. "To my room. I'm not feeling well." Well, at least that part wasn't a lie.

"I know what can help you feel better." Amanda offered an encouraging smile. "We have a celebration coming up, and you can lend me a hand."

"A celebration? For real?!" Lana widened her eyes. It was hard to believe that those serving in Mercy House were capable of experiencing simple joy, let alone celebrating.

"Yes. It will be a charity concert by the Middle Lake theatre troupe. They hold it every year for the girls undergoing the taming sessions. It helps them feel supported and loved by Divine Light."

"It's so ... human."

Amanda chuckled. "See? It's not all bleak. And if you assist, it's a way to earn some extra points."

"That's really kind of you," Lana replied. "I'll do whatever you ask of me."

"Very well. Let's discuss it then." Amanda took Lana by the elbow and guided her back to the garden.

With no opportunity to return to her room, Lana could only wonder what would transpire between Irida and Walter. *I hope they can handle it somehow.*

# A Prank

Irida pressed her hand to her stomach, laughing. Walter, the guardian who used to be so courageous when pressing charges during her arrest, now looked so defenseless! Wrapping his lower body in a bedsheet, he breathed heavily, his face blushing. This view was priceless. Irida couldn't be more grateful for this Divine justice.

"Stop laughing!" Walter waved one of his hands, his other hand holding onto the sheet.

"Or what?" Irida gave him a teasing look. "You're gonna file a complaint?! Oh, right... now it's you who broke the law."

Walter clenched his teeth, giving her a chance to mock him harder.

"Interesting, what will Captain Harrison say when he learns you sneaked into the bedroom of Mercy Sisters like that?" Irida giggled as she collected his clothes from the floor. "I can actually call a senior Sister to witness your naked state. I bet it will be fun."

With his face beet-red, he grabbed his boot from the floor and threw it at Irida.

She dodged, laughing. "Look who tried to attack me! Is it that same guardian who brought an oath to protect people from evil?"

"You're evil!"

Irida raised her index finger, making her point. "It needs to be proved. But your guilt is clear." She stepped closer to the exit door. "Interesting, will you be able to jump from the third floor and get back to your room unnoticed?"

He rushed towards her, but Irida jumped back, closing the door behind her. Luck was on her side, as the door had to be pushed from the corridor to keep it closed. She pressed onto it with her whole body, fighting with Walter who was trying to open it from the inside. Considering he had more muscle power and the Telekinesis Gift which made him stronger, she had to act swiftly to lock him inside. She reached for her pick, the extra one she had in her possession besides the one she had shown to Lana. However, before Irida could stick it in a keyhole, the door flew open, throwing her to the opposite wall. She held her breath, pressing the clothes she had stolen to her chest.

Walter appeared on the threshold, furious. Raising his hand to the ceiling, he used his power, making her float towards him. Irida's feet slid along the floor as she tried to resist the inevitable.

"What the hell is going on here?!" Lana's voice roared, causing them both to stop moving.

As Walter released her from his magic clutches, Irida kneeled on the floor. She raised her eyes to Lana and chuckled. "I had the same question when I walked into our bedroom. What a nice surprise you arranged for me!"

Walter's eyebrows furrowed. "Seriously?! It was just a silly prank?"

Lana batted her eyes, her mouth half-open.

"And it was a good one," Irida teased. She doubted Lana had made him come into the room as a joke, however, she enjoyed adding fuel to the fire.

Walter exhaled loudly, addressing Lana. "So this is how you punish me for being honest!"

Lana finally regained her ability to speak. "It wasn't like that. I can explain."

"Don't waste your time." He moved to Irida and collected his clothes. "I'm not staying in this place any longer."

"Please, Walter! It's just a misunderstanding," Lana pleaded. "Let's talk."

"We have nothing to discuss." He glared at her before leaving. "Now I see why all your relationships end up this way."

Irida watched him walking proudly to the stairs, despite the sheet flapping behind him. Then she turned to Lana.

Her beautiful brown eyes were filled with disappointment. "Was it necessary to act like a child?"

Irida shrugged. "Sorry. I was still mad at him. It was Walter who arrested me, and since then, I was forced to take part in their troublesome missions. Today I just saw him vulnerable and had some fun. I guess I got carried away a bit."

"Yeah, a tiny bit," Lana said with a hint of sarcasm. "I hope it was worth it."

"Oh, it absolutely was!" She laughed.

"Unbelievable. Did it occur to you that you've just ruined our relationship?"

Irida blinked. "You never mentioned you two were in a relationship."

Lana shook her head and walked into the room. She sat on the corner of her bed, her eyes wandering over the peculiar portrait on the wall. Irida narrowed her eyes at the painting, curious about how it looked today.

The interesting thing about that painting was that the woman pictured on it could change her facial expression, and the shades could change from joyful-bright to grayscale. Today, the woman was all gray, her lips pressed tightly together, her eyes glossy as if she was about to burst into tears. Irida had never seen such a painting technique before, so she could relate to Lana's interest in this object.

"Why do you think she is like that today?" Lana asked, nodding at the painting.

Irida shrugged. "I assume it's just a reaction to the weather. When it's cloudy, it takes darker shades."

As she spoke, the sun climbed out of the clouds and lit up the painting. However, the painting didn't change, indicating that her theory wasn't correct. Disappointed, Irida turned her attention to Lana.

Sitting on the bed and hugging her shoulders, Lana seemed so fragile. *Gee, I made her too upset.* Fortunately, Irida could try to fix this. For the sake of her new mission.

Irida sat near. "I'm very sorry about Walter. I thought he was just a fling. Nothing serious."

"It might get serious with time," she said with doubt in her voice.

"Do you want me to talk to him? I can explain it was all my fault. And that I lied by saying it was our prank."

"No. I have much more serious matters to worry about."

Irida nodded, not pushing for more. She had already done enough damage.

Lana gave her an attentive look. "I suppose you didn't find what you were looking for in that archive."

Irida blinked. "How do you know that?"

"You're still here, that's why. You would leave as soon as you get what you wanted."

"How bad do you think I am?" Irida mustered an offended look.

"Enough not to give a shit about anyone but yourself."

"You know what? Since our arrival, I've been doing my best to help you and become your friend, and you never notice it. Maybe the problem is with you?"

"Maybe," Lana agreed, her voice laced with sarcasm. "Alright, if you are such a nice friend, you would agree to help me with one thing. No questions asked."

*She's smart. Clumsy and impatient but smart enough to understand others.* At that point, Irida had to reassure her. "Fine. I'll do it."

Her eyes widened in surprise. "Really?"

Irida smiled. "Of course. But if I agree, I'll expect you to do the same thing. I need you to do something for me without questioning it."

"You still owe me the truth about Mercy House –"

"Hush," Irida placed her index finger to her lips. "Not here. These walls might have ears, don't you know that?"

Her breath quickened. "But I must know."

"I promise, I'll tell you everything once I get what I'm looking for. And to finish it, I'll need your help. So, here is the new deal – I help you now, then you help me, and we talk. How does that sound?"

Lana's face expressed concern. "I won't harm anyone."

Irida chuckled. "No one will suffer, I promise. So, what's your request?"

# 26

# Untamed

Lana walked along the dungeon wall, holding onto Irida's hand. The Gift of Invisibility shielded them, and Lana could see nothing around, not even her own body. Even though the space was barely lit up by the rare torches, they couldn't risk being discovered. The corridor was too narrow, and there were too many turns, so the chance of some guard noticing them was high. Irida led the way, and the pull of her hand was the only guidance. After another turn, Lana squeezed her hand hard, afraid to lose the grip.

"Hey, easy!" Irida hissed.

"Sorry." Lana relaxed her hand, but not too much, so she wouldn't lose her. "How far are those prison cells you said?"

Irida exhaled loudly. "We should be there soon. I visited that place just recently, so just rely on me, okay?"

"Sure," Lana said obediently. She wished it was her, not Irida, who had succeeded in training for the Mercy Sisters. It would have allowed her to freely enter that isolated dungeon for 'hopeless' patients. There, Becca was kept prisoner, and Lana tried not to think too much about the terrible conditions she was in. "I'll see you soon, Becks," Lana muttered under her breath.

The space around them had become brighter as they walked into the hallroom. There, two guards were sitting on the floor by an improvised table – two wooden planks placed on a pile of bricks. They were playing cards and chatting.

Irida's breath warmed Lana's ear as she leaned in. "I'll distract them."

Lana gave her a doubtful look, even though Irida couldn't notice it because they were both invisible. Lana felt another pull as Irida leaned to the floor and collected a pebble, probably fallen from a crack in the wall. *Good. This place is slowly falling apart,* Lana remarked.

From her perspective, Lana watched a black pebble move up and hang in the air. This was how Irida's Gift worked – she could make objects invisible only if she activated her shield *after* touching them. As her power was active, the pebble was still visible to others. The pebble moved back, then flew with force into the corridor as Irida threw it, creating a noise that finally attracted the guards' attention.

"Did you hear that?" one of them asked, putting his cards down.

"Nope," another man answered.

The first guard stood up. "I better check."

His friend waved his cards like a paper fan. "C'mon, don't be a pussy! You're just afraid to lose and owe me twenty."

The first guard glared at him. "What if it's a senior Sister checking on our performance?"

The other man groaned, then stood up, dropping his cards. "Fine."

When they left, Irida opened the door lock, and they walked inside. The dungeons were as dark as an abyss, so Irida dropped her invisible shield and cast her Light, letting its turquoise glow light their way.

As they moved, they passed the prison cells. Most of them were empty, however, Lana noticed a weird pattern – each time the corridor made a turn, there were several unoccupied cells, then two cells with one prisoner in each, followed by several empty rooms. Lana's heart trembled as she glanced at the silhouettes of girls in white robes. They looked like pale shadows of themselves, sitting on the floor with indifferent, empty eyes, not paying any attention to them.

After several minutes of walking, they stopped. Irida pointed at one of the doors. "There."

Lana gave her a hesitant look. "Would you mind opening the door?"

"I can't. Only senior Sisters carry the keys to those locks. And in case you forgot, you've lost my pick."

"I'm sure you have a spare one. Don't you?"

Irida gave her a weary look. "We don't have time to deal with that – those guards will walk to the exit stairs, then back. You have around ten minutes for your talk. Do you really want to spend it opening and closing that tricky lock system?"

Lana shook her head. Not wishing to waste a second, she rushed to the metal rods. "Becca? Becks?"

The movement in the cell made her heart sink. It really was her best friend, Rebecca. As she moved closer, she revealed her bruised cheekbone and a messy chocolate-brown plait. Her hands were cuffed with heavy bracelets, twice as thick as the ones Dorothy, the patient Lana had worked with, wore.

Despite her condition, Becca's blue eyes looked at her with calmness. "I knew you'd find a way to sneak here."

"Of course." Lana pulled her hands between the rods, and Becca took them. Her palms were surprisingly warm. "How are you?"

She smiled. "I'm really close to filing a complaint about their disgusting services."

Lana snickered, tears rolling down her cheeks. "I missed you so much."

"Me too." Becca's eyes gleamed as tears welled in them. "What happened? The last time you wrote to me, you were going to visit Triville in the summer, on your study break."

"Things changed," Lana said in a gloomy voice. She had indeed written Becca such a letter and sent it just before her final exams. "I guess we both had no clue that our plans to enjoy summer were never meant to come true."

"Don't be upset. Putting aside all these awful surroundings, we still met," Becca cheered her up.

Lana exhaled a sigh. It was Becca she knew so well. Even in such terrifying circumstances, she didn't lose her optimism.

"So, you're here to wish me good luck before my surgery?" Becca asked.

Lana winced. "Please, stop joking."

"I'm serious." Becca looked around, as if it would help her prove her point. "I hate this place, and I want to get out of here."

"Is it about Mira?" Lana asked, hoping the mention of her girl-friend would bring Becca back to her senses. "If so, I doubt she would ask you to rush things like that."

Becca's voice grew sad. "It has nothing to do with her. I didn't tell you in my letters, but... Mira left town this winter. Her parents became too suspicious about us, and she preferred to keep it quiet to avoid a scandal."

"So... you two broke up?"

She lowered her eyes. "Yes. But it's okay. She chose to hide who she really is. As do many women."

"That's why you must keep fighting!" Lana said, feeling the dull ache in her chest. Shit, she had to choose her words carefully not to drop dead in front of her friend. "I mean, it's not certain what will happen if you consent to the surgery. As you might know already, nobody ever made it alive –"

"Actually, those rumors aren't true," Becca interjected. "I was full of doubts, too, before I read the letter from one of the girls who went through the procedure successfully."

Lana gave her a puzzled look. "A letter?"

Becca's voice dropped to a whisper. "Yes. My guide, Irida, gave it to me secretly. She went through so much trouble to steal it and bring it here."

"How kind of her." Lana glanced at Irida, who stood fifteen steps away, perhaps eavesdropping. Lana lowered her voice as well. "What else did she do for you?"

"What do you mean? She brought you, exactly as I asked her on our first meeting."

*On the first meeting?* Lana froze, trying to process what happened. *No, it can't be.* Their first session with the patients was a while ago, and it meant one thing – when she had asked Irida to do her 'a huge favor with no questions asked,' Irida was aware of Becca and their connection. She had fooled everyone around.

"Lana, she is a trustworthy person," Becca said, glancing behind her back. "And I'm sure you're worried for nothing."

"I need to see that letter," Lana said. "Now."

"Why?"

"I wish I could tell you," Lana said, taking a deep breath to avoid revealing the deadly truth. "I'm really worried about you, so I want to see that proof with my own eyes."

"Alright. If it helps to reassure you." Becca rushed to her bed and moved her hand under the mattress. After a few seconds, Becca unfolded the paper before her eyes.

Lana had to admit – it looked like a real letter, with the edges lightly greased as if someone had been holding it while reading. The only thing that stood out was the neat handwriting, which looked too familiar. Lana stared at the 'P' and 'L' letters with the same peculiar tails she once saw when Irida gave her their written agreement they made on the day of their trip to Mercy House. *What the actual fuck?!*

Lana glanced at Irida, who shuffled her feet in impatience.

"Wrap it up," Irida whispered. "There is no time for that."

"Of course," Lana said in a hushed voice. Whatever manipulative scheme it was, she would find out soon enough. Now, it was better to focus on reassuring Rebecca. "Becks, please, you shall not trust anyone here."

A disappointment crossed her face. "What do you mean? I showed you the proof –"

"It's bullshit." Lana's breath caught in her throat as a spasm pierced her heart. She clenched her fists around the rods, so her knuckles turned white. "Listen, I'll find a way to get you out of here. I swear. I just need more time."

"But... I hate the idea of being in this prison for too long."

Lana bit her lip. She wished she could explain at least something. Maybe she could try thought-provoking questions? "Have you ever asked yourself why they put you in a dungeon cell instead of a normal room? Like they do in a hospital?"

Becca shook her head.

*To convince you to say whatever they want just to leave this place. It's all thought through.* Lana hoped that Becca would have this epiphany.

Becca frowned. "Alright, it's a good question. Honestly, I have no idea why they do that to us."

Irida stepped behind her back and placed her hand on Lana's shoulder. "It's time. They're coming back."

"A moment." Lana squeezed Becca's hand hard. "Please, think of everything carefully before you make your final decision. Give it at least a week. I need this time to... to make sure you're safe."

"Okay," Becca agreed. "But only because of you."

Irida pulled her back, and Lana let go of her hand.

# 27

# Lesser Evil

Lana followed Irida to the front yard. It was just before dinner hour, so most of the sisters were inside the building, changing into fresh and tidy clothes. There were only two of them outside, allowing them to talk freely without the risk of being overheard. They walked side by side, trying not to raise suspicions.

"So, you got a chance to talk to your friend, just as I promised," Irida said. "Now, it's your turn –"

"Not so fast," Lana interjected. "Firstly, you made the promise to Becca. Then you used me to fulfill the same request. How fair is that?"

Irida shrugged. "It's not my fault that you both wanted the same thing. From my perspective, I fulfilled all my obligations."

"Really?!" Lana gave her a dirty look. "Alright, in that case, I helped you get access to that secret archive. So, whatever the outcome is, you owe me an explanation about the Sorority secrets."

"Whoa, when did you learn to be such a bitch?"

"I had a good teacher," Lana retorted, glaring at her. "So, no more favors until you explain what the hell is happening here."

Irida stopped by the bench and took a seat. Lana sat nearby, hoping it wouldn't be another lie. Her hand was close to Irida's palm, ready to read her in case Irida tried to come up with another excuse.

"So," Irida started, "the thing is, we don't kill anyone. Really."

Lana frowned. "Then why all the secrecy? Why do you keep the patients in the dungeons and treat them like prisoners?"

"When you talked to Becca, you implied that we do it to make them say 'yes' to the surgery. You were right. It's a very effective way to pressure them – nobody wants to sit in those dark caves forever. Sooner or later, they all give in, ready to entrust their lives into the hands of Divine. Imagine their joy when they wake up, realizing they are alive. All of them. It's something they appreciate. It matters more than any possible side effect they might face after the surgery."

Lana frowned. "I don't understand..."

"It's all part of the scheme, as well as the 'rumors' about the possibility of death they hear in schools. We do everything to scare them, which makes them grateful for staying alive," Irida explained. She paused before continuing. "Because we need them to be oblivious to something else we take away."

"You mean... their magic?" Lana recalled the lectures she had attended. "But we only try to suppress their Gifts."

Irida shook her head. "In theory, we are taught that the surgery only burns their magic channels, so they can't cast spells anymore. In reality, it's impossible to separate one's Gift from their body without destroying the whole magic system. The executors burn their channels, rendering them Incapables."

*Incapables...* Lana paused. "You mean... they do that to *all of them*?!"

Irida looked around. "Quiet! Nobody should know I told you about that!"

Lana's heart sank. She placed her hands over her mouth, trying to process the information. There was no doubt Irida was telling the truth. The ugly and scary truth. It explained why nobody with destructive Gifts had returned home – there was no place for people without magic in their society. All of them were sent to small isolated reservations, away from mages and stripped of basic human rights.

Incapables were essentially slaves serving the wealthy, performing housework or working in the fields. Previously, Lana had only heard that it was the fate of ex-prisoners who served their time on Death Island, where the strong magnetic anomaly damaged their magic channels. Now, it was apparent that teenage girls with the 'wrong' Gift were also part of this slave trade.

It now made sense why Mercy Sister Denise had sacrificed her life to bring the diary out of these walls. If Lana were in her place, she would do the same – stopping it was worth dying for. Lana clenched her teeth. It was horrifying, but the worst part was that she had no idea how to stop it. She could try to save Becca, but how? If she attempted to reveal this truth, she would drop dead before she could even explain it properly.

"Lana?" Irida called out. "Please, say something."

"You lie to all those girls, knowing they are all about to be sent away to slavery. They'll never see their families again!"

"And what would I do? This oppressive system is centuries old, so my knowledge would never change a thing. Plus, I'm bound by that stupid oath that won't let me say anything before I fall down with heart failure."

"You knew this all along, even before you took the oath of silence, and you did nothing! Seriously, you're one of the most self-centered people I know. Including men."

Irida gave her a weary look. "Sorry, miss 'I do care.' Perhaps, I just lack that rebellious spirit that you possess. Which is the same reason why I'm still alive."

Lana rolled her eyes. This woman was too selfish to understand why she was supposed to care. Whatever. The most important part was that Lana had learned the truth. Now, she had to rescue Rebecca from their clutches before it was too late. But how?

"Alright, I did what you asked," Irida said, breaking her train of thought. "Now, let's get to the part where we both get what we need – the answers to all our questions."

"What questions?"

"I need to know where *The Book of Life* is, and you need to find a way to help your friend."

Lana exhaled a sigh. She doubted Irida was sincere about helping Becca, but she had no choice but to try to hold onto that hope. "And where is that?"

Irida gave her a sly look. "In Edwina's head."

The dinner time had arrived, and all the Mercy Sisters were called to the dining room. According to their old tradition, they were all fussing around, helping to serve the table and bringing pots of food from the kitchen.

Lana stood by the window, gazing at the spacious front yard through the foggy glass. The sun was hiding behind heavy clouds again, and mist was creeping from the hills to envelop the dark castle, along with its inhabitants and the secrets it held.

A black carriage was waiting at the gates, almost ready to depart. Walter stood by the closed carriage door, conversing with the horseman. In his black uniform, dampened by the mist and clinging to his body, he looked striking. *Have we ever had a chance?*

Lana pressed her palm to the cold glass, silently bidding her farewells. Perhaps she was supposed to speak to Walter. She could explain herself and assure him that the silly incident with Irida was just a misunderstanding. Then, they could work things out and let their relationship unfold. *If only I could tell him everything...*

Her heart bled as the bitter truth washed over her – even if Lana managed to convince Walter to forgive her now, she wouldn't be completely honest with him as long as she was bound by her oath. Eventually, their relationship would crumble like a house of cards, blown apart by the merciless wind. It tore her apart, but it was the right thing to do – to end things here and now.

After all, Walter was a distraction. A wonderful and exciting distraction much needed in times of despair. Lana couldn't afford to waste her time on that, not when her best friend was locked in the dungeon.

Outside, Walter finished talking to the horseman and glanced at the window where Lana stood. Their eyes met, and she exhaled a heavy sigh. Then, she lowered her gaze, turned away, and walked to the dining tables to see if she could be of help.

# 28

# A Hundred of Fires

Irida balanced on the ladder as she attached a garland with paper lanterns to the tree branch. It was the traditional way of decorating the garden for the summer, with each Mercy Sister placing their ball of Light inside the lanterns in the evening to shine with the rainbow of their special energies. This tradition marked the opening of the summer season and coincided with the charity concert scheduled for that night.

"It's looking so beautiful!" Amanda exclaimed as she approached. "I'm grateful for all your help."

"No problem at all," Irida replied with a polite smile before returning to her task. She focused on attaching the garlands while contemplating the timing of her planned mission with Lana – breaking into Edwina's bedroom to read her mind. If all went according to plan, she would soon acquire *The Book of Life*.

Amanda waved her hand, gesturing towards the lush foliage adorned with white lanterns. "It's like they're blooming again, don't you think?"

"Certainly," Irida replied. She descended the ladder and dusted off her hands. "Well, my work here is done, so I should be going."

Amanda's expression turned sad. "Please, don't be mad at me."

Confused, Irida furrowed her brow, trying to recall any reason she might hold a grudge against Sister Amanda. After all, Amanda had always given her good marks and allowed her plenty of freedom, which was greatly appreciated.

"That night when I promised to meet you in the library," Amanda explained. "I was on duty and couldn't leave my desk because of an unpleasant incident."

"You mean when Lana snuck into Walter's room?" Irida clarified.

"Exactly. I had escorted her to your room and saw that you were already there, sound asleep."

Irida nodded. After her unsuccessful search for the book in the secret archive, she had been too upset to remember she was supposed to return to the library and see Amanda. Instead, she had gone back to her room and fallen asleep. "I just finished my work and came back," Irida explained. "It's fine. I suppose that day was stressful for both of us, so let's just forget about it."

Amanda smiled. "Agreed. We have a lot to organize for the upcoming celebration. I hope you can assist me with something."

As Amanda looked at her expectantly, Irida scrambled to come up with a suitable excuse. The last thing she wanted was to be involved in the Sorority activities. "Sorry, I have something else to attend to right now."

"But your schedule is empty for the next two hours."

*And you cared to check it.* Irida gritted her teeth in frustration. "I wanted to use that time for preparations."

Amanda furrowed her brow. "Preparations for what?"

"It's best for me to work with patients when I'm refreshed and full of energy," Irida lied. "I need some rest before the next session."

"Don't worry, I won't give you any difficult tasks," Amanda reassured her. "It's just helping to settle our guests."

Irida sighed inwardly. Apparently, there was no way to escape her 'duties.' At least, she could try to handle them quickly. "Sure thing. Should I show them to the guest rooms?"

Amanda gave her a suspicious look. "We rarely have guests staying at Mercy House. Aren't you curious about them, even a little?"

Irida forced a smile. "I'm eager to hear more."

"Then I'll tell you everything," Amanda said, taking Irida by the elbow and leading her along the garden trail.

They strolled past the orchards. The sky may have been gray, but the day felt cozy and warm. The summer heat was slowly creeping in, causing Irida to sweat under her shapeless robe. Amanda chirped about the upcoming concert and a theater troupe that was scheduled to perform at Mercy House.

Irida's mind was preoccupied with her impending mission. With their successful deal with Lana, she needed to choose the best day to attempt reading Sister Grump. After that, she would meet with David, an Oracle, who had cryptically mentioned something about 'hundreds of fires in the sky.' If only she could decipher its meaning!

"Irida?" Amanda's voice broke through her thoughts.

Blinking, Irida refocused on the present. "Yes?"

"I mentioned that the actresses are about to arrive," Amanda reminded her.

"Of course," Irida replied, nodding. "I'll place them at the far end of the corridor as you suggested, to avoid any potential 'embarrassing incidents.'"

"Very well," Amanda said, satisfied.

Irida gave Sister Amanda a curious look. Perhaps, she might use her to gain some clarity. After all, Amanda had been at Mercy

House for a long time and might have the answer to the question that had been bothering her. "Can I ask you something?"

"Of course, anything."

"I once heard about a prophecy of a hundred fires soaring into the sky. Does that ring a bell to you?"

Amanda's eyes widened in surprise. "Who told you that?"

*An Oracle, with his cryptic messages.* Irida forced a nonchalant smile. "Just a friend," she replied. "No one else knows, I promise."

"Walter, then," Amanda deduced.

*Not exactly, but this explanation will do.* Irida nodded. "Sorry, he might have found out somehow. I was just curious, that's all."

Amanda gave her a stern look. "Fine, I'll explain. But I don't want anyone else to know about this."

"I won't tell a soul, I swear," Irida reassured her, placing a comforting hand on Amanda's. "You know I can keep secrets."

Amanda's voice dropped to a whisper. "Okay, here's the thing – I've prepared a set of lanterns. But these aren't meant to be filled with our Light."

"How will they work then?"

"They have a base that we need to set on fire, so they fill with warm air and fly away," Amanda explained, gazing up at the sky. "I bought a hundred of them, so we can release them into the sky after the concert. It will be spectacular!"

Irida was awestruck. *A hundred fires soaring in the sky!* She had to admit, David was right about one thing – deciphering his riddle had been quite a challenge. But now that she understood it, excitement filled her heart.

"See, even you're thrilled!" Amanda smiled at her.

"Yes," Irida admitted. "I am. And the concert is tonight!" She laughed, unable to hide her relief. The news that their mission would soon be over was exhilarating. She moved closer to Amanda and embraced her. "Thank you for this!"

"You're welcome."

As they pulled apart, Amanda's gaze locked with Irida's. With strands of red hair framing her face and flushed cheeks, she looked alluring. Acting on impulse, Irida leaned in, bringing her lips closer to Amanda's, her voice dropping to a whisper. "I haven't been able to stop thinking about your offer. I really want to see your bedroom."

"Then let's do it," Amanda whispered back, her voice sending shivers down Irida's spine.

"I can't wait."

The sound of arriving horses interrupted the moment, and Amanda stepped back, refocusing her attention. *There are the guests she has mentioned*, Irida realized. *Damn it!*

Amanda turned to Irida. "Let's save that for later. There are too many eyes on us right now."

"Agreed."

Amanda smiled. "And as for the concert, I hope you'll enjoy it."

*I would rather skip that part*, Irida thought to herself.

"One of the actresses used to work here," Amanda continued as three carriages arrived at the gates. "She left when her original contract expired after three years, but she returns every year to perform for the most challenging patients."

"Really?" Irida asked out of politeness.

"Yes," Amanda replied, giving her a sly look. "And the most intriguing part – her name is Melissa Morris."

"Morris..." Irida paused, trying to recall the familiar last name. "Like... Lana?"

"Exactly," Amanda confirmed. "She's Lana's mother."

Irida blinked and turned her head slowly towards the carriages. The door of the first carriage opened, and a woman with nicely styled blond hair stepped out onto the stone pavement. Her petite frame, dressed in a long black dress, bore a striking resemblance to a certain stubborn mind-reader who happened to be Irida's ally.

*Oh, crap!* If Lana found out about the presence of her mother, it could create a serious distraction and potentially ruin their entire mission. Irida really had to find a way to skip the concert and proceed with their mission without any delay.

**29**

# A Voice From The Dark

The evening garden was magnificent – with lanterns of all shades hanging from the glowing trees, it was like being in a fairytale. Becca walked among the trees after the other patients, unable to believe it wasn't a dream. Even with her hands still cuffed, seeing this place after endless darkness and inhaling the fresh air was like a gulp of freedom. The freedom that she might never experience again.

As they arrived at the open space where the stage was, the Mercy Sisters gestured to the patients to take their seats. Becca hesitated at the back row, looking at the girls in white dresses. There were many of them, perhaps around sixty, and all of them had the same expression – utter disbelief.

*Who is that voice from the dark?* she wondered. As she had learned, that girl's name was Sienna, and she was from the Southern Kingdom. Perhaps she had beautiful tanned skin and a warm smile. At least, this is how Becca imagined her during all the hours they spent talking.

"Hey," a voice said behind her, causing her heart to tremble. *The same voice I heard so many times.* Becca turned to see a tall girl with a charming smile. Her almond-shaped eyes shone with excitement. *Gosh, she is even prettier than I thought!*

"I'm Sienna," the girl said. "And you must be Becca."

Becca nodded, taking Sienna's hand. Feeling her warm hand in hers felt surreal. "Yes. It's me. Wait... how did you recognize me?"

Sienna shrugged. "An intuition. You are the only one who stands out. Everyone else is obediently taking their seats, but not you."

Becca smiled at her. "How could I have a seat without seeing you first?"

One of the Mercy Sisters approached. She had gorgeous red hair tied in a knot, her brows knitted. "Take your seats already before I change my mind and send you back to your cells! And no talking!"

Becca lowered her eyes and hurried to the benches, her hand holding Sienna's. They both seated themselves at the furthest spot, hoping no one would see them chatting. As everyone settled, the sounds of violins filled the space, opening the show and providing an excellent cover for a quiet conversation.

Sienna leaned closer, her voice lowered to a whisper. "I don't want to return to that prison."

Becca cast a glance at the Mercy Sisters. They all sat close to the aisle. The red-haired one, perhaps the senior Sister, stood by the exit, monitoring the event. "As long as we keep quiet, we're safe," Becca said. "We have almost three hours to be together."

"Hours..." Sienna gave her a sad look. "What if we could just... be together? As much as we want?"

Becca's heart pounded. "What do you mean? We can't escape. Not so easily. And if they catch us –"

"We're dead," Sienna said in a grim tone. "I'm sorry... I didn't want to confuse you. I just hoped that we might have a chance. You know?"

Becca smiled at her. Since that talk with Lana when she mentioned she used to have a girlfriend, Sienna had started circling around. Not that Becca disliked it. On the contrary, she had discovered herself attached to this mysterious girl who was with her during the darkest times of her life. Unlike Mira, who had cowardly ended things at the sign of danger, Sienna seemed ready to risk her life to be with her. It was encouraging. Only that they never had a chance. Not in this society. Not with their forbidden Gifts.

"I know, it sounds stupid," Sienna spat. "Can you please forget what I just said?"

Becca shook her head. "Never. At least if I die, I will know there was someone who…" she paused, unsure how to continue.

"Who hoped to fall in love with you," Sienna said, her eyes glossy with tears, "knowing how foolish it was."

Becca's heart swelled. "For real?"

Sienna nodded. "I'm sorry."

"Stop apologizing!" Becca moved closer, her breath quickening. "I like you, too. And I wish we both met in a different life where we could be ourselves, but we can't…"

They both went silent. Sitting so close to each other, even knowing what was coming, was still priceless. Who knew? Maybe that surgery would set them free after all. Then, they would become free from all the darkness and all those ridiculous rules of the realm where they simply couldn't exist.

"Maybe there is a chance," Sienna said, breaking the silence.

"I doubt that."

"I just spoke to one of the senior Sisters, and she said that the girls with the strong Gifts like ours are very special. We can think out of the box, and we are never afraid to go beyond the limits."

Becca knitted her brow. "Oh, that's why they eliminate us."

Sienna shook her head. "It's the law, but she is just like us..."

"With forbidden magic?"

Sienna shook her head. "A queer."

"Oh... wow."

"I know, right?" Sienna took both of Becca's hands in hers. "She told me that even if the surgery goes wrong, the worst thing that can happen is we lose our magic."

Becca widened her eyes. "What?! I don't want that to happen."

"Fuck the magic," Sienna said, her expression filled with excitement. "My Gift has only brought me trouble so far."

"Incapables aren't welcome in our world, in case you haven't noticed."

"I know. They live in small isolated communities. But I would rather spend the rest of my life there on my terms than spend it hiding from the authorities."

Becca took her hands away and rubbed her palms. Her cuffs were heavy, and they clinked against each other, causing others to turn their heads at her. Becca couldn't care less.

*Shit. Lana was right about this place – it was built to eliminate people like me from this society.* And if so, there was a question – was it worth it to keep fighting with this whole fucked-up system? With magic or not, Becca never felt too welcomed in this world since she had discovered she was a queer. Maybe giving up was the only way for her to ever be happy.

Becca closed her eyes, a silent tear sliding down her cheek. She was supposed to make a choice, and she had no idea where any of her decisions might lead her. Through the loud pounding of her bleeding heart, she could distinguish the fussing of the patients and the murmuring of their voices. Then all the sounds quieted as the new part of the concert had begun.

A song, coming from the stage, reached her ears, awakening a memory within her. When Becca was a small girl, she sometimes had nightmares. She would wake up alone in her bed, immersed in the darkness of her room and lost in fear. It lasted until her mother brought her to Lana's house, and it was the first time Becca heard a therapeutic story. Lana's mom, Melissa, sang a song, and her soft voice calmed Becca, helping her find her way from the dark.

Now, frozen in her place and completely lost in the abyss of desperation, this voice touched something inside her. Like a thin beam of light, it enlivened her soul, guiding her through the darkness. As Lana's mother told her, hope can never be lost, even in the darkest times. *Because our souls are filled with Light, and Light is hope.*

Becca opened her eyes and wiped her tears. On the stage, there was a woman who had taught her to be brave. Ironically, it was the same woman who had abandoned her own family. And now, she was here. Melissa stood on the stage, singing lullabies for the other girls. *What the hell?*

Sienna poked her shoulder. "So, what do you think?"

"I think there is the only way out, and we must take it," Becca said, clenching her fists. "Let's do that damn surgery."

# 30

## Thieves

The night enveloped the corridors of Mercy House. This time, Irida didn't bother activating her invisible shield – almost all the Mercy Sisters were outside, enjoying the concert, and the guards never ventured to the top floor.

Irida strolled along the main corridor, with Lana trailing closely behind. The expansive windows offered a clear view of the garden where the music was playing. Faint chants could be heard, barely reaching her ears.

"Wait!" Lana exclaimed as they neared Sister Grump's bedroom.

Irida halted in her tracks. "What's wrong?"

Lana gestured towards the window. "I think I heard something from the stage. It sounded like..."

*Your mother's voice*, Irida surmised. "Damn it, we don't have time for this."

"But –"

"I thought you had the courage to do this," Irida interrupted, furrowing her brow. "And now you're backing off like a coward."

Lana shook her head. "Sorry. I guess I'm just feeling a bit nervous."

"It's nothing to be nervous about," Irida reassured. "During dinner, I put some sedative in Sister Grump's soup, so she retired to her room early, believing she was fatigued. She's currently sound asleep in her bed. Additionally, Sister Amanda believes I volunteered to cover her duty, giving her and the other senior Sisters a chance to enjoy the show."

"You make it sound like you did all the work," Lana observed.

"We're a team, and I executed my part brilliantly. Now it's your turn."

Lana nodded, her expression growing confident. "I'm ready."

"Good." Irida smiled as she approached the bedroom door.

Of course, it was locked. However, opening locks here was as simple as cracking peanuts. Irida retrieved her pick and inserted it into the keyhole, applying pressure to the inner spring. With a click, the lock opened.

They entered the room cautiously. Edwina lay on her narrow bed, her wrinkled face bathed in the pale moonlight. She resembled a mummy from the old horror stories that Irida used to enjoy. It felt as though at any moment, Edwina would reach out and grab Irida by the neck to strangle her.

Irida touched the collar of her robe, her heart racing. *It's just nerves*, she reassured herself. Every time she neared her goal, she experienced anxiety. It was a natural part of the process, and she couldn't prevent it. She had to stick to the plan and remain vigilant.

Kneeling beside the bed, Irida placed her hands on her lap, palms facing up, prepared to activate her shield at a moment's notice. As they had discussed earlier, Lana risked waking Edwina with her touch. If that occurred, Irida was ready to shield them both.

Lana sat beside Edwina, rubbing her hands together. Irida nodded in approval – no one appreciated the touch of cold fingers, and with Lana's palms warm, she had a better chance of not disturbing Edwina's sleep.

After warming up, Lana reached out and gently grasped Edwina's palm. Her brown eyes became unfocused, and Lana closed them, entering a meditative state. Her body swayed slightly, her lips moving in a barely audible whisper.

Irida waited patiently, counting her heartbeats. In what felt like an eternity, Lana opened her eyes and gasped for air. Edwina stirred in her bed, shifting to her side. Her eyelids fluttered as she prepared to open them. Irida embraced Lana's shoulders and held her breath as the invisible shield enveloped them.

Edwina's face twisted in irritation, then her eyes widened. She sat up in bed and rubbed her temples.

They both held their breath, frozen in place. Irida placed her hand on Lana's chest, trying to calm her racing heart. *Please stay calm*, Irida silently pleaded, hoping Lana could hear her thoughts. If not, the shield might falter.

Edwina rose from her bed, approaching them with her hands swaying, almost brushing against Irida's head. She then moved to the window and shut it. She stood there for at least a minute, hugging her shoulders, likely trying to warm up. *Old people always feel cold*, Irida mused. *Why doesn't she just return under her blanket?*

Regrettably, Edwina didn't hurry. She scanned the room, furrowing her brow, before noticing the open bedroom door. She walked over to close it and locked it with her key before finally returning to her bed.

Taking advantage of the moment when Edwina was preoccupied with adjusting her bedsheets, Irida stood up and guided Lana to the far wall, holding her hand tightly. With their confinement in the room, it was only a matter of time before her shield weakened. Irida hoped it would hold long enough for Edwina to drift back into slumber. *Old people often struggled to fall asleep*, her inner voice remarked, heightening her nerves.

Lana's breath tickled her ear. "Paralyzing spell. It could incapacitate her."

Irida exhaled slowly. While it was a tempting idea, casting such a spell was too risky. It would drain too much energy, potentially causing their shield to dissipate and expose them to Sister Grump. If they were caught, the consequences would be severe.

"I can do it," Lana offered.

"No. You need both hands to make a spell, and you can't release my hand," Irida reminded her. "Unless you want us to be discovered."

Edwina fidgeted in her bed, as if their hushed conversation was disturbing her.

"Sit down," Lana instructed, applying pressure to Irida's shoulders until she complied and lowered herself to the floor. "Good."

"What are you doing?" Irida whispered, but it was too late. Lana was already crawling back towards the bed, her figure visible in the moonlight.

*Fuck!* Irida bit her lip. She was still enveloped in her shield, which was easier to maintain without Lana's presence. Yet, there was a risk that Lana could jeopardize their plan.

With wide eyes, Irida watched Lana sitting by the bedside. Her lips moved silently as she clasped her hands together, casting a Paralyzing spell – a faint silver glow emanated from her hands, illuminating the room. *We're doomed*, Irida thought, biting her lip until she tasted blood.

At that moment, a brilliant light illuminated the sky. The sight was breathtaking – numerous paper lanterns floated upwards, casting a warm glow over the room. Edwina sat up, her gaze fixed on the window.

At that moment, Lana completed her spell and stood up. Without hesitation, she directed a Paralyzing spell towards Edwina's back, causing the woman to freeze in place. Lana gently guided Edwina back onto her pillow and closed her eyelids.

"Ready," Lana announced, shaking her hands with a smile. "I always knew this spell would come in handy. She'll remain asleep until morning."

"It was a risky move," Irida remarked. "She could have seen you!"

"She didn't. And I'm certain she'll believe she drifted off after watching the lanterns."

"Your spell may not hold for long," Irida cautioned.

"Then we need to get out of here."

Irida nodded and approached the door, her hands trembling as she opened it.

In the corridor, they hurried back to their floor, eager to return to the safety of their bedroom. There, Irida could cast a Muting Spell to prevent any prying ears from the overly curious Sisters and finally find out what Lana had seen in Edwina's mind. Something had clearly frightened Lana, but what?

Their conversation would have to wait, however, as they encountered an actress Irida had met earlier, Melissa Morris – Lana's mother.

Melissa's smile faltered as she noticed them. "Good evening, young ladies."

Lana's expression darkened upon seeing her mother. She crossed her arms and remained silent, visibly shocked by the presence of the woman who had abandoned her.

Irida placed a comforting hand on Lana's shoulder. "Are you okay?"

Lana shook her head, her gaze fixed on Melissa. "What are you doing here?"

"I just came to talk…" Melissa began.

"We have nothing to talk about," Lana interrupted. "Leave me and my friend alone."

Melissa sighed, her gaze shifting to Irida. "What an unusual friendship you two have. When Irida was assisting me with settling in, I mentioned my daughter, who serves as a Mercy Sister here. I told her your name is Lana, and she assured me she had never met you."

Irida felt a lump form in her throat. This woman was on the verge of shattering the fragile trust she had built with Lana. She couldn't allow that to happen. Not now. "Lana told me what you did, and it's clear she doesn't want to see you or speak with you. As her friend, I tried to shield her."

Lana regarded her with skepticism. "Thanks, friend. A heads-up would have been nice, though."

"I was going to tell you later," Irida explained. "I just wanted you to remain focused tonight."

"Focused on what?" Melissa interjected, her brow furrowed. "If you're trying to involve my daughter in any trouble, it's my responsibility to report my concerns to one of the senior Sisters."

"What do you want?" Lana's voice dripped with irritation.

Melissa's tone softened. "I only ask for half an hour of your time."

Lana hesitated. "I can't. The curfew hour is approaching since your show has ended."

"I spoke to Sister Amanda. She granted an exception for tonight."

Lana rolled her eyes. "How generous of her."

"Just half an hour, Lana. Then, you can return to your room and never see me again. Unless you want to."

Irida sighed. Apparently, a much-needed conversation between mother and daughter was inevitable. It was best not to intervene and let them have their moment. As Melissa had promised, it wouldn't be a lengthy discussion.

Irida gently touched Lana's hand, offering her support. "Go. I'll be here, waiting for you."

## 31

The Story We Share

The night garden shimmered in a rainbow of colors – the tree barks glowed green, and countless night flowers illuminated the darkness with shades of red, yellow, and purple. Lana often found herself captivated by the beauty of summer nature, but not tonight.

"What brought you here, mother?" Lana asked in a flat tone. After years of absence, it felt strange to converse with this woman. It was like speaking to a stranger who bore a striking resemblance to someone she once loved dearly.

"We are both here for the same reason," Melissa replied with a smile. "To help those girls."

Bitter tears welled in her eyes. As if abandoning her family wasn't enough, this woman had chosen the most inappropriate moment to intrude – just as Lana was on the brink of rescuing Becca from the clutches of the Sorority. "Oh, yes. I recall our discussions about making a positive impact on the world," Lana forced out, her voice strained.

"I'm glad you remember," Melissa said, reaching out to touch Lana's shoulder. The gesture pierced Lana's heart.

Lana recoiled, brushing off Melissa's hand. "I also remember how you left shortly after that. As if we meant nothing to you. You just discarded us like trash."

"I'm truly sorry if it seemed that way." Melissa sighed, her eyes shimmering with tears. Lana almost believed the sincerity of her regret.

A heavy silence settled between them, punctuated only by the rustling of leaves. Lana regretted agreeing to this conversation outside. Melissa's persistence had forced her hand, unwilling to continue their argument in the corridor where it could attract unwanted attention. Another visit to Sister Amanda's office for reprimand was the last thing Lana needed.

"You were just a teenager when I left," Melissa began. "At that time, a close friend of mine lost her daughter to a 'forbidden Gift.' I was afraid that you might face a similar fate."

"So, you chose to abandon me before my Gift manifested," Lana said, crossing her arms defensively. "To avoid having to deal with it."

Melissa shook her head. "I was terrified for your future. You have always been courageous, Lana, and girls with a heart like yours often possess strong powers. As a mother, I was willing to do whatever it took to challenge the laws that endanger girls like you. I left Triville because I needed to sever ties with my family in order to infiltrate the Sorority. It was the only way to gather evidence against them."

Lana's gaze sharpened. "What evidence?"

"My friend Denise, the one I mentioned earlier, was by my side. Throughout our time there, she meticulously documented everything in a diary. She detailed how the Sorority coerces girls into giving their powers away."

Lana's head spun. It appeared she had been investigating a case rooted in that same diary. "How do you know Denise?"

"She was my best friend in high school. After graduation, she got married and moved to the capital in search of a better life. Her younger brother, Timothy, followed suit. Meanwhile, I met your father, and we settled in Triville. Despite the distance, Denise and I maintained our connection through letters – we became pen pals."

"How sweet," Lana remarked, a touch of sarcasm lacing her words. "Then you reunited and started deceiving the patients."

"We were bound by an oath that prevented us from revealing the truth. We also had little choice but to assimilate here," Melissa explained.

"And what was your objective?"

"Before arriving here, Denise believed that the procedure for burning magic channels was hazardous due to negligence. She wanted to investigate if there was a way to make it safer."

"How quickly did you realize that there was no safe method?"

Melissa's eyes widened in surprise. "So, you're aware."

"Of course I am," Lana spat. "They simply strip women of their power and exile them to isolated communities for Incapables. And the worst part – their claims about female incapability to wield a 'strong Gift' are all lies." This was another piece of information that she had learned from reading Edwina's mind. As it appeared, women could tame all the destructive Gifts just fine. Only that nobody would let it.

Melissa flinched. "Shh. Someone might overhear us!"

"I don't care," Lana declared, her heart racing as she continued. "I just want to know... Why? Why go to such lengths to complicate everything?"

Melissa gave Lana a sorrowful look, lowering her voice to a whisper. "It's always been about power. Men are consumed by their power struggles, vying for dominance in this world. That's why they silence the strongest among us – those with courageous hearts and unconventional perspectives. They want us to serve them quietly, without questioning their oppressive system."

"It's so fucking unfair!" Lana gestured wildly, barely able to contain her frustration.

"I know," Melissa agreed. "And it touches every aspect of our lives. From a young age, we are conditioned to be compliant and forgiving, even in the face of blatant mistreatment. Then, when you manifest your Gift, if it's benign, you're taught to view it as Divine blessing. A reward for being a 'good girl.' That's exactly how I felt when I discovered mine." Melissa raised her hand and gestured over the slumbering flowers, coaxing them to bloom and shimmer in response to her power. "I was fortunate. Once I realized I could manipulate nature, I dedicated myself to aiding orchard farms and fields. I reveled in the opportunity to safeguard crops from drought, diseases, and famine. Using my power in that manner brought me a sense of purpose."

"Then you got married, and everything unraveled."

"Not at all. You were the best thing that ever happened to me, Lana. Watching you grow with your vibrant energy brought me immense joy. However, I never ceased to worry about your future.

That's why I penned a tale for you. The story of a girl with a formidable Gift who became a guardian and even tamed a dragon."

Lana blinked in astonishment. "Wait... You mean my favorite book? You read it to me countless times when I was a child."

Melissa nodded. "I began recounting this tale to help you drift off peacefully. I later discovered it served as a remedy for your nightmares. You were always sensitive, Lana, often restless at night. When you started learning to read, I transformed the story into a book and had it printed. There were two copies – one for my cherished daughter, so you could read it whenever you pleased. The other was intended for a publisher. I hoped this story would empower other girls to embrace their true selves without fear. To believe that they could inspire positive change through their Gifts. How naive I was! When I submitted it for approval, the government rejected and banned the story. In their rejection letter, they claimed it 'threatened societal values.' They confiscated the book and prohibited me from attempting to publish it ever again."

"I still have my copy of the book."

Melissa smiled. "Yes. I'm grateful that amidst the darkness, the story served as a guiding light for you. Lana, leaving you was the hardest decision I've ever made. The only solace I found was in that story. I knew it would bring comfort to you in times of sorrow and uncertainty. Throughout our time apart, that story kept us connected."

Lana's heart swelled. Everything now fell into place. Melissa was simply another woman in this tumultuous world, striving to enact change, even at a great personal cost. "It's alright, mother. It was difficult for me as well, not comprehending your true intentions. But I believe I do now."

Melissa wept. "I'm deeply sorry that you had to endure all of this. I wanted to write you a letter, but I couldn't bear the thought of having a conversation where I couldn't fully explain myself. You understand why."

"Our oath is only meant to last three years," Lana reminded her. "It's been longer than that."

"It doesn't end when the binding spell expires. The confidentiality agreement remains in effect until death. If breached, the authorities punish you by harming your family. Even after I departed and the spell lifted, I couldn't risk your life by revealing this grim truth."

"Then I'm grateful that we are both bound by the same oath. We can finally have this conversation," Lana said with a sigh.

A wistful smile graced Melissa's lips. "Indeed. This is a small breach we can use to communicate with each other."

Lana regarded her mother with compassion. After years of separation, she could finally ask her one burning question. "How have you been all these years? Were you alright?"

Melissa shrugged. "It wasn't too bad. Following my time at Mercy House, I joined a theater troupe and began sharing my stories through live performances. Of course, they aren't as daring as your beloved book. We must be cautious not to arouse suspicion due to censorship. Nevertheless, there is a glimmer of hope within them. Through my experiences, I've come to understand that art is a potent tool. It possesses the ability to mend broken hearts and ignite spirits. Art is a beautiful medium for unveiling harsh truths."

"Indeed," Lana agreed. "I'm relieved you didn't meet the same fate as Denise."

Melissa sighed heavily. "I attempted to talk her out of it, but Denise chose the harsh path. After her initial three years, she opted to remain here, extending her contract to secure a higher position. She dedicated an additional two years to compiling her diary, gathering all the evidence she could. Denise intended to entrust her diary to her brother. She hinted at her plan to him, but tragically, she perished soon after. Her diary went missing. Today, I searched her room, and it wasn't in its usual hiding spot. I suspect the authorities discovered and destroyed her work."

Lana gazed at the foreboding structure of Mercy House. *How many lives did it shatter?* Regardless of the risks, she was determined to take action to halt this injustice. "Her diary wasn't destroyed so swiftly, mother. She eventually managed to pass it on to her brother, Timothy, and I happened to read his thoughts. That's why I'm here – to continue Denise's mission."

Melissa shook her head. "Please, don't tell me you're considering stopping them."

Lana regarded her mother wearily. "No, I'll simply allow them to continue their actions. By the way, Becca is next in line to be labeled as Incapable."

"You mean... our Becca?"

Lana nodded. "Yes, my closest friend, Rebecca Turner, the most genuine person I've ever known. She happens to possess a Fire Gift and, unfortunately, she trusts the Sorority."

Melissa massaged her temples. "That's too bad. She must escape from there."

"The issue is, she won't heed my advice if I ask politely. And I can't disclose the truth without risking to drop dead."

"Then she'll listen to me. Unlike you, Lana, I am no longer bound by the deadly spell."

Lana furrowed her brow. "No offense, but why do you believe Becca would trust your word? After everything you did... the way it appeared?"

"Leave it to me." Melissa's eyes gleamed as she began formulating a plan. "I used to be a trusted Sister, so tomorrow morning, I'll request one of the senior members to visit the 'hopeless' girls. It's

not uncommon for us to offer words of encouragement and brav-
ery. This is how I can talk to Becca and warn her."

Lana had to admit – Melissa's plan seemed more practical than
her own. Initially, she had considered a solo venture to the basement to persuade Becca to flee, which could potentially trigger a
fatal heart attack. "If you proceed with this plan, what happens
next?"

"We'll guide her out and conceal her in my carriage until we depart. I'm leaving tomorrow afternoon," Melissa outlined.

"How will you explain the presence of 'the patient' to your
troupe?"

"Don't fret. They are aware of our cause," Melissa reassured.
"The only hurdle is acquiring a key from Becca's cell and facilitat-
ing her escape."

"I'll get the key, and I'll handle that part," Lana assured her.

"Then it's settled."

Lana smiled. Before she honored her promise to Irida to deliver
the book, she could seek a few more 'favors.' It was time to return
to her room and set her plan in motion.

# 32

## Sweet Lies

Irida paced the room, periodically glancing at the time crystal on her wrist. It glowed bright red, indicating that it was midnight. "What the hell is taking them so long?" she asked for the hundredth time, facing the door. The silence was her only response.

As she glanced at the painting on the wall, Irida noticed that the woman depicted in it seemed to be wearing a cunning smile. It was as if she was up to something, her eyes gleaming in the dark, causing Irida to shiver. Shaking off the unpleasant sensation, Irida moved back to the window and narrowed her eyes, hoping to catch a glimpse of the silhouettes of the two women. However, there was no one to be seen. Their bedroom faced the front yard, with its narrow road leading into the endless forest. The tree trunks shimmered like emeralds, shaded by the foliage.

*Probably, they walked to the garden,* Irida decided. It made more sense – from the back side of the building, their chances of being seen were very low. Plus, Lana loved night flowers and nature in general. She had a surprisingly amusing trait – the ability to see the beauty of the world despite its ugliness. Irida exhaled a sigh. It had been enjoyable getting to know Lana. She would miss her.

With her naivety and courage, Lana stood out from the crowd of other women. Generally, the women Irida met were hopeless and desperate. After years of living in this harsh society, most of them had submitted to their fate. Their inner Light was dimmed, and their voices quieted. Irida never considered herself to be one of them. She was still a fighter, but life had taught her to fight for her own interests. Perhaps that was why she found Lana so interesting – she had that spark, too. Much like Irida in her younger years, Lana was a dreamer.

A quiet knock on her door made Irida startle. She hurried to the doorknob and opened it widely, ready to pull Lana in and start questioning her. However, it was a different woman standing before her.

"Amanda?" Irida asked, taken aback.

Amanda gave her a charming smile. "Yes. Did you expect someone else?"

Irida shook her head, regretting opening the door so wide. If Amanda walked in and discovered that Lana was still not there, they would both be in trouble.

"Why isn't your door locked?" Amanda inquired.

Irida blinked, trying to come up with a suitable explanation. Nothing came to mind. *I must improvise*, she decided.

Irida moved into the corridor, almost stepping into Amanda's embrace. Amanda didn't retreat, merely watching her with curiosity in her wide-open eyes.

"Why did you come?" Irida asked. "Has something happened?"

"Yes. And I believe you know exactly what."

Irida's heart sank. Earlier, Lana's mother had mentioned that Amanda had allowed their late meeting, but only if it lasted no longer than half an hour. It was well past that time. This would be the second time Lana had broken the sorority rules, a solid reason for banishment from the place.

It was the only possible reason Amanda could be paying a visit – to give her a warning about her roommate. *How could it happen tonight, when I was so close to acquiring The Book of Life?!* Irida clenched her teeth in frustration.

"Will you say anything?" Amanda whispered, her minty-chamomile breath reaching Irida's face.

*Shit.* Irida forced herself to breathe deeply. The last thing she needed was to screw up her mission because of Lana's sloppiness. *Can I possibly fix this?* Irida narrowed her eyes at Amanda, recalling their recent conversations. They never had a chance to make out because something always came up. Perhaps it could serve as a distraction. "Fine. I'll tell you something."

Amanda's eyes gleamed in the moonlight. "I'm listening."

Irida lowered her voice, trying to sound more seductive. "I can't stop thinking about you. But it seems like you're always too busy to notice my efforts. It's as if you're not interested anymore."

"I'm sorry I gave you that impression," Amanda said, locking eyes with Irida. "But I actually came here to see you."

*How intriguing.* Irida licked her lips. "Really?"

"Yes. I promised to sort things out after the concert, so here I am."

*Shit, that's why she came.* It meant that Lana wasn't in any trouble, and she might be on her way back any minute. Unfortunately, it also meant that Amanda needed to be dismissed before she became an obstacle on Irida's path to freedom. Irida put on a worried expression. "I appreciate it. But if Edwina finds out –"

"She's not a threat. Not to me." Amanda reached out and caressed Irida's cheek, sending pleasant goosebumps across her skin. "Is that clear?"

"Crystal clear."

"Good." Amanda stepped back. "Then be wise. This door won't stay open for too long."

Irida's heart raced in her chest, filled with excitement. It was too difficult to resist the opportunity to spend her last night at Mercy House in Sister Amanda's bed. *Lana has so much to discuss with her mom,* Irida reasoned with herself. *She might not return until sunrise.*

Blinded by irresistible temptation, Irida moved closer, her lips pressing against Amanda's. Amanda responded eagerly, her body ignited by the same flames of passion. Irida trailed her hand along Amanda's spine, her fingertips brushing against the straps of her tight corsage under her robe. *Does she always wear something surprising underneath?*

"We can take it slow," Irida whispered between kisses. "If you want."

"I only want one thing right now," Amanda replied with a sly look. She then walked towards the stairs and glanced back. "What about you?"

# 33

## Morning Prayers

"Let Divine bless the food on our table and the hands who cooked it," the chorus of Sisters' voices sang as they sat at the long dining table, holding hands. The morning prayers were a regular ritual that Lana had grown accustomed to. After expressing their gratitude, they were allowed to break their fast and enjoy the first meal of the day. Today, it was oatmeal with blueberries, which wasn't a bad option.

Lana grabbed a spoon and looked around for Irida. That night, when Lana returned to their room, she initially thought Irida had fallen asleep. Sometimes her Gift of Invisibility worked against her will in a certain stage of sleep, causing Irida to disappear. However, she did not reappear in the morning.

At sunrise, when Lana woke up, she realized that Irida had not spent the night in their bedroom. This violation of their strict discipline raised a question – What made Irida take such a risk? Lana's anxiety was pushed to the edge when Edwina, upon opening the room without using her key, expressed dissatisfaction. Naturally, she lashed out at Lana.

Now, Irida was calmly sitting at the far end of the table, close to Amanda. They were both laughing as if nothing had happened. The oddest part was that Amanda's eyes gleamed as if she had just spent the night with a lover. Lana narrowed her eyes at both of them, and a realization hit her. Amanda's lover was the same woman who had gone missing that night and caused her so much worry.

"Irida!" Lana stuck the spoon into her porridge with force. The metal clanked against the bottom of the plate, causing the Sisters to turn their heads.

Irida gave her a confused look. "What?"

Now that the voices around them had quieted, Lana could talk to her even from the opposite edge of the huge table. She wished she could say all the things that were on her mind and point out Irida's recklessness. Unfortunately, Lana couldn't afford to be direct, mainly because she still had a mission to accomplish. "It's good to see you're fine," Lana said in a plain tone. "I was worried."

Irida chuckled. "There is no reason to worry that much."

"I see." Lana gave her a sharp look. "I guess some matters aren't that important, and they can wait for a better timing. Right?"

Apparently, this reminder about their common business of stealing the book snapped Irida out of her careless state. She shook her head. "Of course not. We need to get back on track as soon as we finish our breakfast."

Amanda eyed them with curiosity. "What are you two up to?"

Irida didn't take her eyes off Lana as she replied, "Nothing. We were just discussing our Sister's duty."

"By the way, today is a big day," Amanda said cheerfully. "After the concert, many girls expressed their wish to undergo the procedure, even those with less strong magic. Edwina mentioned she had to schedule them for the afternoon to handle the volume."

This remark almost made Lana choke on her meal. She swallowed her oatmeal and pushed the rest of it aside, having lost her appetite. Then, she stood up.

"Where are you going?" Amanda asked.

"Back to my duty. Where else?" Lana replied in a grave voice. "You said it's been busy."

"Not for us," Amanda said with a chuckle. "After the procedure, all the patients go to after-care, sleep, so it's none of your concern anymore. I would say it's a more relaxing day for all of us, so we can take our time –"

"Still, I'll check on the rest of the patients," Lana interrupted. "Just to see how they are doing."

Amanda shrugged. "Fine."

Becca opened her eyes to see the flickering light of the burning torches on the black ceiling. She raised her hand, surprised by the lightness of her movements. It was real – her palms were free of the cuffs, and only the fresh burns on her fingertips reminded her of the surgery she had undergone.

As she recalled, Sienna had been taken first, followed by the Mercy Sisters coming for Becca. They had placed her in a procedure room where she had taken a potion meant to numb her pain, and then everything had gone blank.

Becca sat up, her head spinning. She gripped the edge of her bed, trying to focus her vision on her surroundings. This room wasn't as dark as her cell – the exit door was made of metal rods, offering a view of the round corridor. The torches lining the corridor provided enough light for her to see around.

The room was spacious, with four beds occupied by patients like herself. The other girls were sleeping soundly. Becca lifted herself and slowly walked along the wall, watching the other patients and trying to find Sienna. That girl was the only person who could understand her now. After all, they both agreed to give their magic away to be together.

Sadly, Sienna wasn't among the girls in this room. *Where the hell is she?*

"Hey," Sienna's quiet voice called from the corridor, making Becca flinch.

She rushed to the door, forgetting about her dizziness. Just before reaching the exit, she stumbled and fell to her knees. It took Becca an effort to hold onto the metal rods and sit upright while trying to focus her blurred eyes on the corridor. There was a tall female figure in a formless gray cloak standing in the middle, a hood shading her face. No doubt, it was one of the Mercy Sisters.

"What's happening?" Becca asked. "Where is Sienna?"

The Sister came closer, removing her hood as she approached.

Becca's heart sank as she recognized the girl who had spoken to her in the darkness, the one who had held her hands and professed love with tears in her eyes. Sienna. *How could she do that to me?*

Sienna smiled at her. "I'm so glad you embraced the will of the Divine and –"

"Oh, stop this farce," Becca said, her voice laced with disdain. "You lied to me?! All this time you were one of them?"

"Ah, you're still at the stage of anger. I guess I'll see you later." Sienna sighed and turned to leave.

Becca swiftly moved her hand between the rods and clenched onto Sienna's robe. "No! Don't go, please. Just tell me what's happening."

Sienna stood motionless. "You chose to become free. So, now you are free to be yourself."

Becca's fingertips ached, and she released her grip on Sienna's robe. Her palm pulsed. Perhaps, her wounds were still healing from the surgery. Without magic, it felt like a void forming deep inside her, filled with despair. "They took my magic away. Because of you."

Sienna turned to Becca, her eyes filled with compassion. *Is this her other role to play?* Becca couldn't know for sure; she just hoped that, at least this time, Sienna was sincere.

"I'm very sorry I lied to you," Sienna said. "Now, I'm telling the truth. You're right; this was my task – to become your companion and find a way to persuade you to consent."

Becca's eyes tingled. Shit, it hurt even worse than the physical pain in her hands. Tears rolled down her cheeks, and she didn't even bother to wipe them away. "I hate you. All of you."

Sienna nodded. "I understand. But please, hear me out – all this time, it was also something bigger than that."

"What do you mean?"

"You cleansed yourself of the Gift that could have endangered the lives of all those you love. Through your sacrifice, you saved them. Be grateful for that opportunity. I understand you may feel a deep emptiness now that your magic is gone, but remember – it's up to you to decide how to fill that void. You can choose the path of anger and destruction, which may ultimately lead to your demise. Alternatively, you can choose to fill it with love and compassion. Becca, you are embarking on a new chapter of your life, and you have the power to do so much good!"

"I'm freaking Incapable now."

"So what? You'll live in a community where people have no magic, but they hold dear the same values. They have more open views on relationships and many other matters that aren't allowed in our society." Sienna raised her hand, revealing the black marks left from the cuffs she had worn as part of her 'work.' Sienna clicked her fingers, and a gust of wind blew from the corridor, causing the lights to shiver. "I have the ability to control the wind, but I found it quite useless. That's why I chose to dedicate my life to serving the Sorority and helping people like you find their true path. The one they can explore once they become free from the ties of this unwelcoming realm. You can try to do the same – to find your purpose and be helpful."

Becca shook her head, unable to make sense of it all. The truth was, there was no way back for her, not after she had lost her Gift. She had no idea what awaited her in the future. It was scary, but she had no other way but to discover what Divine had prepared for her.

# 34

## When Magic Ends

Lana sprinted down the corridor, desperate to reach the dungeons as quickly as possible. However, her efforts were in vain as she arrived at the dungeon doors to find her mother, Melissa, waiting for her with a somber expression. There were no guards in sight, likely occupied with delivering the 'patients' to the executors who stripped them of their powers.

"We need to hurry," Lana urged, feeling a sense of confusion at her mother's frozen demeanor.

Melissa shook her head. "It's too late."

"Don't say that!" Lana exclaimed, shaking her mother's shoulders. "You came here to speak with Becca, right? Let's go together and talk to her."

Melissa swallowed hard and grasped Lana's hands. "I'm so sorry. I just found out what happened. I didn't anticipate them taking the girls at sunrise. If only I had known... we could have..." Her voice trailed off as she broke into sobs, unable to complete her sentence. However, her expression conveyed the truth to Lana. Becca had lost her magic.

A heavy silence enveloped them, causing Lana to tremble like a leaf. *No, it can't be. Perhaps, it's all just a misunderstanding.* "Mother, what do you mean?" she asked, her voice barely above a whisper.

"Becca... she's not there," Melissa replied, gesturing towards the dungeon doors.

"Maybe she is," Lana suggested optimistically. "Let's check again."

"I've already looked three times and called out for her. Sister Edwina confirmed that she was taken first."

Lana's heart sank as she took a step back, her hand instinctively covering her mouth. She couldn't fathom her best friend meeting such a fate. Memories of their shared past flooded her mind – their childhood adventures, the time they had solved their first crime case, and Becca's unwavering support during Lana's darkest moments. They had dreamed of spending the summer together in Triville, indulging in seasonal fruits and picnics by the river. Lana also longed for their horseback rides, where Becca's infectious smile could chase away all worries.

*Will I ever see her again?* The absence of Becca felt like a cruel illusion, a nightmare from which Lana couldn't escape. A tear trickled down her cheek, leaving a chilling trail on her skin.

"I'm still reeling from the shock," Melissa's voice sounded distant, as if coming from far away. "But we have to keep moving forward."

Lana looked up at her mother, her voice filled with anguish. "Moving forward? What do you mean?! They're doing this to all of them, and you... You're just standing by and letting it happen!"

Melissa let out a heavy sigh. "It feels like no matter what I do, it's never enough. Like trying to fill a bottomless pit with just my hands."

"Then take my hand!" Lana's voice rose almost to a shout. "It can't be like this! It just can't!"

"I know. Unfortunately, there's nothing we can do now. Becca willingly gave up her magic to be taken away. And now, she's beyond our reach."

Lana wiped her eyes with the back of her hand and paced along the wall, determined to regain her composure. As Amanda had mentioned during breakfast, the girls were still in the castle's aftercare facility. If Becca was among them, she might finally learn the harsh truth. Which meant Becca could potentially serve as a witness to the Sorority crimes. Lana only needed to find her. "Where is Becca now?"

"I don't know. And it doesn't matter at this point." Melissa's gaze bore into Lana's. "You must escape this place with me, so we can help others. We can travel across the continent, sharing our stories to warn and empower other girls. You can learn how to make them believe –"

"I don't need that!" Lana cut her off. "With Becca by our side, we can go to the Guardian House and reveal the truth. Don't you see that?"

"No. It's a suicide mission. If you speak a word, the deadly spell –"

"Becca can speak freely. She isn't bound by any oath. And if you're not willing to help, you can leave. I'll do it on my own."

"Lana –"

"I've made up my mind," Lana asserted. "I'll do it regardless."

Melissa took a deep breath. "Fine. As your mother, it's my duty to caution you. But I know you well enough to understand that you're too stubborn to give up."

"Exactly," Lana agreed.

"Alright. Here's what I know – after the procedure, the girls are still under the effects of a sleeping potion. It's a narcotic to alleviate their pain. They are then placed in a secluded chamber, typically for twenty-four hours, before a carriage arrives to transport them to the Incapables community. During this time, as per the contract they sign before the procedure, they are prohibited from disclosing what transpired."

*How fucking organized!* Not content with deceiving the 'patients' about their supposed inability to control their Gifts, the Mercy Sisters didn't even afford these girls the opportunity to bid farewell to their families. Not a single goodbye letter! While there was a concern about potential information leaks, it seemed as though these girls had been dehumanized.

"I don't know the location of that chamber," Melissa said. "But we could attempt to intercept them on the road."

"With the armored guards?" Lana's brow furrowed. "No. I'll handle it. You just need to meet us on the road."

"It's too risky. If they discover she's escaped, they'll track us down within hours!"

"Then we'll separate," Lana proposed.

Melissa nodded in agreement. "That might work. Escort Becca to the old theater in Middle Lake. I'll arrange for someone to meet her there and assist her in reaching Triville."

"Alright." It was a daring plan, but at least they now had a course of action to pursue.

"I'll be waiting for you in Triville," Melissa said. "I'll speak with Bernard and try to make him understand."

Lana blinked in surprise. "You're going to talk to my father?"

"Why not? We may've gone our separate ways, but we're not enemies."

Lana couldn't forget her father's anger when Melissa had left them, saying she must pursue her dream of becoming an actress. "He was... very upset with you."

Melissa offered a small smile. "There's no room for grudges when our only child is in grave danger. Besides, after you took the Sorority oath, I have nothing to lose by breaking the confidentiality agreement. I can speak to him candidly."

"I hope you know what you're doing."

"Me too." Melissa embraced her daughter. "Please, be careful."

# 35

# The Book of Life

Irida was in her room, looking at the painting. The woman in the painting brought her palms together, as if she was praying. Besides her appearance, there was something odd about it today – the frame was slightly shifted, while the main picture was aligned with the wall. Irida moved closer and extended her hand to touch the frame.

The entrance door opened, distracting her. She turned to the visitor and let out a sigh of relief. "Lana."

"Irida." Lana gave her a sharp look, mirroring her expression.

*Is she still upset with me for my absence last night?* Irida wondered. "Come on, you can't stay mad at me forever."

"Oh, I'm absolutely furious right now." Lana's eyes flashed, indicating her seriousness.

Irida swallowed. "I know... You have every right to be angry with me."

"Do I?" Lana asked sarcastically, then sat on the corner of the bed, perhaps waiting for an apology.

"Listen, I'm sorry." Irida approached her. "Was Edwina upset with you this morning?"

Lana gave her a weary look. "It doesn't matter now."

"True." The most important thing was their mission from the previous night. The one they were on the verge of completing before Melissa showed up, followed by Sister Amanda's unexpected arrival. *And it's not something I should dwell on now*, Irida reminded herself as her cheeks began to flush. The memory of Amanda's sweet screams as they lay together under the sheets, naked, would always remain etched in her mind. It would provide comfort on lonely nights in her spacious beach house. Finding a serene place to live by the seashore was the first thing Irida planned to do once she was free. And to achieve that, she needed to retrieve the book and leave this place behind.

"How was she?" Lana asked.

"Who?"

"Amanda." Lana locked eyes with her. "Was she worth it?"

Irida smiled. "Absolutely."

Lana scoffed. "Unbelievable."

"What?" Irida gave her a hesitant look. "I waited for you last night, but you never showed up. So, I kept myself occupied."

"This is the thing about you – you think that the world revolves around your persona," Lana accused.

"It isn't revolving around you, either," Irida retorted.

"I know that." Lana sighed. "And I also know that there is a small group of people who define the world order. The men. They dictate to all the women how they must live, and they silence the ones who dare to speak up."

"This is very unfortunate," Irida said, not quite understanding why Lana chose to bring up this topic now. She sat on the bed beside her, prepared to feign interest as a good listener. This tedious discussion about the 'dark side of the patriarchy' wouldn't last long. Soon, she would obtain what she needed and deliver the manuscript to David, the Oracle. She had no doubt that David was eagerly awaiting her arrival with her payment. *Interesting, does he know how long Lana will continue to torment me here?*

"And you just don't care about it at all," Lana spat, interrupting her thoughts. "You're the most selfish person I've ever met."

"I think you've already shared this thought," Irida remarked.

"Then it wasn't enough, apparently," Lana replied. "And in case you didn't get it, this was a brief summary from *The Book of Life*."

Her heart skipped a beat at the mention of the long-awaited manuscript. "You found it?!"

Lana nodded. "I found it, and I read it until sunrise. The group I mentioned – they manipulate educational programs to instill obedience in us. They control everything – from the literature we read to the doctrines preached in churches. Additionally, they established these dreaded Mercy Houses to eliminate the courageous young women who could potentially bring about change in society."

"Why would they silence us?" Irida inquired, merely to keep the conversation going. It seemed that Lana needed to voice all her concerns before she could be of assistance.

Lana exhaled a sigh. "Because we think differently. Unlike the men in power, we strive to make this world a better place. We advocate for fair laws, equal access to healthcare and education, and a decent standard of living for everyone. These ideals... they pose a threat to their status quo. All they care about is their wealth and maintaining control. They want to perpetuate a society where the common folk are trapped in poverty and discouraged from seeking a better life. They aim to uphold a system where ordinary men are consumed by the struggle to make ends meet, and women are burdened with the responsibilities of child-rearing. Such people are never given the opportunity to question the order of things."

"Okay," Irida responded calmly. "So where is the book?"

"Don't you see?" Lana prodded her forehead, causing Irida to recoil. "You're just a slave to this system. Driven by your financial struggles, you're willing to betray your fellow women in pursuit of the stability and freedom you crave! But let me tell you – true freedom will elude you until you stand up for what's right."

"I'm glad you've never experienced poverty," Irida shot back. "I simply desire the same for myself."

With the demeanor of a patient mentor, Lana continued to challenge her. "Okay. Let's say you obtain your money. What then?"

"Then... I can do whatever I please."

"Such as?"

Irida shrugged. "Firstly, I'll purchase a home by the sea. I'll relish the sunrises and sunsets on the shore, and I... I'll eat all the foods I desire."

"Suppose that dream comes true. What next? Will you continue to age, savoring delicacies, and gazing at the sun?"

"Maybe." Irida shrugged. Honestly, she hadn't thought that far ahead, but it was an intriguing notion to contemplate. "Okay, perhaps one day I'll consider starting a family."

"How exactly? According to the laws of all the Seven Kingdoms, you wouldn't be able to marry a woman."

"Well, I could explore a relationship with a man. I've had such experiences before, and I'm completely comfortable with it. Although I tend to avoid them due to the risks and the hassle of contraception. But for the sake of starting a family and having a child, I'll find a suitable partner."

"How clever," Lana teased. "A child... what if you have a daughter?"

Irida smiled. "That would be wonderful."

"Not so wonderful if she gets a Gift of Fire."

Irida stared at Lana as if she had just demolished the beautiful sandcastle she had built. And she didn't appreciate that feeling.

Lana nodded, finally content with her role as the buzzkiller. "There you have it. I trust you now understand that if this manuscript falls into the wrong hands, we are all doomed."

Irida furrowed her brow, her thoughts drifting to Captain Harrison and his insatiable ambitions. He was certainly not the 'right person,' but it was too late to backtrack and abandon her aspirations for a life of prosperity. "Okay, I see your point," Irida replied, attempting to convey respect.

"Good." Lana rose from her seat. She approached the frame covering the painting, deep in thought. Then she turned back to Irida. "By the way... where is the secret chamber?"

"What?"

"The one where they imprison the girls after stripping them of their powers."

"Oh, that," Irida pondered. It had been some time since she had perused Denise's diary, but she distinctly recalled references to that room in several entries. Denise had even provided a detailed account of the room's location and its security measures. "If I recall correctly, the entrance is in Amanda's room."

"Why there?"

Irida shrugged. "I have no idea. Perhaps because she is a teacher, and it would be less suspicious... Actually, why do you need to know?"

Lana gave her a weary look. "Guess."

*Fuck... Her friend must be one of the captives.* Irida nervously bit her lip. *No, no, no... I can't deal with this now.* "Listen, I just want to get this over with quickly. I've shared all the information I have and then some. Can you already reveal the book?"

"Of course." Lana grasped the frame with both hands and removed it. Surprisingly, the frame and glass were detached from the main painting.

Lana then pulled the portrait, and it took Irida a few moments to comprehend why the canvas was so thick and concealed within the wall. It wasn't a canvas at all; it was a book. *The Book of Life* that she had been tirelessly searching for.

Irida gave Lana a puzzled look. "It was here all this time?"

Lana grinned. "I know, right?! They really played us, Irida. This is just another reason why this place needs to be shut down."

Approaching her, Lana handed the book to Irida. She accepted it, feeling the weight of it in her hands. Like a small gravestone, it seemed to gleam, causing her heart to sink. *It's just a book*, Irida reassured herself. *Just a damn book. But someone is willing to pay a hefty price for it.*

# 36

## The Future Starts Today

The horse puffed, galloping along the forest trail. Irida held the reins, pressing her body to the horse's neck, the wind whistling in her ears. The narrow path, surrounded by the thick forest, finally widened. The area where the trees parted became visible, luring her with the beautiful golden light of the setting sun. Irida slowed down her horse and enjoyed trotting to the road fork.

Here, the paths split – one led to the Middle Lake city where she dreamed of building her career as a doctor. There, her dreams were shattered by the stark reality. She then started building a different life piece by piece, trying to survive as a thief. Eventually, she met Captain Harrison, and even though it brought a lot of trouble, a new, bright dream shimmered on her horizon. It was like the sun that dispersed the heavy clouds after the storm.

Irida never planned to return. Now, she had the other road to take – out of the Lake Kingdom, back to the south where her roots were. It would be the place where her best future would finally begin. *It will be a great life*, she decided.

At the crossroad sign, there was a carriage. A man in a hat stood by its side, leaning on the tree and chewing on a long grass stalk.

Two horses were resting at the roadside, but there was no horse-man in view. *Did he come here by himself with an empty carriage?* she wondered. Knowing David just briefly, she wasn't surprised by his seemingly illogical moves. After all, he was an Oracle, which meant everything he did made sense.

Irida neared him and dismounted her horse. "For how long have you been waiting?"

"Long enough to give my horses proper rest." He grinned. "I assume you succeeded in your search."

"Of course I did," she said, trying to sound nonchalant, but it only made his grin wider.

"Good job," his green eyes gleamed at her. For a few seconds, their color turned acid-green as it usually happened when he was using his Gift.

Irida folded her hands, waiting. It was a good thing she didn't carry her bracelet on her. Otherwise, she risked getting a burn. As she had learned, it was how time crystals responded to the Gifts of Time.

"Interesting," David said as he finished reading her.

"What did you see?" she asked, curious to see what awaited her next.

He gave her a sly look. "You go first."

Irida nodded and opened her roadbag. The book was resting there, its constantly changing cover now in gray shades. It looked like the woman on the cover was mourning, her eyes expressing deep sorrow. Irida pulled it out and held it in her hands, not quite ready to let go of it. She bit her lip, her heart full of doubts. *Shit, Lana really managed to get into my head with her farewell speech.*

David frowned at her. "What's the matter?"

"Just one question." Irida shuffled her feet, her head spinning. It felt unnatural just to give this book away. "What will happen to the book after Harrison gets it?"

"You never asked such things before. And you shall not ask them now."

She pressed the book to her chest. "I won't give it away until you answer my question."

"Then I'll take it by force. Trust me, even your magic stands zero chance against mine, so it's better to do it the easy way."

She stepped back. "How do I know if you give it to him?"

David nodded to the carriage. "He is here."

"Oh." Irida glanced at the window – it was shielded with a black curtain, but she could swear she saw a movement inside. Now it made perfect sense why David arrived here with two horses and a carriage – he was a horseman, not a passenger. "I want to speak to him first."

"About what?"

"I need to know what he'll do with it."

"It's none of your concern." David extended his hand, palm up. "Come on, give it to me already. Then, you'll get your money and live happily ever after."

Irida swallowed. She craved for that money and a chance to be free from all of this. But how could she be sure if that mess wouldn't end up ruining her life? "Will I really be happy?"

He shrugged. "Yes. Well, until you have a child."

Her heart sank. Now everything that had concerned her during the conversation with Lana became petrifying. It was one thing when a regular woman said such a thing about her future, but when it was told by the Oracle, it changed everything. "Is it... she?"

"The girl, yes," he confirmed, revealing a crooked smile. "Although, you'll need to give me the book first. This is the only guarantee you'll make it that far."

She squeezed the book in her hands, her knuckles turning white. "My girl... What about her Gift?"

"The Gift is a choice that the spirit makes. And I can't predict this choice."

She sighed. Everything he said didn't bode well. Irida took another look at the book. Now it turned pale, like a painting exposed to the sun for too long. *Is she scared?* Then it hit her – the book indicated the mood of the person who looked at it, that's why it behaved so weird.

Using her hesitance, David took the book from her hands. "Here we are. The money's at the nearest motel that you plan to hit next. Under the bed."

"You can't help making quests, huh?"

"That's right." He grinned. "If you choose to leave the Kingdom tonight, you'll never see me again. And there will be no more quests."

She paused. "What do you mean '*if* I leave the Kingdom?'"

He didn't answer. Instead, he took a pause as the carriage door squeaked open and Captain Harrison walked out.

Harrison frowned at Irida as he approached. "What takes so long? Did you get your further instructions?"

She gave him a look full of disdain. There was no way Harrison would use the book to change anything for the better. He was just too selfish for that. "What's your plan regarding *The Book of Life*?"

Harrison stepped closer, so Irida felt small and vulnerable against him. "My plan is to keep things in order," he declared. "There was a risk some women could cause distortion in the system, so now I'll keep the book close to me."

"So nothing will change, then?"

"That's right," he confirmed with a nod.

"Wait... what have you just said about distortion?" The thought of Lana being in danger made her throat dry. David was right in saying that people had free choice, but there were also people like Harrison who didn't leave them such a choice. He would just get rid of all the obstacles, treating them like weeds on his lawn.

Harrison grinned at her. "I think we both know the answer." He raised his hand, revealing his wrist decorated with expensive watches with the time crystals in it. "Don't waste your time thinking about it. You would rather hurry up to get your money before someone else checks into that motel room and rips you off from your dream life."

David gave Irida a teasing look. "Damn choices, huh?"

She didn't respond.

"We're done here," Harrison announced before getting back to his carriage.

David nodded and took his seat at the front. Then he shook the reins, and the horses started trotting to Middle Lake, the city where Irida's brightest dreams were crushed.

In a minute, she was alone on the crossroad, her heart aching in the depth of her chest. *I must hurry up.*

## 37

✤

# Meet The Queen

The lock clicked, sealing Lana inside her bedroom. She stood before the door, straining to hear the fading footsteps. Then, silence enveloped her.

Tonight, it seemed good luck was on her side. Sister Edwina had been surprisingly lenient with her. Irida also had played her part perfectly – she had requested permission to visit the nearby village, citing a shortage of ingredients for the potions needed for new patients. Of course, Irida cared little for the patients; she had only used the excuse to mask her departure from Mercy House, granting Lana one more night before she would arouse suspicion.

Lana had to make the most of her limited time. With Irida likely already en route out of the Lake Kingdom and her mother en route to Triville, there was no one left in the castle she could rely on, except for Becca.

*Becks...* Lana took a deep breath, attempting to steady her racing heart. The knowledge that her best friend was imprisoned somewhere in the secret dungeon filled Lana with a seething anger. Above all else, Lana longed to storm into Amanda's bedroom and

234

rescue Becca. Unfortunately, she couldn't afford to be too impulsive. She couldn't risk jeopardizing her carefully laid-out plan.

As Lana checked her time crystal for the hundredth time, it finally glowed a salmon-pink hue. *Eleven o'clock.* It was time to act. Lana retrieved a small pick from her pocket, a parting gift from Irida. She then donned her black rain cloak. Lana had discovered that wearing dark clothing allowed her to blend seamlessly into the shadows of the dungeon corridors, remaining unnoticed.

Before departing, she stole a quick glance at the window – the night had descended into near darkness, the sky obscured by thick storm clouds. "Please, let my luck hold out for as long as this night," she whispered, gazing out at the horizon.

A flash of lightning illuminated the sky, like a spark of Divine blessing that ignited hope within her heart. The subsequent rumble of thunder reverberated through the forest, and the first raindrops began to pelt against the window glass. *Perfect.* The storm's cacophony would mask her footsteps, giving her a chance to succeed.

The door to Sister Amanda's bedroom swung open, allowing Lana to slip inside. The raging storm outside masked any sounds that could potentially wake the sleeping person, however, she needed more to make sure nothing would disturb Amanda's dream.

Lana pressed her palms together, channeling the silver energy of the Paralyzing spell into a sphere that hovered between her hands. Moving silently, she crept towards the bed, intent on finding Amanda and administering the spell to her chest. With the spell poised in her right hand, Lana inhaled deeply and yanked back the bed covers.

The lightning flashed, briefly illuminating the empty, rumpled white sheets on the bed. Lana's heart skipped a beat. Amanda wasn't in the room. *What the hell?* Lana took a deep breath, thinking of a reasonable explanation to this mystery. Given what Lana had discovered about Amanda, she wouldn't put it past her to enjoy her night with another Mercy Sister. However, it meant that Lana couldn't proceed with her original plan now; Amanda could return at any moment.

"Looking for someone?!" Amanda's voice rang out from behind her, causing Lana to jump in surprise. Slowly, she turned to face Amanda, who stood just five steps away, brandishing her own Paralyzing spell. The silver light of the spell cast a strong, bright glow on Amanda's grinning face. "I could ask what you're doing in my bedroom, but I think it's clear we no longer need to play games," Amanda stated, her tone sharp. "Drop your spell. Now."

Lana's mind raced with potential escape scenarios. She could attempt to cast the spell at Amanda now, but she wasn't quick enough. Amanda could easily evade the spell, putting Lana at a disadvantage. Furthermore, the Paralyzing spell had a side effect of numbing magic channels, rendering Lana unable to use her powers for a period of time. If Amanda retaliated with her own spell, Lana would be incapacitated for even longer, as Amanda's spell was of superior quality. It seemed she was trapped.

Amanda's stern voice broke through Lana's thoughts. "I said drop it! And if you dare to pull any tricks, I'll ensure your friend from Triville never reaches the safety of the Incapables community."

The mention of Becca's safety compelled Lana to lower her hands and release the spell. It slipped from her palm and landed on the wooden floor, leaving a delicate circle of frost on the planks.

"Good girl," Amanda remarked, her voice sending a shiver down Lana's spine.

*How could I've missed it?* Lana pondered as the realization dawned on her. When Lana had delved into Edwina's thoughts, she had been taken aback to discover the old woman's fear of Sister Amanda. This senior Sister was a master manipulator, a stark contrast to Edwina's timidity. Confident and unafraid to push boundaries, Amanda had skillfully ingratiated herself with Lana, always appearing at the right moment to earn her trust. Through these interactions, Amanda had gleaned Lana's fears, doubts, and hidden intentions. The adage of keeping friends close and enemies closer rang true in this hostile environment.

The truth was clear to Lana now – Amanda was the boss here, not Edwina. Lana met her gaze head-on. "You used Sister Edwina as a pawn to instill fear and maintain discipline among us. All the while pretending to be the one we could turn to for support."

Amanda's smile widened. "Exactly."

Lana flashed a grin. "I'm glad Irida stole your precious manuscript. Now, your secrets aren't safe anymore."

Amanda laughed. "She did me a huge favor. *The Book of Life* could serve as proof against us, and honestly, I would gladly destroy it myself if I could. All this time, only Edwina knew where it was, and she was bound by the oath to keep this secret until her last breath. Imagine my joy when Edwina reported its absence shortly after Irida's departure!"

Lana sighed. It now made perfect sense why Edwina had hidden *The Book of Life* in their bedroom – she never wanted Amanda to learn its location. "I'm surprised you didn't kill Edwina to achieve your goal faster."

"Kill?!" Her eyebrows twitched. "I can't do that to other Sisters. We are bound by the sacred Oath, in case you forgot."

"So... you kept her alive because of the damn oath," Lana concluded. At least, now she knew that Amanda wouldn't kill her, so she had a chance to get out of this situation. "Alright, that part is clear. But what makes you think the book will be destroyed?"

"Because I know the man who hired Irida. She gladly placed *The Book of Life* in the hands of a man consumed by greed, who will do nothing to alter the course of events."

Lana cursed inwardly. She had hoped Irida would at least make one correct decision. "What's next? Are you going to arrest me?"

Amanda's response was matter-of-fact. "Of course not. Your father, as the guardian, holds the key to helping you evade punishment. I have a different plan in mind for your future."

"So, you're the one determining my fate now?" Lana challenged. "Since when do women have that authority?"

"*The Book of Life* you stole doesn't reveal the complete picture. The truth is, it's not solely about gender. It's about who wields the power to control others, regardless of gender. There are few women in such positions, myself included. I've spent two decades here, determining the fates of those in the mage society – who can continue living their lives and who must be silenced."

"Why do you subject us to this?"

Amanda gestured around the room. "Because of all this. I'm the queen of this castle, and people obey me. Here, I have the freedom to act as I please."

Lana regarded her with pity. "I see. You've chosen to exist in this prison because it's the only way you can be with other women. You can never truly be yourself in a society of mages."

Amanda winced. "You've turned everything upside down."

"The truth may be bitter, but it has the power to heal," Lana remarked.

Amanda rolled her eyes, a hint of irritation in her voice. "I find solace in this place, and you won't infiltrate my mind and disrupt that."

Lana gave her a weary look. "So, what do you have in store for me?"

Amanda toyed with the Paralyzing spell in her hands, a sinister gleam in her eyes. "You will be stripped of your magic and sent off to become the wife of an Incapable man."

The thought made Lana shudder. "And what makes you think I'll remain silent about this?"

"This process only goes smoothly if every step is executed precisely. However, there can be side effects in some cases, such as the loss of speech."

Lana shook her head in disbelief. In her darkest nightmares, she could never have fathomed that a woman could be capable of such cruelty. And the worst thing – she wouldn't be the first person to face such a horrific fate. *How many others perished in their quest to challenge this inhumane world order?* Mia, Oliver's sister, was killed when she attempted to escape. Denise had lost her daughter, too, so later, she sacrificed herself to pave the way for those who would follow. Poor Denise had given her life to expose the Sorority secrets. And for what?

Now, with Irida using her diary for personal gain, the cycle of destruction would continue, snuffing out lives and extinguishing hope. Lana doubted whether Irida would ever muster the courage to do what was right. It meant that all the women who had died fighting for change had done so in vain.

"Don't be so despondent," Amanda's voice interrupted Lana's somber thoughts. "The loss of speech is merely a potential consequence. If you agree to behave and keep silent, I'll request that they treat you with leniency."

Lana regarded Amanda with a solemn expression. "You're a woman as well. How can you stand by and allow this to happen? Don't you feel any remorse?"

"Freedom comes at a cost, and I am willing to pay that price, no matter what it entails."

"You can't achieve your own freedom by sacrificing the lives of others."

"It seems that I can, and I will," Amanda retorted as she aimed her hand towards Lana. "All I need is your word. Just say you agree to remain silent. That's all."

Lana took a step back, nearly stumbling over the bed. "Never!"

Amanda glanced upwards, as if addressing her own conscience. "May Divine bear witness that I've tried!"

"You should have tried not to be such a bitch."

Amanda chuckled. "I'll miss your sense of humor. Well, it's time to rest."

Lana closed her eyes, resigned to her fate. If this world was truly as fucked up as it seemed, she had no desire to keep being a silent bystander. Not any longer. Despite the potential loss of her magic and ability to speak, Lana still could use her hands to reveal the truth. She would write about her experiences and send letters to all the Guardian Houses, ensuring that they could no longer turn a blind eye to the injustices the women like her had faced.

Amanda's attempts to justify her actions did not sway Lana's resolve. She didn't need reassurance of her righteousness. Lana knew she had always lived her life as a mage with integrity – showing kindness to others and sharing her Light generously, offering solace to those navigating their own challenging paths. Neither Amanda nor any other powerful figures in the world could extinguish that Light within her.

The Paralyzing spell twisted in the air, and Lana froze. *That's weird.* She had never experienced being shot by such a spell, but she knew from her studies that it would feel like a cold touch on her chest followed by an inability to move. She didn't feel anything like that.

Lana attempted to move her fingers and found that she could. Opening her eyes, she saw Amanda frozen in place, the Paralyzing spell glowing in her hand as if she were about to throw it. Lana shook her head in confusion. "Is this a dream?"

"Nope, it's me," a familiar voice answered. Irida emerged from behind Amanda, a proud smile on her face.

Lana's eyes widened in disbelief. "You... you came back for me?"

"Yes," Irida confirmed, pulling Lana into a hug. Even through her cloak, Lana could feel Irida's icy-cold fingers. It became clear that Irida had used the Paralyzing spell on Amanda first, rendering her motionless.

"We don't have much time," Irida urged as they separated.

"But your magic won't work for a while," Lana pointed out.

"I'll stay here and immobilize Amanda, tying her to the bed. It will buy us more time to escape."

Lana nodded and glanced towards the fireplace, where the small door to the secret dungeons was now visible. "I'll be right back."

"No," Irida interjected, her expression filled with concern. "Amanda has alerted the guards, and they are patrolling the corridors. I barely managed to make it here, and I've nearly depleted all my magic."

"What do we do then?"

"There's another door you must use once you're out of there. It leads to the loading area where they dispose of the garbage."

"How fitting," Lana remarked sarcastically. "Couldn't they have a separate dock for the women they've stripped of their powers?"

"We can question that later. For now, we need to focus on escaping."

"Agreed. I need to get Becca out."

"Good. Let's stick to the escape plan. The guards change at midnight, so simply give Becca the key. She will get out at that time."

"What if she bumps into a guard?"

"All of them are preoccupied searching for you in the main corridors. They wouldn't station more than two guards there. We can use that to our advantage."

"Got it. And what about you?"

"I'll replenish my power and make my escape. Don't wait for me. Once you find Becca, continue on your planned path."

Lana looked at her with gratitude. "Thank you, for everything you've done."

"I wish I could do more."

Lana smiled. "See? It's never too late to do something good for someone else."

Irida's cheeks flushed, and she waved her hand dismissively. "Go. We're running out of time."

"Of course," Lana said, pausing before moving to embrace Irida one last time. "I'll never forget what you did for me."

Irida clapped her back. "Me too."

# 38

## The Chase

The rain poured into Irida's face as she ran along the narrow forest trail. The path beneath her feet quickly turned to mud, causing her to slide and stumble before falling into a puddle.

Breathless, she sat up and looked around. The forest shimmered green through the curtain of endless rain. It seemed she had managed to escape, but it could be just an illusion. It was only a matter of time before the guards from Mercy House would start chasing her. They had a significant advantage with their hounds and horses.

Irida checked her bracelet, which glowed orange. It had been an hour since she left Amanda tied to her bed and fled. She hadn't risked retrieving her horse because her invisibility shield was almost depleted and the guards were everywhere around the black castle, including the stables. She had been running non-stop since then.

The only silver lining was that Lana had managed to escape. Irida hadn't seen her or Becca on the hilltop as she passed it, so she hoped they had safely fled the cursed place. Now, all Irida needed to do was keep running. With a groan, she rose to her feet, feeling the acid in her muscles.

"I can't get caught," she muttered, trying to convince her body to keep going. At that moment, a sharp tip of steel poked under her rib, causing her to freeze.

"How does that feel?" a voice asked. It belonged to a young woman, not a man, which was a relief. It likely wasn't a Mercy House guard, but perhaps just a forest thief looking for her mostly empty purse.

"Take my purse and go," Irida said. "I'm not looking for any trouble."

"Then why are you running after me?" the young woman asked, circling around to face Irida. The hood of her black cloak was up, casting a shadow over her upper face. *The cloak... it was black, matching the one Lana had worn that night. It even had the same initials on the sleeve. L.M. What the hell?*

The woman pulled her hood off, letting the rain water her pale face. Her big blue eyes glared at Irida. It was only then that Irida recognized her. "Rebecca? What happened? And where is Lana?"

Becca narrowed her eyes at her. "Why are you chasing me?"

Irida blinked, trying to make sense of the accusation. It appeared that she had been unknowingly running along the same trail that Becca had chosen for her escape. "Okay... I think it's just a misunderstanding. I wasn't –"

"Stop lying!" Becca pressed her knife closer, its tip painfully touching Irida's skin.

Irida gasped for air. *That's why I never help anyone. There are too many complications that I don't need.* "I don't lie, I swear."

"Oh, really?!" Becca's face twisted into a sarcastic expression. "Then you can go, I guess."

Irida stepped back, rubbing her sore side. "I assume you won't let me go so easily."

Becca twisted the knife in her hand. "That's about right. And don't even try to escape because I'm really good at throwing knives."

Irida gave her a small smile and slowed her breath. Then, she stepped aside and became invisible. Becca stood still, her face puzzled. *You didn't expect that, right?* Irida thought with satisfaction. It was empowering to have control over the situation.

Remaining silent, Irida waited in case Becca decided to follow through on her threat to throw the knife. It was likely that Becca was on edge after the loss of her magic. *This girl is vulnerable now*, Irida realized. *That's why she's so defensive.* Irida wished she could do something to ease her pain.

Stepping behind a tree, Irida spoke from her shield. "Listen, I'm truly sorry about everything. I'm not here to harm you."

"Then why can't you just leave me alone already?" Becca asked, lowering her hand. Surprisingly, she seemed open to reason.

"I honestly had no idea I was following you. I was trying to escape after helping Lana."

"Suppose you're telling the truth…" Becca paused. "Then why did you lie before? To all of us? Why did you claim that the surgery for removing a Gift was safe?"

Irida felt her cheeks flush with embarrassment. She had no justification for her previous deceit. She didn't want to lie anymore. "Firstly, I didn't want to accept the truth that every girl loses her power after undergoing the procedure. I suppose I felt too scared to confront it. So, I simply tried to ignore it."

"What changed?"

"Your friend, Lana. She somehow got through to me, and I couldn't continue to turn a blind eye."

"Yes, she has a way of doing that," Becca agreed.

Irida smiled. At that moment, her invisible shield blinked and faded away. Perhaps her powers had worn off too quickly due to exhaustion, but it no longer mattered – there was no need to keep hiding. Irida stepped out from behind the tree. "By the way, where is Lana?"

"It was chaotic shortly after I left. Lana and I had to split up and head in different directions," Becca explained, sheathing her knife. "I need to go to Middle Lake alone."

"We should stick together now," Irida suggested. "It's safer."

"Fine. There must be a village nearby where we can find horses to steal and maybe some food."

The idea sounded appealing to Irida. She hadn't eaten since breakfast. However, it was a risky move. "A village is the first place they'll search."

"Then we won't enter the village. We'll just take the horses and some food, then continue on to Middle Lake. There, we'll part ways and disappear."

Irida smiled. "Sounds like a plan."

The bright sun teased Irida's eyelashes, prompting her to turn to her side in an attempt to avoid it and catch a few more minutes of sleep. The bedsheet tickled her sides, reminiscent of lying on a bed of hay, and her muscles ached as if she had been fleeing a pursuit. The memory of the stormy night and her sprint through the forest quickened her heart rate, jolting her fully awake.

Confirming her suspicions, she found herself lying on a bed of hay. Irida distinctly recalled them choosing one of the remote barns to rest and recover their energy. However, Becca was nowhere to be seen. *Has she left without me?*

Standing up, Irida made her way to the single window and peered outside. To her relief, Becca was sitting in the shade, eating what appeared to be a loaf of bread with a jug of milk by her side. With a mix of relief and annoyance at being left behind, Irida walked out of the barn.

Becca greeted her with a cheerful smile. "Look who finally woke up."

Iirida ignored the comment. "Where did you get this food?"

"Sorry, I was going to offer it to you once you woke up," Becca replied, taking another bun from a towel and handing it to Irida.

The aroma of freshly baked bread wafted to her nose, causing her stomach to rumble and overriding her caution. Irida took a bite and savored it greedily.

"I've always loved the way they bake bread in villages," Becca remarked. "It's a special scent... It reminds me of the wild fields and endless skies."

Irida nodded in agreement. "True. Life in the city made me forget how good it is. So, where did you get it?"

"There's a village about a ten-minute walk away, and a woman was setting up a breakfast table in her garden. She kindly shared her food with us."

Irida nearly choked on her food. "You... Did you talk to her? Did she see your face? If she did, then we need to run –"

"Relax," Becca interrupted, chuckling. "I'm just messing with you. I took the food when she went back inside. She didn't even see me."

Irida let out a sigh of relief. Becca certainly had a mischievous side. "It's not wise to joke like that, given our situation –"

"Considering you lied to me all the time when I was a 'patient,'" Becca interjected, raising her hand and using two fingers to emphasize the air quotes around the word 'patient,' "I think it's my right to tease you a bit."

Irida sighed. After Becca lost her magic, she didn't have the moral high ground to question her harmless joke. "I'm truly sorry."

"Don't be," Becca replied, taking another bite of the bun. "You know, one of the Mercy Sisters worked undercover to get my consent. She said that everything that happened to me was the will of Divine. I just need to come to terms with it."

The mention of Divine's will sent a shiver down Irida's spine. It was all a lie to justify the worst human actions – the deceit, the murders... all to maintain the wealth and safety of a few while the majority of people suffered. *Shit, I've become another Lana,* she thought with concern. "Any chance you can forgive me?"

Becca gave her a weary look. "Asking for forgiveness without the intention to change is a form of misery."

"I'm helping you right now, if you haven't noticed," Irida retorted.

"How exactly?" Becca questioned skeptically. "It was me who brought us here and stole the food."

"And I'm grateful for that. But stealing the horses will be more challenging. I can use my magic to help with that."

"Because you have one?!" Becca spat, then immediately shook her head as if regretting her words. "Sorry... I just... I try to imagine what my life would be like without it. To be Incapable. I'll never be able to create my Light ball to help heal my wounds."

Irida gave her a compassionate look. "Incapables... I mean, people without magic, they find ways to cope. I've heard they are less affected by potions and more resilient to harmful magic. It could be an advantage."

"Yeah, I'll need a mountain of herbal tea to relax after a tough day. What a joy! Sometimes, I wonder if such a life is even worth living."

Irida fell silent. There were no words that could offer comfort in such a dire circumstance. After all, Becca was stripped of her powers and was supposed to be sent to a place where she was a complete stranger. Legally, Becca wasn't even allowed to live among the mages. This raised a question – what was Lana thinking when she helped Becca escape?

Becca met her gaze. "I only wanted to see my family again and tell them what happened to me."

"Will they listen?"

She shrugged. "I can only pray they let me speak before sending me to the Incapables community."

Irida nodded in understanding. "That might work. But considering that you escaped Mercy House, now you might not get away with it. If the guardians learn that you spread the truth, they'll silence you."

"You mean... they'll kill me?"

"Exactly," Irida said, looking up into the cloudless sky. "Maybe it's better for you to return to Mercy House. If you beg Sister Amanda to forgive you, she'll give you a chance to keep living among Incapables."

Becca widened her eyes. "You seriously want me to beg that woman? After everything the Sorority did to me?"

"It's the only way to make it safe."

Becca paused. "I guess I have two choices right now – to stay alive but become a slave of this system or to put my life at stake for the slim chance to stop the Sorority and save countless other girls like me."

That was about right, and Irida already knew she would do everything in her power to help this girl, whatever choice she would make.

"Honestly, I hate my options," Becca said, rising to her feet. "But here is what I know for sure – I would rather die fighting than keep living on my knees."

Giving Becca an agitated look, Irida asked, "Where did you say you need to go? Is someone helping you get to Triville?"

"Lana told me to go to the old theater in Middle Lake. From what I understand, there's a group of women there who are working to help stop this situation."

"Then I'll make sure you get there safely."

# 39

## The Order

It was late at night when they finally arrived in Middle Lake. At the old theater, they dismounted their horses and hugged before parting. Irida stayed under the shade of the tree to watch Becca walking up the stairs and knocking on the tall doors. The door opened, revealing a plump woman in round glasses. Seeing Becca, she smiled and hugged her, as a mother would hug her long-lost child.

Irida smiled. Her mission was accomplished, at least this part of it. Despite all her worries, it seemed like Divine will that Becca talked about had worked. Like a shield, it had saved them during their journey – they hadn't encountered the guards of Mercy House or the guardians.

Now, she could return to Captain Harrison and try to collect her payment for *The Book of Life*. After all, he owed her that much for all the hard work she had done for him. And if he didn't comply, she would make him pay for all his lies. It wouldn't be an easy task – he held a high rank and was well-guarded. Though he had a teenage son who could be approached. Irida bet she could try to use him as a pawn. Maybe Harrison would even resign to save him...

Irida turned on her heels, ready to walk directly to his house, when the dark silhouette of a man separated from the nearest building. She took a deep breath, trying to calm her racing heart and pull her invisible shield on. But it was too late. His eyes shimmered bright green, and the time crystal on her hand burned her skin, making her forget about her attempt to hide.

"David!" she yelped, rubbing her wrist. She might have admired his Gift once they met, but right now, it was annoying. "Stop it!"

He grinned at her. "You chose to save Lana instead of being rich. It's difficult to surprise me, but right now, I'm truly impressed."

She folded her hands. "It was only a small delay. I'm not leaving this city without my money."

"Here we go. The old Irida is back." He chuckled. "I advise you not to go near Harrison, though. He can't wait to arrest you."

"For what?!"

David gave her a weary look. "Shall I really say that he knows Sister Amanda? The one that you tied to the bed and held captive, so Lana and a prisoner could escape Mercy House?"

Irida blinked. Shit, it made a lot of sense – last night, just before she rescued Lana, she was eavesdropping by the door, waiting for the proper moment to knock off Sister Amanda. As it appeared, all this time Amanda was helping Irida to complete her mission. Her own goal was to give that book away to bury those secrets forever. "It's hard to believe she didn't know the location of *The Book of Life*."

"It was secret information. Only Edwina knew it, and her mission was to make sure it wouldn't go into the wrong hands."

Irida sighed. "Well, sadly she failed."

"Not at all. Before we gave it to Harrison, there was another person who read it. And that was all that mattered."

She batted her eyes, trying to make sense of it. Then, the realization hit her. "Lana."

He smiled. "Yes. I wasn't completely honest with you, Irida. It wasn't the book that I was looking for all this time. It was the right person who was capable of making a difference. That manuscript was only a tool. And you were her guide. You were the person whose destiny was connected with hers on so many different levels. You challenged Lana, however, she would never make it through without you."

Irida swallowed. "Did you know I would go back and rescue her?"

"No. In fact, the chance of that was very small. As I've said multiple times already, I can't predict human choices. You truly surprised me, Irida."

"What if I didn't do that?"

"Lana would never stop trying to change the world order. You only made it easier for us, which I appreciate."

"And I have no money now," she reminded him. "How am I supposed to survive?"

"Here." David took a purse from his belt and gave it to Irida. "Take it as my 'thank you' gift. It's not as much as Harrison promised you, but it will be enough for you to start a new life. Just take it and go South. They wouldn't look for you there. I checked."

Irida opened the purse and smiled. The gold inside shimmered in the emerald light of the trees surrounding them. It was enough money to make her forget about Harrison and restore her dream of a decent life somewhere in the south. She would buy a small beach house, exactly as she planned, and then... the conversation with Lana popped into her head, spoiling her mood. She raised her eyes at David. "What about Lana? Will she be safe now?"

He shrugged. "Changing the order is a complex task. It involves a lot of people, and all of us must make the right choices."

Irida winced. "I didn't understand a thing."

"Okay, I'll explain." He pointed at the theater building. "You've just seen the woman who let Becca in. She must be strong and brave to deliver her to Triville safely. Then Becca will talk to people who need to make their own choice."

"Her parents, you mean?"

He nodded. "They might be scared of law enforcement and give her away to the guardians. Or they could choose to fight for her. At that point, Becca will become the case that will cause a ripple effect and eventually lead to shutting down all the Mercy Houses."

"What if they betray her?"

"If it happens, I'll need to play this game again. Only the stakes will be higher."

Irida felt her heart swell. It was crystal clear now. This is what she must do from now on – to fight injustice. It sounded much more exciting than sitting on a beach and drinking piña coladas all day long. "How can I help?"

"You already helped a lot. Right now, it's better for you to flee the city." He thought for a moment, his eyes shimmering with green sparks. "If I need you, I'll know how to reach you."

"Fine," she agreed. David was right – she had to go now. However, she still had a question, and it might be the only chance to ask it. "Why do you do it?"

He looked up into the sky. "The life of an Oracle is a form of torture."

She scoffed. "Seriously?! You can predict what people say or do, and all the treasures of the world can be yours if you want."

"Still, there is the thing that was beyond my reach until now. My daughter's happiness."

Irida widened her eyes. It was hard to imagine this man being a family guy. "You have a daughter, then."

He nodded. "Sadly, she is an Incapable."

"Ouch."

"I know." He gave her a sly look. "There is no greater love than the love for your child. For their future, we are ready to do unimaginable things. Knowing that this society isn't made for her makes me think of ways of rearranging it. And trust my word, one day I'll be there."

# 40

## A Sacrifice

Becca stood in the barn, surrounded by silent shadows. She used to visit this barn often when she helped stack hay for the horses and rabbits. It was a bit far from their house, so Becca often stayed until late and lit her way home using her Light. She raised her hand, looking at the healing burns on her palm. There was no more Light left in her, but she was still alive. And as long as she breathed, she would keep trying to tell the truth about Mercy House she had learned in such a hard way.

"Rebecca?" The voice called, causing her to flinch. It was a voice she had known for as long as she could remember, but now it sounded hostile. It wasn't surprising – since she had returned to Triville, it quickly became clear that she wasn't welcomed here.

She turned to see a male figure in a black cloak, his lower face hidden behind a black scarf. Clearly, he was a Gift Hunter, a Guardian whose role was to catch girls like Becca and arrest them. It was a big surprise that he happened to be the one she knew so well. Maybe it meant she had a chance to convince him to take her side. She gave him a smile. "What is all this masquerade for? I know you –"

"I came to stop you," he interjected, making her go silent. "You've broken too many rules already."

"These rules broke me first." She raised her hand, showing her burned fingertips. "So, now it's my turn."

He shook his head. "You've always been too rebellious. Starting from dating that girl from your school to getting the Gift that you can't carry."

"As it turns out, I had a chance to master my power. Did you know that all those stories about our Gifts are a lie?" Becca asked. It was what she had learned from the woman she had met in the old theatre. "With proper training, we can learn to control even the strongest magic –"

"Nobody ever allows that."

"Why not?" She questioned. "There were several studies showing that women can tame all kinds of magic. The only problem is that all these study materials are forbidden."

"And there is a reason for it."

She knitted her brow. "And what reason is that?"

He paused. "I don't know. But if this law exists, I must trust the ones who created it."

Becca laughed, walking around the figure in black as she spoke. "So, just like that? You'll keep following these rules blindly, knowing how many lives it has ruined? You're just going to embrace their absurd explanations without even giving it a second thought?"

He sighed. "I'm sorry I disappointed you, but –"

"But what?"

"I must think of your family now. By escaping Mercy House and coming here, you've put everyone in trouble."

She shrugged. "I didn't stay at the house to avoid being a nuisance."

"That's not what I meant. If someone discovers that your family was aware that you were hiding in their barn, they will face consequences."

Becca crossed her arms. "Oh, I see. They must report on me, huh?"

"Exactly. Otherwise, everyone who was aware of the situation will be executed."

She swallowed hard. "You must be kidding me."

"I'm serious."

Becca stared at him, waiting for reassurance. His eyes remained fixed on her with a mix of pity and disdain. She exhaled a sigh. "So, what's your suggestion?"

"I know that someone's helping you. Turn yourself in and tell us everything you know about those women who aim to shatter the existing order. If you do so, your family will be safe and you'll stay alive. I'll make sure to send you to the Incapables community where you can live –"

"No."

"Shall I remind you what's at stake?"

"No," Becca said, turning away and gazing out the night window. There, a silent crescent moon was rising above the black silhouettes of the tree crowns, bearing witness to their conversation. "I believe that everything that happened to me was the will of the Divine. Before Mercy House, I would never have believed that those people could take the magic from all of us. But now, after experiencing it myself... After witnessing everything... I do believe it now. I managed to escape to see the people who know me and to tell my story, so everyone will know the truth."

"This truth won't change a thing."

She shrugged. "I'll be happy if it saves another naive girl who has just discovered her forbidden magic. I believe we can start a movement to teach them to control such power. Over time, it might render all these ridiculous laws obsolete, and most importantly, it will save countless lives."

He shook his head. "That's why I can't let you continue. You're too ambitious."

Becca's heart sank. *Is that what Irida warned me about? Is he going to kill me?* No, this man wasn't capable of executing such an order. Not him. "And what are you going to do if I may ask?" Becca's voice trembled slightly, but she kept speaking. "Will you silence me just like you do with all the other innocent girls?"

"I won't have to if you agree to our terms."

Becca grinned at him. "I've come too far to stop now. So, my answer is 'no.'"

He gave her a look full of pity. "Right now, you may feel invincible and believe you're doing the right thing, but in reality, it was simply good luck that allowed you to escape that place without being caught. And as for your movement... you have no idea how to handle it. So, drop these foolish thoughts and turn yourself in before it's too late."

She lowered herself to the floor, maintaining eye contact. "If you want to stop me, you'll have to kill me. Otherwise, leave."

He paused, contemplating. Then, he raised his hand, whispering a spell. His fingers ignited as he cast a Fireball – a spell forbidden among regular mages and often used by the Guardians to intimidate criminals. Becca had never imagined she would be on the 'dark side' of the law. As it appeared, it was intimidating and also strangely invigorating.

As the flames illuminated the space, Becca remained seated. "Is that a threat?"

"Wanna sit here?" He shouted. "Sit for as long as you wish. But once you get out of here, scared and weak, remember who you are and do what you must." With that, he threw the Fireball at the wall behind Becca.

The hay quickly caught fire, filling the barn with smoke and making it hard to breathe. Becca covered her mouth with her sleeve, her eyes stinging as she watched his silhouette walk out of the barn, leaving the door open.

*Does he really think I'm going to give up so easily?* Her heart pounded as the smoke reached her nose, causing her to cough. The fear of death washed over her, but Becca remained seated. She hugged herself to dispel the fear. It was only a primal instinct – an impulse to run away to survive. Clearly, it was his tool to manipulate her into giving up on her ideas. She couldn't let it happen. Not anymore. Becca had to stay strong and prove she was serious. Otherwise, all the sacrifices she had made would be for nothing.

She couldn't just get out and name all those women who helped her come this far. They all lost too much to be betrayed like that. They deserved a chance, even if the price of it was her own life.

The smoke made her choke, so Becca lay on her back and placed her hands on her chest. *Will the Gift Hunter return for me?* She hoped he would. However, even if that man didn't come back to save her, it wouldn't mean he had won.

The beginning had been set. Becca still had an ally – the woman she had met in the theater. She had left her a letter to warn Lana in case something unexpected happened. Also, Becca had shared the whole story with her. This story might have a tragic ending, but it would live on in the hearts of all the other girls accused of having the 'wrong' power.

Becca closed her eyes, letting the warmth of the fire surrounding her carry her soul away.

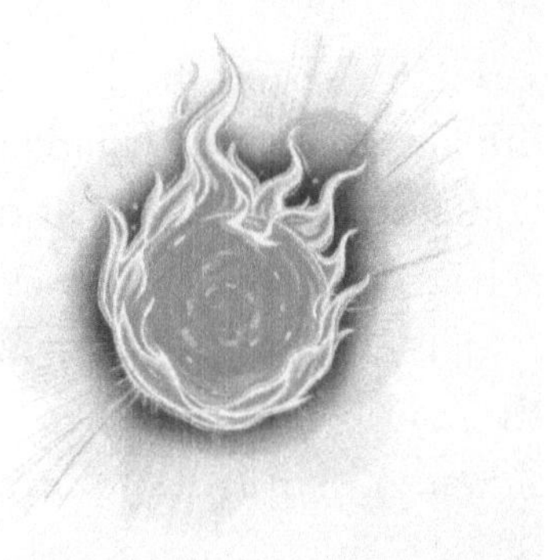

# Epilogue

The flames danced in the fire pit, casting shadows on the surrounding trees. Lana sat on the ground, reading a letter, her mouth covered with her palm. It was a farewell letter from her best friend, Rebecca. The letter wished her all the best in her life and advised her not to be too upset that she was gone. *No, it can't be...*

"I'm so sorry," Melissa, her mother, said in a grave voice. She sat on the opposite end of the fire pit, her hands on her lap as she crumpled the hem of her dress. "Someone left that letter by our door, and we grew suspicious once we read it. Bernard checked around, and he found Becca in the burnt barn. I mean, he found her body... The experts said it was an accident."

Lana stood up, walking around the glade. *Becks...* No way she would believe Becca had made such a long way only to get into some sort of accident. Someone must have found her and silenced her. Forever.

"What really happened to her?" Lana asked.

"I don't know. The experts said it was a fire in the barn, and she didn't survive."

"A fire?" Lana repeated, refusing to accept this awkward lie. "She had the Gift of Fire, so she was immune –"

"Exactly. She *was* immune when she used to have magic. After it was taken away from her, she became just an ordinary human being."

*This is all so fucked up.* Lana gritted her teeth, tears welling in her eyes. "If I'd only been a bit faster, I could have protected her."

"You took the long forest road because the guardians are looking for you," Melissa pointed out. "That's also why I came to meet you on the way. Lana, we can't return to Triville. After everyone learned about Becca, the chief issued a warrant for our arrest."

"We can't just leave. I have to find out who killed her. I have to stop those people."

"How will you do that if you can't even speak a word of truth without getting a heart attack?"

Lana gasped, feeling the grip of the deadly spell on her neck. Her mother spoke the truth – she couldn't afford to speak frankly with anyone but her.

"Listen," Melissa continued. "Rebecca wasn't alone when she came. I never had a chance to meet her or her helper, but someone had sent that letter in the morning after her death. It means that Becca had a trustworthy ally. She will keep working on our plan."

"Then I must find her ally and do my best to help her. She might already know the truth if Becca spoke to her, so my oath wouldn't kill me."

"You'll get arrested once you show up in the town."

"I'll take my chances."

Melissa raised her eyes to her. "Do you know what they do with female prisoners?"

Lana shook her head. She really had no idea.

"They don't try to convince us like they do in Mercy Houses. They'll just strip us of our magic and send us away to live among the Incapables."

Lana breathed heavily. *No way.* It was the same scenario that Amanda had promised her, and she thought she had managed to escape it, only to fall into the same trap.

Melissa rose to her feet and approached her. "Lana, please, listen to me now. Your father managed to buy us some time by sending the guardians to places where you are less likely to show up. But you can't tempt fate like that. You need to get out of here."

"Where?" She asked in a hoarse voice.

"To the High Canyons, then to the port. Together, we'll travel far, far away. Preferably to the other side of the continent."

"I'm not really in the mood for traveling."

"You aren't in a position to choose."

Lana dropped her hands, obeying her plea. At least, for now. "Fine. But I'll come back once the dust settles."

Melissa nodded. "Of course. Let's give it three years to make sure your words won't kill you."

"Three years?!"

"I know, at your age it might seem like a lot, but please, understand – it is the best strategic move we can make right now. Then, when the time comes, you'll be back and find out what happened to Rebecca. We will use her case as leverage to make the change possible."

"We will," Lana promised, glancing at the silent trees surrounding them. "I'll be back, and I'll show them what our power is worth."


*To be continued...*

## *THANK YOU, DEAR READER!*

Thank you so much for reading the second book about Lana!

This story was tricky to write. I guess it happens with all tragedies. However, no matter how badly the author wants to give their story a happy ending, tragedies keep happening in real life. So, this story was written to honor the memory of all the women who have become victims of the system in which they happened to live.

Tragedies are points of no return. They allow us to see clearly what is at stake and understand the real reason why we should never give up on fighting for things such as equality and human rights.

Now, when Lana has lost her best friend due to the oppressive system, she is determined to do her best to change the order of things. And, of course, she won't stop until she reaches her goal. The next story about Lana, "Ghost," is set three years after the events happening in this book. Please feel free to explore it and find out how her story ends. A little spoiler – this time, the tragedy won't be repeated.

By the way, if you liked this book, you are welcome to give it a good rating. To do that, just check the store where you bought it and give it the stars you think it deserves!
Your support means the world to me!

Sincerely yours,
*-Lubov Leonova*

# What will happen next?

## GHOST

### *Chapter 2. The Favor*

*3 years later*

Lana climbed the stairs and walked through the front yard. Guided by a gentle breeze, the daffodils swung toward her like curious children. In front of the house, the bright morning sun fell on luscious green grass and round flower beds framed by river stones. Lana stopped at the white door and took a deep breath before she knocked three times. She listened carefully, but it was quiet inside.

"Is anybody home?" Lana called out.

There was no reply but the quiet rustle of the grass behind her. Lana turned to the yard. The dirt in the flower beds was wet, which meant that the daffodils had been recently watered. *It hasn't rained for a couple of days, so the witch must be somewhere nearby,* Lana concluded. *She is most likely avoiding unwelcome visitors.*

Lana knocked again, louder this time. "I'm not going away, Meredith!"

Quiet footsteps approached. The door opened, revealing a woman not as old as Lana had imagined her to be. White streaks accented her dark hair and nascent wrinkles framed her bright green eyes. She wore a simple beige cotton dress.

"Are you lost, girl?" Meredith asked.

"No. I need your help."

Meredith narrowed her eyes. "I don't know you."

"But I know about you, Meredith."

Meredith sneered. "All right, what do you want?"

Lana clasped the purse hanging on her belt. "To make a deal."

"I don't help strangers." Meredith started closing the door.

"Wait!" Lana put her foot on the threshold.

Meredith raised her hand, and a fireball spell grew in her palm. "Don't mess with me."

Lana raised her arms. "Listen, I'm not asking for myself. I'm only helping my friend."

"Which friend?"

Lana hesitated for a moment. Why would the witch need the name? It didn't matter; she had nothing to hide from her. "Rebecca Turner," she said.

Meredith gave her a suspicious look. "Rebecca died three years ago."

Lana sighed. Even after three years, it wasn't easy to think about Becca's death. But somehow, the witch knew her friend. "I know, and I'm here to find out why."

Meredith clasped her hands together, and the fireball disappeared. "What's your name?"

"I'm Lana. Lana Morris."

The witch stepped back. "Come on in, then."

Lana stepped into a spacious living room; its curtains opened wide to let the daylight in. The walls were lined with shelves holding little glass bottles filled with liquid–probably potions. There were also books, old ones with leather covers. These books had to hold knowledge of the art of magic on their fragile yellow pages. Lana couldn't resist picking up a folder with a smooth green cover and neat golden letters: *The Agreements*. Interesting. Who else had been in the witch's house to sign these papers?

"Don't touch anything!" Meredith said.

Lana flinched, almost dropping the folder. She placed it back on the shelf.

Meredith had already put two steaming cups of tea on a round coffee table, so Lana sat on the sofa and took a teacup. The drink smelled of raspberries, reminding her of the sunny summer days.

"If you want me to help you, you must be completely honest," Meredith said, looming over her like a thundercloud.

Lana took a sip of tea and put the cup on the table. "Of course."

"How did you know Rebecca?"

Lana rested her hands in her lap. "I knew her all my life. Our fathers are guardians who work together in Triville. Three years ago, when I was a Sister in Mercy House, Rebecca was brought in. No one there knew of our previous acquaintance."

"What was her Gift?"

"One of the most dangerous ones – she could create flames. As it happens with all new Gifts, Becca couldn't control it properly, and after an accident in school, she was sent to Mercy House."

Meredith scowled. "And you let them take her powers away."

"Of course not!" Her eyes tingled at the memory of her last meeting with Becca. "I mean, I tried to stop the Sorority, but I was too late. When I found out they had taken all of her magic, I helped her escape. I thought that if her father saw her like that, he would do something to shut this facility. But he preferred to stay out of it."

Meredith nodded. "I see."

"On the night of the escape, Becca and I split up. I thought she was safer without me – she lost her magic, so Searching spells didn't work on her. I was wrong. I was on my way home when I received a message about Becca's death." Lana's voice trembled. "The experts said it was a suicide, but I knew – someone killed her, and after that, I... I just couldn't come back home. So, I went hiding for three years."

Meredith sat down on the sofa next to her. "You did the right thing – you might have been in danger."

"I was."

"Then why did you decide to come back?"

Lana clutched the teacup, chasing the chill from her hands. "Things changed. The Sorority has stopped looking for me, and the oath of secrecy I brought to Mercy House has worn off. Also, my father has recently become a guardian chief. He suggested I help him with the archives in Triville, and I agreed."

"Hmm, a chief. Why don't you tell your father everything?"

"It's not that easy. Even if he believed me, he would do nothing. He's tied with his Guardian Oath, so he can't disobey their rules without putting our lives in danger."

"Then what are you going to do?"

"I'm not tied with such an oath and have nothing to lose. When I get proof that the guardians murdered Rebecca, I'll make her case go viral. They won't be able to hide the truth about Mercy House any longer."

"Proof?"

"Yes. I need to steal Rebecca's case file."

"That's interesting," Meredith said. "Go on."

"I started working as a secretary in the archives a week ago, and so far, I figured out that Rebecca's file is being kept in a secret archive. As you might understand, nobody would place a suicide case in that archive, so once I find it, I'll have the truth they're trying to hide."

"Well, I hope your plan will work. How can I help?"

To find out how Lana's story ends, read *Ghost.*
The story is available at multiple online book stores!

**Amazon Book Store:**
http://author.to/lubovleonova

**Check all my books on my official website:**
https://www.magical2worlds.com/books

I always loved reading. I guess all the books I've ever read impacted me greatly - they let me expand my worldview and inspired me to pursue my dreams despite the obstacles.

Born in Russia, I immigrated to Canada in 2014, where I faced multiple challenges, including building my own life from scratch and figuring out what career path would let me use my full potential. My searches led me to feministic studies in college and volunteering in female support groups.

My experience slowly formed into ideas for my fantasy series *TwoWorlds*, where females shape the sphere of justice using their natural talents.

Today, I live on the East Coast of Canada with my husband, Alex, and my bunnies - Boris and Flora. Recently, we also welcomed a cat named Grayson into our family.

# LET'S CONNECT!

Do you want to win Giveaways for my books and receive daily inspirational content? Yes? Then follow me on any of these platforms on your preference:

**Instagram - author's official page**
https://www.instagram.com/authorleonova/

**Instagram - 2 Worlds Series**
https://www.instagram.com/magical2worlds/

**Facebook**
https://www.facebook.com/magical2worlds

**Twitter/X**
https://twitter.com/LeonovaLubov

Also, I have a **Goodreads** account where you can always get the newest updates on my stories release:
https://www.goodreads.com/author/show/21216748.Lubov_Leonova

www.ingramcontent.com/pod-product-compliance
Lightning Source LLC
Chambersburg PA
CBHW030809210726
48290CB00002B/502